IN THE SHADOWS
THE ORION PROPHECY
BOOK ONE

CAROL MCDONALD

Copyright © 2023 Carol Hellier

All rights reserved.

No part of this book may be reproduced in any form or by any electronic or mechanical means, including information storage, retrieval systems and artificial intellegence, without written permission from the author, except for the use of brief quotations in a book review.

This is a work of fiction. Names, characters, places, and incidents are either the product of the author's imagination or are used factiously, and any resemblance to actual persons, living or dead, business establishments, events or locales is entirely coincidental.

Cover Design
Francessca Wingfield @ Wingfield Designs

Formatting
TBR Editing & Design

*As always to my children and grandchildren.
There is nothing as precious as family.*

And to Cathy, my very good friend, over the years we have had some laughs and heres to the next lot, but not mince pie making!

A SPECIAL THANKS

Back in time is a quaint little diner situated in Victoria road, Chelmsford, Essex, UK. It boasts an American themed menu with plenty of choice for both, children and adults.

The toy train still runs around the top of the restaurant, and the clock at the front still goes backwards.

I have eaten here many times with my children and with friends. Without a doubt it still is, today, one of my favourite restaurants.

With thanks to the owner for allowing the restaurant to be included in the story.

PROLOGUE
SUNDAY, 31 OCTOBER 1996

As the car pulled out of the 'Back In Time' restaurant car park the heavens opened. Destiny noticed Phil could barely see out of the windscreen, which on its own made her nervous, but the fact that the rain was making such a racket as it smashed onto the roof of the car, she had an eerie feeling too. She felt it was unnatural.

"Wow this is like one of those tropical storms you read about." Phil remarked as he turned the windscreen wipers up high.

"Don't you normally get those in tropical countries and not England?" Vanessa replied. "Drive carefully, Phil."

"Do you think we should wait it out?" Destiny asked as she tried to look out into the darkness. She could hear the worry in her mother's voice, she was worried to.

"Nope, no way. I am not sitting in my car on the side of the road after leaving the cosy restaurant that had music and a bar, we will be home in no time, now buckle up, sit back, and relax birthday girl." Phil replied.

The rain continued to get heavier causing the roads to instantly turn into mini rivers. Pressing her forehead against the window Destiny breathed onto the glass and watched as the condensation formed, she then wrote her name in it with a little heart underneath.

"Darling have you had a lovely birthday?" Vanessa asked, her voice a little shaky.

"Yes, thanks mum, and thanks for the money and meal." As birthdays went this one wasn't so bad.

Back In Time was her favourite restaurant, boasting a full American dinner menu. Ribs, Burgers and of course chicken. Although the place was small it was packed with atmosphere. It had a toy train that ran all the way around the top of the walls, on a track, and at the front there was a clock that went backwards. Her mum always said it was the closest thing to her hometown, which of course was the United States. Other than that bit of information Vanessa never talked about her past. Only that she had moved to the UK where she had given birth to Destiny after her husband had died. Destiny guessed it was too painful for her mother to talk about, so never asked. Destiny rubbed her tummy, maybe she had overdone it with the marshmallow sundae, but it was her birthday after all. She had also been given money, that she would bank tomorrow in her lunch break. She planned to going travelling. She had been saving up since she had first started a paper round at the age of thirteen, and four years later she had managed to save a pretty penny, thanks mainly to her job in the patisserie.

Destiny jumped when she heard the loud crash of thunder, it was accompanied with a lightning bolt that struck the car causing a blinding light.

Destiny closed her eyes and gripped the door handle so hard her knuckles turned white. Her heartbeat fastened and she struggled for breath. As the car flipped onto its roof and started sliding back across the road, Destiny held on tight. Her eyes were still closed as the car came to a standstill in a ditch. As it lodged itself in at an awkward angle. Destiny heard the crunch of metal and then the windscreen shattered. She could hear her mother screaming as the glass shards flew back into the car. Everything had happened in slow motion and yet at the same time a hundred miles an hour. As she hung upside down her chest tightened and a knot formed in the pit of her stomach, her mother had gone quiet.

"Mum……. Mum are you ok……Mum!" Destiny cried. She

pulled and twisted at the seatbelt, but it wouldn't budge. "Mum?" She called frantically as she continued to fight to get free. She needed to get to her mum. She needed to make sure she was okay. As she fumbled with the clasp, she could feel her eyes growing heavy and her movements were slowing. It was like being under water, everything was harder, like there was an invisible force holding her back. She struggled against the feeling and attempted to release the belt one last time before everything went black…..

CHAPTER 1

Destiny stood at the graveside and watched as her mother's coffin was lowered into the ground. She stood emotionless; she had no more tears left to cry. After waking up in hospital two weeks after the crash, only to be told her mother and stepfather were both dead, Destiny had cried for almost two weeks; her whole life had been ripped from her. Now here she stood saying goodbye for the very last time.

She looked around the group of people that had turned up to pay their respects, it was weird that her mum or Phil had no family, just a few friends and neighbours. They had always kept themselves to themselves, very private people, which didn't really match her mother's personality. Venessa had always seemed outgoing, but when it came to friendships, she had kept people at arm's length. It was one of the things her mother had taught her. 'You can't trust people Destiny; they will take what you tell them and use it against you somewhere down the track. Protect yourself.'

Destiny wished she could hear her mother's voice one last time, feel her arms around her one last time, hear the words, I love you baby, one last time. But of course, there would never be a one last time. Destiny swallowed down the grief and gazed at the single white rose she held; her hand trembled. How could she go on?

The vicar coughed to gain Destiny's attention, causing her to turn her head towards him, there he stood looking sombre, but Destiny knew it was an act. He didn't know Vanessa, he didn't know her stepfather, and he didn't know her pain. Destiny looked down at the white rose she had brought. White roses were her mother's favourite flower. Vanessa had always said they were magical and would ward off evil spirits. She always had vases around the house full of them. Destiny used to laugh at her mum, every now and again she would talk about magic like it was real. Well she wouldn't be talking about it anymore, and Destiny doubted she would ever laugh again either. She threw the rose onto the coffin and watched as it fell, her last gift to her mother.

AFTER THE SERVICE Destiny was taken back to her house, where she held a small wake for her mother and stepfather, she had used part of her savings to lay on a little spread for the people that had paid their respects, she felt it was the least she could do.

"Hello, my dear, I'm so sorry for your loss, if there's anything I can do for you or help you with then please let me know." Mrs Richards told Destiny.

Mrs Richards had lived next door to Destiny for as long as Destiny could remember, she was the one constant in her life that hadn't changed. Destiny smiled at the plump, old women, she reminded Destiny of a nan, an old-fashioned nan, which baked cookies and gave good cuddles, the only weird thing about her was her smell, she smelt like bonfire. "Thank you, Mr's Richards, that's very kind of you. Please help yourself to something to eat." Destiny made her way to the kitchen and popped the kettle on, she needed a cup of tea, her throat felt like it had closed up. She stood at the window and looked out at the garden, wondering what she was going to do next. There was no way she could afford to keep the house; she would have to put it up for sale, but then what? Where would she go? Suddenly she caught movement from the side of her eye, it was coming from the magnolia tree, turning sharply she squinted trying to make out what the movement was.

"Now what?" She sighed as she grabbed her coat and walked down the garden. It was now December, and the weather had a nasty nip to it. The grass crunched under her feet as she approached the Magnolia tree, she inspected it closely. Whatever was out there had gone. All she could see were the wooden bare branches. About to turn around and head back in doors she was stopped by a small voice.

"Hello Destiny." The voice called out.

"Who's there?" Destiny spun around in panic. The garden looked deserted. Slowly stepping backwards towards the house, she stopped when she heard the voice again.

"All the answers are inside the house; you need to look for them."

"Answers to what? What do I need to look for? Who are you? Show yourself." Destiny began to shiver as her eyes scoured the garden. She couldn't see anyone. Was she going mad with grief, was that even a thing, she was sure it was. She turned to walk away when the voice spoke once more.

"We will meet soon, find the answers, I will be waiting for you."

"DESTINY!" Mrs Richards called. "Come inside dear, you'll catch a chill out there, it looks like it might snow."

After she looked around one last time, Destiny made her way back indoors, still unsure whether she had been hearing things or daydreaming. "I just needed some fresh air Mr's Richard's, I'm gonna make some tea, would you like some?"

"Yes dear, that would be lovely."

FINALLY, the last of the mourners left, Destiny looked around the kitchen at the mess. Mrs Richards tea sat on the table untouched. "Well that was a waste." She mumbled, as she tipped it down the sink. She made her way to the lounge and flopped onto the sofa, kicking off her shoes at the same then wiggled her toes at the freedom, she had never liked wearing heels, and neither did her toes. Today had been hard, no doubt the hardest she had ever lived through. She lay her head back and closed her eyes. There was a lot of tidying up to do, but she decided to leave that until the morning. She also needed to go and see her boss; she had been off work since the accident and was hoping her job would still be available. Reluctantly she dragged herself off of the sofa and made her way up the stairs. Tonight she hoped she would sleep well, lately her sleep had been broken, waking in the early hours for unexplained reasons. She always woke with a feeling of being watched, it was a scary thought at 2am or 3am in the morning.

Throwing off her clothes she slipped into her pyjamas and made her way to the bathroom, ready to clean her teeth. She scrubbed lazily as she looked at her reflection in the mirror. Destiny noticed the dark circles around her eyes, she needed a good night's sleep, maybe then she would stop hearing voices. "Yeah, you're not going mad girl, you're just tired." she told herself. Bending down she rinsed her mouth and spat out the water. Wiping her mouth on the towel she looked back at her reflection and froze. There on the mirror, written in toothpaste was the words - *look for the answers* – Destiny looked behind her, someone was in the house, the same person who had spoken to her in the garden. Turning back to the mirror, again she froze when the writing had disappeared. "What the hell is going on?"

After inspecting the mirror, which was perfectly clean, and having a quick look on the landing, Destiny put it down to fatigue, it had to be, there was no other logical explanation. As she climbed into bed, the feeling of being cocooned in the warmth was welcoming as she snuggled down and pulled the quilt up around her head. She still had the strange sensation of being watched but Destiny's eyelids grew heavy as she gave in to the much-needed sleep.

CHAPTER 2

Destiny woke after a few hours; she had the same dream she had been having ever since the night of the car accident. It always started with Destiny running through a forest, scared and alone. And it always ended with a huge black wolf padding towards her. Then she would wake up, she could never remember the start of the dream, and she never slept long enough to find out the ending. "I'm officially going mad." She mumbled as she reached for the bedside lamp, Destiny fumbled for the switch, it clicked on and lit up the room. She lay back and thought about her dream, it was possible that running through the forest scared could mirror her feelings now. She was scared and lonely, she had no family, no real friends, as the funeral proved - There was no one there to support her. But what does the wolf mean? It was the most beautiful creature she had ever seen, truly a magnificent beast, obviously it wasn't real, it was way too big to be a real wolf, it was nearer the size of a bear than a wolf, maybe it was showing her what she had to be. "A beast?" Destiny shook her head and laughed. "Maybe it means brave, I have to be brave, and maybe I should stop talking to myself before I get carted away in a straight jacket."

Destiny yawned as she reached for her dressing gown at the end of her bed she grabbed it and stood up, wrapping it around her middle and tying it tight, she then slipped on her slippers and made her way downstairs to grab a cup of tea. She couldn't help but look at the Magnolia tree, as she filled the kettle, she thought back to the voice she had heard or thought she had heard. It sounded so real and there had defiantly been movement around the tree, why else would she have gone out there. Suddenly Destiny noticed a tiny flicker of light, almost like a candle flame, and it was coming from the tree. "What the hell?" Dropping the kettle into the sink she ran to the kitchen door, unlocking it and threw it open before she rushed down the garden path. "Who's there? Show yourself, before the police get here, I mean it, show yourself now." Destiny stood looking at the flickering light that seemed to be hovering just above the branch. She raised her finger, noticing her hand shaking and poked at the tiny flame, but as her finger drew near, it vanished. "That's it, it's official, I've gone mad." Destiny made her way back indoors and rescued the kettle from the sink then continued to make her tea. Confused by the unusual events, she decided to go to her mother's bedroom, as the feeling of loneliness hit her. She was on her own. How could she go on living when she had no one? But her biggest question was why did she survive the crash, why couldn't she have died to? As she lifted the cup of hot tea, her hands were trembling, causing the tea to spill slightly onto the work top. "Pull it together Destiny, please." She whispered. Her heart was still thudding in her chest. She knew it was silly running outside like that. What if it was someone playing tricks on her, or worse, a madman waiting to jump on her. Destiny shook the thoughts from her head and decided to head up to her mother's room, hoping to find comfort.

She made her way up the stairs then stopped when she got to the closed door. She hadn't been in there since returning home from hospital, and even now she didn't feel strong enough. "You can do this." She told herself. Digging deep for all her courage, she pushed the door open and took a small step in. Holding her breath as she stood and looked around the room, she released it when she realised it was exactly as it had been left the night of her birthday. Venessa's makeup lay scattered on the dressing table, and her cardigan was thrown over the back of her chair. Destiny walked over and picked it up, burying her face into it. She stumbled backwards onto the bed and curled up tight into a ball, hugging the cardigan too her chest. Destiny closed her eyes as she felt the familiar sting of tears, while the memories of her birthday and that fateful night flashed through her mind. Why did they have to go out? Why did Phil insist on driving when the weather was so bad? Why did they have to die? The questions whirled through her mind like a hurricane, and the answers all led to the same thing. All she wanted was Vanesa there with her. Deciding to spend the rest of the night there, snuggled on her mum's bed, she breathed in her familiar scent. Destiny's eyes soon started to close as her body relaxed, until she heard a faint scratching coming from above her, followed by a tweet. She squeezed her eyes shut tighter in order to ignored the noise, she even pulled a pillow over her head and held it firmly in place. But when the noise got louder she could no longer ignore it. Destiny huffed as she climbed out of the bed and made her way onto the landing. She looked up at the loft hatch. It was secure. She decided it had to be a trapped bird, no way anyone could get into the loft and even if they did, why would they tweet? She made her way downstairs and grabbed a pair of rubber washing up gloves and her mother's flour sieve, then put on her coat, pulling the hood up securely. Ready to catch the culprit, she passed the hall mirror, taking a glimpse at herself as she did so. Destiny almost laughed, she looked ridiculous. Grabbing the loft pole she pulled down the hatch and waited as the steps slid gracefully down, only stopping when they landed at her feet. Destiny flicked on the light switch and watched as the loft came alight. After taking a few deep breaths she braced herself, ready to come face to face with the feathered fiend. Up she went, one step at a time, preparing herself for what was waiting. When she reached the top she poked her head in first to get a good look at the little fella. But to Destiny's surprise there were no signs of life at all, in fact there were no signs of anything other than an old chest that looked antique. It was standing proudly in the middle of the loft. She gradually climbed further up the ladder and stepped into the solid loft floor, then she took a good look around. It was the first time she had been up there. Why was it empty though? Where was all the stuff her mother had said was up there? More importantly what made the noise? Taking a closer look at the chest she felt goosebumps cover her body, knowing the way her life had gone recently she expected to find a dead body stashed in there.

"Get a grip and be the wolf." Destiny shook her head. "Seriously, now I'm listening to a dream." After running her fingers over the top of the chest she realised just how dusty it was, which was strange as the rest of the room was dust free. She blew the dust off causing a succession of sneezes that seemed to last forever, by the time they did stop she sucked in a lungful of air as she was left gasping. As she refocused on the chest, she noticed the carving on the lid. It was of a woman, in a long flowing gown, standing next to an extra-large wolf. They were both standing next to a weird looking tree, both staring up at it. "What is it with wolves?" She asked herself. "I wonder what colour it is.......Oh my god, you find a creepy chest in your mothers loft, and you wonder what colour the wolf is, seriously! Focus Destiny, focus." Destiny grabbed the latch and tried to pull it open but on further inspection it needed a key. "Great, just great. Why can't anything be simple?" Destiny climbed back out of the loft and into her mother's bedroom. "Now where would I hide a key?" As she scanned the room her eyes rested on an old jewellery box, Destiny felt a little startled as she had never seen it before, she was certain it wasn't there earlier. It seemed her mother had secrets; did she really want to find out what they were? *You can't stop now.* She tried to ignore the little voice in her head, but she knew she was just too damn nosey, just like her mother, to let it go now. Destiny opened the jewellery box and was amazed to find it empty, she looked at the intricate carving on the top, it looked similar to the chest in the loft. Carrying the box, she went back to the chest and compared the carving, it wasn't just similar, it was exactly the same. This had to be the answer to opening the chest, she just didn't know how. As she stood there contemplating what to do next, the loft ladder sprung back up causing Destiny to scream and drop the jewellery box, she watched as it hit the floor, smashing into pieces.

Destiny shook as she looked around her, the thought of someone in the house frightened her more than being trapped. A knot had formed in the pit of her stomach, and she found herself glued to the spot. Had someone pushed the ladder back up, could the loft hatch be open from inside? Well there was only one way to find out. Her feet felt like they were made out of lead, each step she made took all her strength. She approached the hatch cautiously, half expecting it to drop open any second. Kneeling down she placed her ear near the hatch and listened. There were no sounds coming from below, in fact the only sound she could hear was her heart beating in her chest so wildly, it sounded like it was trying to escape itself. Cautiously she pushed on the hatch, Destiny tried to free it, but it wouldn't budge so she stood up and jumped on it, but still nothing. She slumped back down on the floor and wrapped her arms around her knees, she had no idea what the time was. Was she stuck here forever, who would find her, she had no one. She placed her head in her hands and started to sob. She was trapped and all alone. As she wiped at her eyes she glanced back over to the chest, and the broken jewellery box, sighing to herself she decided she may as well attempt to get the damn thing open, after all, if she was going to die, she may as well die not wondering about a mystery chest in her mother's loft. She wiped at her eyes with the back of her hand then crawled over to the chest and started to pick up the pieces of the jewellery box, the feeling of guilt overriding her senses. She knew it didn't make sense to feel like this, her mother was gone, she wouldn't need it where she was now, and to be perfectly honest it was an ugly looking thing anyway. Reaching down for the last piece, she spotted a key laying underneath it. "Bingo!"

 Destiny grabbed the key and tried to insert it into the keyhole. Her hands were shaking which made it harder to aim. She took a deep breath and closed her eyes. "Focus Destiny." She told herself. When she opened her eyes she attempted to open the chest once again, this time with success. She pulled up the lid, it was a lot heavier than she had expected, and took all her strength to open it. Once open she peered in. "Is that it?" She exclaimed, almost in disgust. In the chest was a bag. Just a bag and nothing else. And not only that, but the bag also looked empty. She reached in and pulled the bag out, and just to be on the safe side, she ran her hand across the bottom of the chest. Indeed, it was empty. She sat back on her knees feeling disappointed, while holding the bag out in front of her so she could study it. It wasn't even a nice bag, which only added to the disappointment. Destiny didn't know why, but she opened the bag and stuck her hand in anyway, her hand brushed against something large, startled she flung the bag away. Destiny scrambled away to the far wall, her eyes firmly on the bag as it flew through the air. How could she feel anything, it was empty. She focused on the bag as it landed against the wall and then dropped to the floor, with a loud thud. It didn't sound like it was empty. As the bag hit the floor a piece of paper also came floating out.

"Okay, this is some creepy shit." Desting crawled towards the paper, grabbing it and then the bag, and went and sat back down with her back resting against the chest. She held the piece of paper up, so she could examine it, it was a letter, the page was torn off at the bottom right-hand corner. She focused back on the top and started to read.

Dear V,

I'm glad you managed to get away safely. Magnus is tearing the town apart looking for you and his daughter. You may think of him as a monster, but one thing is for sure, he loves Destiny, with all of his heart.

It's no longer safe for you to write. A darkness has fallen over the town, I fear we are all cursed, but then you knew what would happen when you took away his
   grand
   I wish
   love

Mum
xx

Destiny stared at the letter. "Magnus? But my dad's dead." She focused on the missing corner. "What did you take away mum?"

Destiny Sighed. "That's got to be granddaughter, does that mean I have a nan? She signed it mum. I must have a nan, wait, I was a baby, could she be dead? Could Magnus be dead? Mum what have you done?" Destiny dropped her head into her hands. She didn't want to know.

After thirty minutes of self-pity Destiny glanced back at the bag, it was pointless just sitting here waiting to die, so she decided to hunt for the other part of the letter. She grabbed the bag, sticking her hand in and wished for the missing corner, but instead of finding the missing corner, she pulled out a neat pile of unopened letters that were neatly tied up with a white ribbon. "How is this possible?" Filled with confusion, she rubbed her head and started going through all the things that had happened since the accident.

The voice.
The toothpaste message.
The light on the tree.
The creepy chest.
The empty bag, that apparently isn't empty.

Making herself comfortable once again, she decided to read through the letters, maybe the answers she needed would be in there. Undoing the ribbon, Destiny pulled out the first envelope and read the address.

MRS E DARK
414 MOON CRESCENT
VALLEY FALLS
PORTLAND
MAINE

USA

Destiny ripped open the envelope, and pulled the letter out, it was dated only a few days before her seventeenth birthday.

> Dear Mum,
>
> I hope you are well. I know I write every year, just before Destiny's birthday, but I never send them, just like you said. No more contact. But I can't help myself, it makes me feel better. I still miss you so much.
>
> Destiny has grown into such a beautiful young woman, it's hard to believe 17 years ago she came into the world. Only another year until I have to tell her the truth, but at least she will have had 17 years of normality. I just hope she takes it well, it's not every day you find out you're a witch.

"What?" Destiny whispered. "This can't be true, it's a dream, yeah like the wolf thing, just a dream." Destiny pinched herself. 'Ouch, okay, it's not a dream…... a joke then, a not so funny joke." Destiny returned to the letter.

> Mum you would be so proud of her too, I wish you could meet her, you would love her as much as I do. Anyway, I guess I should get going.
>
> I love and miss you so much,
>
> V
>
> XX
>
> P.S. I hope Magnus got over the loss, I know we

didn't get on, but so much time has passed, things are different now, I wish him no harm.

Destiny looked at the other unopened letters, there were sixteen of them, she guessed it was one for each year of her life. Reaching for the first one, she sat back ready to read them all.

CHAPTER 3

Destiny woke to the sound of the phone ringing, she sat bolt upright and wondered how she had managed to get out of the loft, the last thing she remembered she had been trapped up there. Had it been a dream after all? The phone fell silent as she looked at the clock, 11.30 am, she had certainly made up for the lack of sleep lately. So, just a dream then, she smiled, relieved at the thought as she flung the quilt off and jumped up, catching the side of the bedside table, and knocking off a pile of neatly stacked letters that were tied together with a neat white ribbon. "Shit!" Bending down she reached for the letters and discovered the bag next to them. "So, it wasn't a dream."

She scooped up the letters and placed them back into the mysterious bag. Destiny trudged downstairs to make a cup of tea, picking up the mail that lay on the front door mat, as she went. There was a ton of brown envelopes that could only mean one thing…... Bills. "Great!" Destiny threw them onto the worktop and continued to make herself a cup of tea. She found herself throwing glances out of the window, towards the magnolia tree, like it held all the answers. Maybe it did, that's where all this hocus pocus stuff started. She returned her attention to the bills after she poured her tea and viewed the pile. "Right what have we first, water rates, phone bill, gas bill and a letter from the bank, well isn't that just great."

She opened the bank letter first, Destiny discovered that the mortgage was in arrears by eight months, and they were going to reposes in five days' time. They needed her mother or stepfather to phone them. "I guess it's up to me then.... Hello Mr Bank manager, my names Destiny Black, my parents are dead and I'm a witch that makes cakes and if you take the house, I'm gonna turn you into a frog! .... That's not gonna go down well!' Destiny let out a little laugh. The voice had said all the answers were in the house, well maybe there was something here that would get her out of this mess. She reached for the bag and pulled out the pile of letters, the last letter, the one that would have been written around the time of her first birthday was the one she looked for. Her brain was on overload and the information she had learned last night was slowly coming back to her. Magnus Black was her dad, he was a warlock, Mum was a fae so was nan, what was a fae? And why did mum say Magnus was a freak, actually the fourth letter announced Magnus as an evil freak, what had he done to earn that title? The more Destiny found out the more questions arose, the biggest question being, how did she get out of the loft? Sighing to herself she reached for the bag, hoping against all odds that she would find something inside this magical bag of emptiness, which would help her find the answers she needed. Destiny plunged her hand in and felt around, but she felt nothing, overwhelmed with frustration she picked the bag up raising it above her head, ready to throw it across the room. "Just give me the answers?" Suddenly the bag became heavy causing Destiny to lose her balance, she stumbled backwards landing in a heap on the floor. "Seriously, I'm done with all this magic crap!"

Standing up Destiny grabbed the bag with both hands and hauled it to the table, before plunging both hands in, to pull out a large, antique looking, leather bound book. Undoubtedly the book was old, it had a smell to it just like a junk shop, old and in need of a clean. Destiny studied the front cover, in bold writing across the front was the title -

'WICAN HISTORY AND KNOWLEDGE'

Then on the inside cover it had: -

SPELLS
WITCHES AND WARLOCKS
WEREWOLVES
VAMPIRES
FAE, ELF, PIXIE, AND SPRITES
TROLLS.
DEMONS

Destiny sat with her mouth gaping as she re-read the words again, saying out loud "Werewolves and Vampires.... No, no way do they exist, impossible." Slamming the book shut, Destiny stood up and marched around the table three times clockwise and then twice anti-clockwise. Occasionally stopping and shaking her head at the book, as if it single handedly was the cause of all her problems. Sighing loudly she pulled out a chair and sat down again then opened the book, flicking through as she looked for Fae.

"Aha! .... Right Fae are Faerie, more recently renamed by humans to be known as Fairies. Legend has it if you tell a Fae your name, they will hold power over you and possibly complete control. You must never tell them, however if you know their name and say it, they will leave you alone. Fae have magical powers.... Did you have magical powers mum?" Destiny wondered out loud as she closed the book. She sat back letting out a slow breath, and turned her attention back to the bag, was it possible the book appeared because she had asked for it, she guessed it was worth a shot, after all, she had already lost everything, there was nothing else she could lose. "Show me what I should do next." Destiny put her hand in the bag and searched around, but it was empty. "Well a fat lot of good you are.... Five days, I have just five days to find somewhere to live."

Destiny put her head in her hands and started to sob, at only seventeen years of age, and although she had prided herself on acting much older, this was one situation she couldn't handle, at least not on her own and yet she was exactly that, on her own.

By the time Destiny finally sat down, it was late afternoon and she had spent the day tidying up the house after the wake, everything was back in its place. She had the book in her hands and decided to have a look at the spell section, if she were a witch then surely, she could magically make things better, couldn't she? Maybe magic up some money or put a cloaking spell on the house. "Seriously, just listen to yourself, a cloaking spell?" Fumbling through the pages she came to a levitation spell; it looked pretty straight forward. "For the spell to succeed, like all magic, you have to visualise it. Right, ok television, let's see you float." As she focused on the tv Destiny started saying the words. "Read the words that are wrote, make it light and let it float." Her eyes burned into the tv, as she imagined it floating. With a shaky start the tv rattled and gradually started to hover just above the floor. Destiny blinked, screamed, and then jumped behind the sofa, covering her eyes with her hands. This couldn't be happening. No she wouldn't allow it. There is no such thing as witches, werewolves or warlocks. There can't be, can there? Destiny slowly peeked from behind the sofa, the TV looked okay, no damage. "Okay, let's try again, just to make sure." Destiny sat back on the sofa and focused her attention on the TV. "Read the words that are wrote, make it light and let it float." Destiny almost shouted the words, and as she finished the tv shot up to the ceiling and smashed into pieces before raining back down into a heap of glass and plastic. "Shit, it worked!" Unable to stop herself she burst out laughing, but it wasn't a normal laugh, it was a nervous cackle. Almost hysterical. She must be a witch, she did a spell, ok so it might have gone a little wrong, but she still did it. Destiny continued to flick through the pages stopping at Werewolves.

A man with an inner wolf, A wolf with an inner man. A mighty predator, fast and strong. Able to smell an enemy coming from a couple of miles away. Loyal to their pack.

The Alpha is the strongest in the pack, followed by the Beta, who is the second strongest.

Normally this would be the Alphas best friend or brother, as it would be someone he can trust above all others.

Gamma is the third strongest and in charge of the warriors.

Werewolves mate for life once they find their one true mate, while the mate of the Alpha becomes Luna and helps look after the pack.

Omegas are the weakest of the pack and are normally servants.

"Well that's shit, being a servant because you aren't strong." Destiny flicked through to Vampires next.

The undead. Those that do not have a heartbeat and drink human blood. Thought to raid villages for their victims to feast on, vampires now tend to buy blood or hunt animals. With only rogue Vamps hunting people.

Destiny skimmed through the paragraphs, until her eye caught the word baby.

The Alpha Vampire is able to mate with a human to produce living vampire offspring, which can feast on blood and food.

"Urgh disgusting. Right what's next... Trolls, seriously, how could a troll live in the human world. No way."

Trolls have always been regarded as violent, but truthfully, they have a kind nature, all but heavy handed, which has given them their bad name.

Destiny's eyes were drawn to the word Demon, she felt a cold chill sweep over her as she read the paragraph.

Demons are the things that escape from the underworld, occasionally plaguing the earth, it is the responsibility of the werewolves, to protect the human world from such beasts. Demons come in many shapes and sizes, sometimes they are impossible to spot, which is why werewolves have such great sense of smell, it's there number one protection against their enemy's, and a great way of finding them.

Feeling unsettled, Destiny flicked to the last page, and there written at the very end of the book was an inscription –

NO OTHER EYES MAY SEE BUT THEE - DESTINY BLACK.

CHAPTER 4

Destiny was walking along the sidewalk, taking in all the little shops, the town was tiny and rural compared to Chelmsford, Essex, where she lived in the UK. She stopped in front of a small patisserie and as she stood there the door opened and out walked Mrs Richards. What? What's Mr's Richards doing here?

"Hello dear, I'm so glad you decided to buy the Patisserie, with your cake making skills I'm sure you will make a success of it."

"Thank you, Mr's Richards, I hope I'm as successful as you have been." Destiny looked at the sign at the end of the street.

Welcome to Valley falls, Maine, USA
the land of the White Pine and the honeybee

As she read the sign something caught her eye in the trees on the edge of the road, a large black thing was moving. Destiny walked towards it, breaking into a run as it disappeared further into the trees. She called out. "Wait!" Coming to a standstill at the edge of the forest, Destiny froze as the big black mass turned and faced her, it was the wolf from her dreams, and it was staring at her. Suddenly it bared it's teeth and snarled as it took a step closer to her, unable to move Destiny stood as the wolf lunged.

SITTING up in a pool of sweat Destiny wrapped her arms around herself to stop her body from shaking. She looked around the familiar room, glad that she was in her own bedroom. "What the hell was that?" She couldn't understand why Mr's Richards had appeared in her dream, it felt so real, she could even smell the old woman's bonfire smell mixed with the lavender perfume she wore. But more to the point she could feel that beasts hot breath against her neck as it lunged for her. Was that even a real place?

Destiny got up and grabbed her dressing gown, she decided to turn on her mother's computer and do some research. Once the computer sprang to life she typed in, 'Valley Falls. Maine, USA' then sat and watched as pictures came up of a small town. As Destiny scrolled through them, she came across a picture of the same sidewalk she was walking down in her dream.

"No frigging way!"

Scrolling down further she looked at a picture of the forest that was lining the road leading to the town, and there hidden partly by the trees was a large black shape, she couldn't quite make it out but as she went to scroll down, she was sure she saw two eyes, only briefly but definitely there were two eyes. Destiny closed down the computer and looked at the bag once more. "Give me answers, please?" Just as she stood up there was a knock at the door, so she made her way out to the hall. Destiny wondered if things would ever become clear as she opened the door. "Mrs Richards, what can I do for you?"

"I thought you might like some company dear." Mrs Richards greeted with a smile.

"Oh, Mr's Richards, that's lovely but I was just about to have breakfast." Destiny stared out into the street; it was still dark.

"No dear its teatime, look at the clock, it's 6.30 pm." The old woman walked past Destiny and into the kitchen."

Destiny followed her through, dazed at how it could be evening time when she was certain she had gone to bed hours ago. Something was wrong.

"Look I appreciate you checking up on me, but I'm not really great company at the moment." Destiny watched as the smile fall from the old woman's face, causing her to immediately feel bad. "I'll put the kettle on."

Mr's Richards smile returned. "Lovely dear. So tell me, anything happened lately?"

Destiny stopped and turned around. "Happened, like what?"

"Well like, the house, you said you were going to sort it out. Have you decided what you're going to do?"

"It looks like the bank is going to take the house, so I won't have anywhere to live, I suppose that's the first thing I need to do, pack."

Mr's Richards sighed. "You know dear, to get the right answers you need to ask the right questions."

Destiny looked at the old woman suspiciously. "What happens when you don't know what answers you want?"

"It's not about what you want Destiny, it's about what you need, and what you need to know." Mr's Richards smiled. "I'll leave you to it, just ask the right questions child and all will become clear." And with that the old woman made her way out, while destiny stared open mouthed after her. She was still staring at the closed door five minutes after Mrs Richards had left, she had the same question playing over and over in her mind. Does Mrs Richards know about the bag? But how could she, it was hidden in the loft, by her mother.

Destiny walked into the lounge, picked up the bag, and asked the one question that had been playing on her mind since her last dream. "What do I need to know about Valley Falls?" Reaching into the bag destiny pulled out a photograph of a large black wolf and by its side standing proud was a tall, well-built man. Destiny felt like she knew this man, it was a weird feeling. Next to him was a slim woman, elderly with white, silver hair, her hand was resting on the man's arm. Destiny's eyes almost popped out of her head when she noticed in the background Mr's Richards. Destiny stared at the photograph, it didn't make sense, Mrs Richards looked just like she looks now, how could that be, she's been here for as long as Destiny could remember. Without bothering to get dressed, Destiny charged towards the front door, she yanked it open and stormed out, marching to the next house, like she was ready to go into battle.

"OPEN THE DOOR!" Destiny shouted as she banged on the front door of the old women's house. "OPEN UP MRS RICHARDS, NOW!" Destiny continued to bang until a young women opened the door holding a small child in her arms.

"What's going on? why are you banging? Who are you?" The woman asked looking at Destiny like she had just been let loose from the asylum.

Destiny took a step back, startled for a second. "Where's Mrs Richards? I need to speak to her."

"Who? I think you've got the wrong address love; I live here and I'm not Mrs Richards."

"Mrs Richards has lived here for years, COME OUT, I KNOW YOU ARE IN THERE." Destiny pushed past the women and ran into the front room, but there was no sign of Mrs Richards.

"If you don't leave, now, I'm gonna call the police." The woman picked up the phone and started to dial.

"Okay, okay, I'm going." Destiny backed out of the house, slowly, while watching the young woman's confused and frightened face. "I'm sorry, I...." Destiny trailed off; she didn't know what to say. There was no logical explanation she could offer, other than she was going mad.

The woman slammed the door, causing Destiny to jump, she took one last look at the house that wasn't Mrs Richards then looked at the houses either side. Making her way back in she felt her head start to swim. She shut the door behind her and rested back against it, closing her eyes to stop herself from crying. "I miss you mum." Destiny was pulled from her thoughts when she heard a noise coming from the kitchen, making her way through she stopped abruptly when she saw Mrs Richards standing there, humming.

"I think we need to talk Destiny, why don't you put the kettle on." Mrs Richards turned and continued to hum, while all Destiny could do was stand and stare.

"Now dear would be good." Mrs Richards prompted.

Destiny jumped to it then took the hot steaming cup of tea and placed it in front of Mrs Richards. Still dazed by all the events that had led to this moment, Destiny was unable to think straight.

"I'm sure you have a million questions dear, and I'm going to give you the answers that you need." Mrs Richards told her.

Destiny's mind suddenly sprang to life. "Who's the woman living in your house?"

"It's not my house dear, I've never lived there, I've been here since the funeral, I only found you when the cloaking spell stopped working, obviously your mum didn't get a chance to renew it."

"What are talking about? I've known you all my life." Destiny opened her mouth to say more but Mrs Richards held up her hand to stop her.

"Look dear, I know it's hard to take all of this in, especially when your mother has lied to you…"

"Don't talk about my mother, I've read the letters, she was protecting me,"

"Protecting you from who Destiny? Your own father? A father that tore a whole town apart looking for his baby daughter. No child, your mother was selfish, her actions caused more harm to a whole town than an army full of demons could do."

"Look Mrs Richards just say what you need to say and then go." Destiny put her cup down and turned away from the old woman. She didn't need to listen to her talking about her mum.

"Ok, I will start from the beginning. Your mother was fae, your father a warlock, which is a male witch, only more powerful. They were very much in love, they married and ten months later you were born. At the time of her pregnancy your mother didn't know about the tradition of your fathers family, which was the first-born daughter was given to the Alphas first born son. It's been like that for centuries, anyway, to cut a long story short, your mother ran away with you, and no one could track you, your mother had the foresight to stick a cloaking spell on you both, so it wasn't until she passed away, and was obviously unable to update it, that the spell broke and then I found you."

"And what happens now? I'm not going to marry a dog, that's for sure." Destiny looked at the old woman with defiance.

"How about we go home, and you meet your father for starters, you won't be forced into marriage child, it would only ever have been consensual between you both, something your mother would have known if only she had asked."

"Don't blame my mum, she did what she did to protect me…. Why do I think I've known you all my life?"

"It's a spell deary, I have powers too, a simple memory spell you can make people believe anything, I turned up the day before the funeral, made you believe you had known me for as long as you've lived here."

"Where have you been living?"

"Here. You just couldn't see me, who do you think put the toothpaste on the mirror, the flame in the tree, everything that has happened has been my doing, however, I needed you to find the bag before you found out who I am. Now Destiny, I think we both need a good night's sleep, tomorrow we sort the house, and get everything in order, before it's too late." Mrs Richards turned and walked to the hallway.

"Too late? Wait Mrs Richards, too late for what?" Destiny ran to the hall, but Mrs Richards had vanished into thin air.

CHAPTER 5
APRIL 1997

Jaxon King stood out on the training ground and watched his Gamma as he trained his warriors. He stood tall at 6ft 5 and with his extremely muscular body he was everything an Alpha should be. His jet-black hair swept back from his handsome face, showing off his piercing grey eyes and chiselled jaw line. He had become Alpha four months ago when his father had been killed in a freak car accident, along with his mother, on All Hallows' Eve. He hadn't had time to grieve, he had a role to fulfil. Those around him thought he was heartless, and he guessed they were probably right. Jaxon had until the summer solstice which was the 21st of June to choose his Luna. This worried him, despite him having a different girl almost every night, he wanted his Luna to be his one true mate, he wanted what his mother and father had, not a loveless relationship. Time was running out, he knew he needed his true mate to be able to have an air to the pack, this worried him even more, his line would end with him. He was twenty-one, now normally by this time a wolf had met his mate, generally if he hadn't then he probably wouldn't. He blamed Magnus, as did his father. It was his daughter that was promised to him, not that he wanted to be with a witch, but it would have given him offspring. With the magic of Magnus and that of his daughter, if Jaxon didn't meet his true mate, then it was a backup plan, rarely used but in place just in case. So now here he stood, worrying about the future of his pack, and trying to work out which pack bitch to take as his Luna.

"Hey… trainings going well." Carlton Cane shouted over as he made his way to stand by Jaxon's side. Carlton was Jaxon's best friend and Beta, second strongest in the pack. As he approached, he pushed his hair away from his face, it annoyed Jaxon, as he liked to be well groomed, whereas Carltons hair was like another entity, an entity that was totally out of control.

"You need a haircut." Jaxon told him, meaning every word.

"Hey, don't let my wolf hear you say that" Carlton laughed. "Besides the girls love running their fingers through it."

Jaxon rolled his eyes. "You need to think with your head instead of your dick." Jaxon laughed as he watched his friend trying to tame his hair as the wind picked up. "Maybe get yourself a hairband."

"What do you think of the newbies Alpha?" Alex Cane, Carlton's brother asked as he walked over and joined the men. Alex was Carlton's double, apart from the fact he had his hair cut short, both men were 6ft and had muscles in all the right places. Both had mousey brown hair and green eyes. Carlton was the eldest at 21 with Alex a year younger at 20.

Jaxon took one last look at his warriors and nodded. "Not bad." With that he turned and made his way back to the pack house. The pack house was huge, boasting twenty double bedrooms on three floors plus another ten single rooms in the attic. Jaxon's bedroom was on the second floor and was larger than the rest, although his parents room was the largest. It stretched from the front of the house to the back. Jaxon's father had said it was important to be able to see around the pack grounds. Of course being a pack house the rooms had to be large enough to hold the fifty pack members. The kitchen had a table that ran full length and could seat them all. Not that it was used that much. Pack members would eat when they were hungry and quite often would have their food cooked on an open fire, although meat was always cooked rare. Jaxon could hear Carlton behind him, he knew what was coming. Another lecture on letting his hair down and having fun. Carlton didn't quite get the whole Alpha thing, probably because it had happened over night. One day they were messing about having fun, and the next Jaxon's in charge and fun had gone out the window.

"Jax, look I know you're under a lot of pressure, but you need to let your hair down. Let's go into town tonight, have a few drinks, a game of pool. You never know, we might both get laid." Carlton looked at his best friend with pleading eye's. "Come on it will do you good."

Jaxon sighed, getting pissed wasn't going to help him, but then again, maybe there'd be some new eye candy to chase, not that he had to chase anyone, they always chased him. "Yeah sure, see you at 7pm." Jaxon made his way up to his room and flopped down on the bed, he stared blankly at the ceiling. What would it be like to meet a girl that he had to chase, his father always said despite him and his mum being true mates, she still made him work for her affections. He guessed he would never know, tonight he'll go into town, get pissed and screw the prettiest girl in the bar. Just as he closed his eyes there was a knock at the door, he knew who it was, wolves could smell who approached long before they saw them. "Not now Gene, I'm busy." Jaxon shouted without moving.

"O, come on Jaxon, we haven't had any fun for ages, open the door." Gene replied.

Jaxon stood up and flung the door open, "I said not..."

There standing in the doorway was a scantily clad Gene showing a lot more than she should have. "But I made such an effort." Gene fluttered her eye lashes and twiddled her long blue hair between her fingers.

Jaxon grabbed her hand and pulled her into his bedroom, slamming the door behind him. He knew he shouldn't, he knew it would give her false hope, but any single red-blooded wolf would have done the same thing.

"So……" Carlton paused, "I hear you had a busy afternoon. Gene seems to think she's gonna be Luna?"

"No. She's not, and I know what you're gonna say, and yes you're right, but she turned up practically naked at my door." Jaxon sighed. "You would've done the exact same thing."

"You're my best friend Jaxon, I love you like a brother, but dude, you're playing with fire, she's not gonna take rejection laying down, I mean I know that's her favourite position but mate, think, if you take someone else then there's no telling what she will do, I'd fear for the Luna you chose."

"Look I'll talk to her…… tomorrow, okay? Right now, I'm gonna shower, meet you in an hour." Jaxon walked back upstairs to his room, he looked at the state of the bed. In temper he ripped the sheets off, took them downstairs and threw them on to the front lawn, he caught Gene watching from a window, so to make it loud and clear to her and everyone else at the pack house, he then proceeded to set fire to them. "I have not chosen my Luna, and I will not have anyone spreading rumours." And with that he stormed back towards the pack house, stopping briefly when he caught a scent, wild honey suckle with a mix of cupcakes, he breathed in the sweet aroma but as quickly as it came it was gone. For some strange reason Jaxon's pulse started to race, shaking himself he put it out of his mind and continued up the stairs to get ready for his night out.

CHAPTER 6

Destiny's first glimpse of Valley Falls was the sign she had seen in her dream.

    Welcome to Valley falls, Maine, USA
    the land of the White Pine and the honeybee

Before she knew it, she was looking at the rows of quaint houses as the taxi sped through the town, stopping outside a little bed and breakfast. As she exited the taxi Mr's Richards appeared, standing at her side.

"Oh Mrs Richards, were did you come -"

"This is your hometown Destiny, you was born just down the road in a little cabin, on the outskirts of the forest, I'll show you around tomorrow dear, let's go in and get settled first." Mrs Richards rudely cut in.

"I thought you lived here. Why are we stopping at a bed and breakfast?" Destiny asked as she looked up at the sign.

"This is where I live dear, it's my business, now come on, it's getting dark, let's get you settled and I'll treat you to dinner, we have a bar down the street that does the best ribs in the county, not that I can eat them with my teeth." Mr's Richards waved to the taxi driver and smiled at Destiny before she led her in.

Her room looked dark and dingy, Destiny decided it needed a complete makeover, it was like something from the 1700's it was a pleasant surprise however when Mrs Richards flicked on the light switch. She really wasn't expecting the place to have electricity.

"Bathrooms down the hall dear, now, get yourself cleaned up and we will leave shortly."

Destiny stood and watched the old woman leave, not knowing what to do. The place gave her the creeps, she didn't want to stay here on her own. Suddenly overwhelmed by the situation Destiny started to cry. She wanted her mum, she wanted her bedroom, she wanted to go back to the UK, the only place she knew as home.

Destiny was grateful for Mr's Richards help, not only had she helped her sell her parents' house, which gave her a little bit of money in the bank, she also talked her through her families traditions, and taught her to control her magic. Destiny could now do some spells without speaking, she was taught to defend herself and taught when and why to use magic. Mr's Richards told her never to use it for bad and never give it away for free. If someone wanted a spell from you, they had to pay. Normally in body parts or things that would be handy for future spells. Destiny didn't like the sound of that, but she was most defiantly a witch, so she would at some point have to do what was expected. She had continued having the dreams, always ending the same way, the black wolf lunging towards her, and she would always wake up in a pool of sweat. But she never told Mr's Richards, she didn't know what to say. Although the dream scared her, she wasn't afraid of the wolf.

Once the house was sold and the plane ticket was bought, Destiny packed up her few belongings, her family photo album, and the few clothes she had and headed off to a new life, a different life and a life that still held so much mystery. The hardest part was leaving her mum, okay so she was dead, Destiny reasoned, but she was there, buried in the local church yard. It was a place to visit, and she had many times. Destiny would sit on the cold ground and tell her mother of her days events, even asking for advice. But none came, nothing but silence in her head. Destiny swallowed down her sadness. She had to remember her mother was in her heart and that was where she would keep her.

"Are you ready dear?" Mr's Richards called up the stairs. "It's 7pm we need to get going so we get a table."

"Just coming." Destiny gave herself the once over in the long mirror and smiled, content with her appearance, she slipped on her shoes and went to join the old woman.

Jaxon walked to the bar and grabbed a stool, shouting over to the barman for a bottle of whiskey, being a wolf, it took a lot to get him drunk, so he always bought by the bottle.

The barman gave Jaxon the bottle and slid two glasses in front of him. "Enjoy Alpha." He called as he walked away.

Jaxon noticed Magnus at the end of the bar, drunk as usual, he didn't know if he had ever seen him sober. He understood he had lost his daughter, but at the end of the day he was a mighty warlock. He should have known what was going to happen before it did. But the main thing was as a mighty warlock he should have kept his families promise and delivered his daughter to the Alpha. Jaxon felt his temper rising, so he focused back on the whiskey, he poured Carlton and himself a large measure, just as the door opened and he smelt the same sweet smell he had been smelling on and off all day, wild honey suckle and cupcakes.

Mr's Richards ushered a shy Destiny through the door. As Destiny stumbled in, she stopped dead, all eyes were on her. Everyone stopped talking and just stared. Destiny spotted the drunk at the end of the bar, 'there's always one' she thought. Then she watched as a man turned around to look at her. His face was perfect, sculpted by the gods, as her eyes dropped to take in all of him, she could see his body matched his looks. As she looked back up his face was neutral, no smile, no frown, nothing. She was surprised to smell pine forest and freshly fallen rain, with a hint of musk, she knew it was him, but she didn't know why she could smell him. Must be a witch thing, she decided. She took a deep breath, then followed Mr's Richards to the middle of the floor.

"Everyone, I would like to introduce Destiny... Destiny Black, your daughter Magnus, and your property Alpha." Mrs Richards announced.

Destiny watched in horror as the drunk, which was obviously her father, attempted to slide off of the bar stool and stand up. Only he ended up in a heap on the floor. That's when the room erupted with laugher, and that's when Destiny lost her temper. As she stormed towards her father her anger rolled off of her in waves causing the lights to flicker. "Firstly Mr's Richards if you've brought me here to make a laughingstock of me and him." Destiny pointed at Magnus, who was attempting to right himself. "Then you have seriously messed up, and secondly, as far as the Alpha is concerned, I am no one's property, least of all a dogs." Destiny bent down to her father's side and looked at him. "When you're sober, if that's even possible, come and find me Magnus."

JAXON WATCHED as the girl stood up, she was beautiful, and he knew before she had said a word, she was Magnus's daughter. Her smell had filled his whole body, it was confusing him. Was this a witch trick? He knew witches were never to be trusted. His anger grew, not only was she trying to put him under a spell, but she had also just called him a dog in front of half of his pack. He couldn't let that slide. He couldn't be seen to be weak, plus she was a witch. He hated witches, they always took more than they should. Jaxon stood up and walked over to Destiny just as she stood up. "Firstly young lady, and I use that term loosely, I do own you, but don't worry, I certainly don't want you, and if you ever refer to me or any of my pack as dogs again, I will rip your throat out, and that's your one and only warning, now get out of my sight." Jaxon watched as Destiny marched out of the bar and then took his seat next to Carlton. "Another bottle Jim."

"Wow, that's the most entertainment we've had around here like in ever!" Carlton commented. "Fancy her coming in and announcing magnus is her dad and she isn't your property, and who was she talking too?"

"I don't know, and I don't care, now can we talk about something else." Jaxon necked his drink and poured another.

"Okay what's going on Jaxon, if any other person were to call you a dog you would have killed them there and then on the spot." Carlton took a swig of his whiskey before continuing. "You like her."

Jaxon realised it was a statement and not a question. "No I don't now drop it." Jaxon poured another glassful ready to neck it but before he had a chance Carlton continued.

"Well if you don't, I might have a crack at it."

Jaxon grabbed Carlton and threw him across the floor and started to shift.

"Jesus Jaxon, stop man, what's going on." Carltons face was a mixture of shock and hurt, which stopped Jaxon from attacking him. Instead he bound through the door and out into the street, he ran, only stopping when he caught up with Destiny.

DESTINY TURNED and looked into his eyes, she knew who the wolf was, after all she had seen him many times in her dreams. "Decided to rip my throat out after all then?"

Jaxon surprised her by shifting back to his human form, Destiny watched with horror as his body changed, the sound of bones cracking filled her ears, finally he stood up naked. "Omg cover yourself up, omg."

Jaxon rolled his eyes. "Haven't you seen a naked man before?"

"NO! I'm seventeen for Christ sake." Destiny turned around so she could no longer see him, but she couldn't shake the image from her mind, she had seen smaller baguettes in the bakers, she knew he was big but to be that big all over, quite honestly it took her breath away.

"It's covered now witch." Jaxon replied as he placed his hands over his penis.

Destiny turned around and glared at him. "Witch?" As she looked down her anger turned to embarrassment. "I thought you meant you had clothes on."

"Well as you can see I haven't. Anyway, the reason I'm here is to tell you you've got 24 hours and then I want you gone. You don't belong here." Jaxon then turned, shifted, and sprinted off into the distance while Destiny watched.

Fighting back her tears, which she put down to anger, Destiny ran up the steps and through the door slamming it shut behind her, she leant back closing her eyes as the tears dripped from her cheeks.

JAXON SHIFTED and made his way back to the packhouse, he knew he would have to apologise to Carlton, he planned on doing it in the morning, tonight he wanted to think about Destiny, but before he got a chance he caught Carltons scent, coming up the stairs towards his door. Jaxon leapt up and opened his bedroom door then stood back allowing Carlton access.

"What the hell happened tonight, Jaxon? We've been friends since we were kids and we have never fallen out." Carlton stood opposite Jaxon waiting for a reply.

Jaxon looked at his best friend, his Beta, the one person he trusted more that anyone. But how could he tell him the effect Destiny had on him when he didn't know himself. "It's complicated Carlton."

"No, it's not, just speak to me, it's the girl, has she put a spell on you?"

"NO! no that's not what's going on, look give me time to process it, I need to work it out in my own mind first." Jaxon sighed. "I need a good night's sleep. Carlton, we can speak tomorrow."

"You're in denial Jaxon, when you trust me again and can be honest with me then let me know, until then don't bother." Carlton went to walk out but Jaxon grabbed his arm stopping him.

Jaxon shook his head. "She's mine.... My true mate."

CHAPTER 7

Destiny rolled over in bed, she hadn't slept much, after Mr's Richard's came home, Destiny had questioned her on her motives for bringing her here and why she had disappeared from the diner. Why she had shown Magnus up like that and why she had announced she was the Alpha's property. None of it made sense. Didn't she say Destiny got to choose if she mated with the Alpha, so why the announcement? And then there was the Alpha, one-minute threatening to rip her throat out, the next exposing himself to her, and then kicking her out of town. Well she wasn't going. Alpha or not she would never be pushed around by a dog. "Dog, dog, dog." She called out and then smiled. No, she wouldn't be told what to do. She turned her attention to her future. She needed a job, a job and somewhere to live. As kind as it was for Mrs Richards to put her up, she couldn't shake the feeling that bad things had happened here. It was a feeling that unnerved her enough to barricade the door when she went to bed. Today she would have a look around and see if there were any vacancies' going, for work and accommodation. And then she would go and look for Magnus, he was her father after all, even if he were the town drunk, and in need of a wash and of course, is a total embarrassment.

Jaxon had been running for just over an hour. Carlton thought it would do him good to go for a run together, in wolf form. When they came to the clearing in the forest further up the hillside, they both stopped and shifted back to human form.

"Feel any better?" Carlton asked as he lay on the ground next to his friend. "So who is she?"

"She's the first-born daughter of Magnus, well his only daughter as far as I know. She's a witch and she was promised to my father for his first-born son, which is me. It's something that was started centuries ago, to keep the blood lines of wolves going. If we don't find our true mates we can't have pup's, but with a witch we can, a spell was done that can never be broken, but then when she was born her mother took her away, it drove Magnus mad. My father blamed him, but it wasn't his fault, it was her mothers."

"Wow Jaxon, that's huge, so she's your Luna?" Carlton sat up and looked down at his friend.

"I can't stop thinking about her, one minute the witch part disgusts me, the next minute I'm getting a raging boner…... I always thought about her as the backup plan, and here she is, the main and the back up." Jaxon shook his head. "I don't know what to think or do, all I know is if another man touches her, I will kill him, so she has to go."

"Sounds to me like you should get to know her before you make any decisions, either way, she's here and you have that mate bond, whether you like it or not she's your only chance of having pup's." Carlton rested back on his elbows.

"It's not that straight forward Carlton, I would never have a witch as my Luna, no matter how desperate I was." Jaxon stood up and looked across the clearing. "Even Gene would make a better Luna than her."

"You don't have feelings for Gene though, do you. Just think about what you're doing, don't make any rash decisions. Okay?"

"Okay." Jaxon replied, more confused than ever.

"Anyway, I'll race you back." Carlton jumped up and started shifting with Jaxon following suit, the sound of cracking bones rang out in the forest as both men landed on four legs.

DESTINY WALKED down the stairs and straight out of the front door. As she continued down the sidewalk she came face to face with Mr's Richards. Stood next to her was the tall, elegant woman that was in the photo, she was the one holding on to Magnus's arm. Her hair was the same colour as Destiny's, and it was put up in a neat chignon bun. She looked wealthy; her clothes certainly weren't from the local store.

"Destiny, just in time, this is your Aunt Edna, your fathers sister, Edna, your niece, Destiny."

Destiny stared at the woman, annoyed that she had been cornered yet again. "Look I'm sorry but I'm in a bit of a hurry, maybe we could be properly introduced later." Destiny side stepped the two women and headed off on her mission to find a job. She let out a deep sigh, how many more people were gonna pop out of the woodwork, she had enough just dealing with her drunken father and the up his own arse Alpha. Destiny giggled at the thought, she was sure if he could, he would. He loved himself, standing there in front of her naked. She bet he did that with all the girls. Feeling slightly jealous she berated herself, whatever he did was of no concern to her. She felt a hand on her arm, bringing her out of her thoughts.

"Destiny, sweetheart, please. I'm your dad's sister, Edna, come and have a coffee with me, just fifteen minutes out of your day." Edna smiled, a warm friendly smile.

Destiny felt uncomfortable, not because of Edna, but because of herself. Edna seemed nice; she could sense that she was being sincere. "Fine, fifteen minutes and then I really must get on, but I don't like coffee, I like tea."

Edna smiled broadly and then led Destiny to the little coffee shop, it was the one from her dream, it didn't even surprise her, nothing would surprise her anymore. "I dreamt about this place, its exactly how I saw it in my dream." Destiny looked at the selection of cakes in the window, there wasn't as many as the shop she worked in back in the UK. Destiny could feel Edna studying her.

"Would you like a cake to go with your tea?" Edna asked.

"Okay, I'll have one of those cream doughnuts please." Destiny hadn't planned on eating anything, but she couldn't help herself, cream cakes were her weakness plus she hadn't eaten since the airport. Destiny looked around the quaint room as she walked inside, it was larger than it looked from the outside, and had eight round tables dotted around. The counter was wooden painted white to match the walls, and had glass displays underneath, showing off all the delicious goodies on offer. The flowery curtains that lined the windows were full of colour and matched the tablecloths that dressed each table. Each table had four white wooden chairs neatly tucked underneath and had the same matching pattern on the seat cushions. The finishing touch was a little dish with white pinecones in, placed in the centre of each table making the place smell like a pine forest. Destiny wondered if they picked fresh ones daily, to get such a wonderful aroma.

Edna led her to a table and pulled out a chair for her. "Thanks.... It's a lovely coffee shop." Destiny sat and continued to take in the room until the drinks arrived.

"Here you go deary." the elderly shop assistant said as she placed Destiny's cup of tea in front of her, followed by the cream doughnut.

"Thank you." Destiny looked at her aunt. "What do you want from me?" She watched as Edna looked a little shocked.

"You're my niece Destiny. Surely it's obvious?"

"Not to me it isn't, Aunt Edna, so please enlighten me." Destiny took a huge bite of the cream doughnut and felt the cream slide off of her chin. Sighing loudly, she grabbed a napkin and dabbed at the now spreading stain.

"I want to get to know my niece, I've missed out on seventeen years, so has Magnus, your father." Edna smiled as she watched destiny rub at her dress, making the stain bigger.

"He looked like he was coping well, last night, you know, when he fell on the floor." Destiny looked pointedly at her aunt.

"Right young lady you can drop the attitude right now, when you disappeared your father spent the first five years trying everything in his power to find you, he drove himself almost insane.... That's when he started drinking, to blot out the pain of missing you and your mum. He loved her too you know." Edna looked away as the tears pricked her eyes.

Destiny had the good grace to look ashamed. She could see the tears forming in her aunts eyes. God she could be such a spoilt bitch at times. "I'm sorry, I guess it's been worse for you, I've only had to deal with this recently, I know I feel resentment towards my mum for having lied to me."

"Don't resent your mother Destiny, she did what she thought was right, she loved you as much as Magnus, it's just unfortunate, someone lied to her and that's why she went. Anyway, I don't want to go over the past, I want to build a future with you.... So, what are your plans for today?" Edna sipped her coffee.

Destiny could see Edna watching her over the rim of her coffee cup, she was definitely drinking in more about Destiny than she did her coffee. "I need to find a job, that's first on the list, then I can find somewhere to live, while I stay here, I'm not sure how long that will be." Destiny picked up the doughnut ready to have another bite but stopped when her aunt spoke.

"What did you do before you came here?" Edna asked.

"I baked cakes in a little tea shop, a bit like this, I always thought I would end up owning my own one day, but that's not gonna happen now."

Edna clapped her hands together "I think it's your lucky day! Do you see the woman that served us?"

Destiny nodded.

"Well she is retiring at the end of the month, how would you feel about working here, you would have free reign to bake whatever you like, and there's a flat above the shop you can have, what do you say?"

"You can't just offer me a job, what will the owner say?" Destiny stared at her aunt. "Wait…. You are the owner?"

Edna nodded, the grin spreading across her face. "I will be here when its busy, helping, but you will, as I said have free reign, what do you say?"

"Okay, deal." Destiny picked her doughnut up and took another huge bite, the cream splodged around her mouth and stuck to her nose this time. Before she had time to wipe it away the door pinged open.

Jaxon entered the coffee shop with Carlton following close behind. He spotted Destiny, of course he knew she was in there, he could smell her before he even got to town. Seeing her startled with the cream all around her mouth he smiled. "You don't look so dainty when you eat then?" Laughing he turned to the old woman and ordered two coffees. All the time wishing he could walk over and lick the cream off of her beautiful face. Once finished at the counter the two men joined Edna and Destiny at their table, without being asked. "Edna." Jaxon nodded. "Nice to see you."

"Alpha." Edna returned the nod. "It's always a pleasure to see you."

Turning his attention to Destiny and her now clean face he smiled. "So have you packed yet?"

"Packed?" Edna asked, looking at Destiny.

"Oh didn't I mention the Alpha here has banished me from this town, I have 24 hours to leave." Destiny glared at Jaxon and then smiled at Edna. "Of course I'm not going though."

"You don't belong here." Jaxon argued. "We already have a warlock, not that he is much use. I don't need any more dead weight in this town."

Before she could answer Edna replied. "Oh that seems such a shame Alpha, Destiny already has a new job."

"New job. So, you're planning on staying then?" Jaxon could feel his heart racing at the thought of her defying him, on the one hand he felt anger but on the other he felt relief.

"Only for the time being, until I decide to leave." Destiny put on a fake smile and made sure he knew it.

Before Jaxon could answer he stood up abruptly and took a deep breath. "Stay in here, do not go outside. Carlton?"

Carlton nodded. "Blood suckers."

Destiny looked at her aunt confused. "What, leeches?"

"Yeah, the two-legged kind, now stay in here. Edna, watch her." Jaxon walked out onto the sidewalk and watched as a black Sudan pulled up, with Carlton standing by his side.

Destiny watched out of the window, despite Edna trying to pull her away, she watched as two men, and two woman exited the car. "Aunt Edna, who are they?" She whispered.

"They are vampires, Destiny come away from the window, please."

"Why aren't they going poof in the daylight?"

"That's a myth, as long as it's not direct sun they are fine, now please Destiny, they will see you, come away."

"Are all vampires that good looking, even the men are beautiful?" Destiny scrunched her face up to get a better look at the vampire who was driving. "He's almost as good looking as Jax...." Destiny stopped herself from finishing the sentence, embarrassed that she was caught out. She turned to her aunt and noticed the smug smile on her face. "What?"

"Oh, come on Destiny, I could see from the moment he walked in the door you liked him, and him you. Look child, what will be will be, as Doris Day would say Que Sera. Sera."

"Who? Please tell me she's not another relative." Destiny rolled her eyes; these relatives were coming out of the woodwork everywhere.

Edna laughed. "She's a famous singer from the sixty's, was in a lot of films too, we will have to watch one together."

"Oh great, sounds fun." Destiny rolled her eyes and then refocused her attention on the group outside. The driver was handsome, and dressed in a suit with a matching tie, he reminded her of a film star, what was his name, ahh yeah, Luke Perry, whereas Jaxon was more of a Brad Pitt, but with more sex appeal than any film star could possibly have. Destiny found her insides tingling at the mere thought. Shaking herself, she tried to concentrate on what they were saying and not how sexy Jaxon was, but her lip-reading skills were null and void. "Aunt Edna, is there a spell so I can hear what they are saying?"

"Yes, there is, but I'm not teaching it to you now. Now come away Destiny, this looks serious."

CHAPTER 8

Jaxon was standing face to face with the vampire that had been driving. "I thought we agreed you would stay in the main town William."

"Jaxon, it's good to see you too." The vampire laughed. "It's not a social call, can we talk. I see we have an audience." William nodded towards the coffee shop window. "Maybe we could speak in there? I'm sure she wouldn't mind."

Jaxon cursed under his breath, why couldn't Destiny just sit down and shut up, of course the blood sucker would have heard every word she said, he had too. That was one of the perks of being a supernatural, wolves not only had a superior smell they also had superior hearing, it was just unfortunate that the bloodsuckers did too, although not as good as a wolves. "You can come in, but the others can stay out here." Jaxon mind linked to Carlton "Watch the others, I don't know them."

Carlton nodded and stood watching them.

Destiny jumped when she noticed the vampire looking straight at her. Stepping back she tripped and started to fall backwards when two strong arms caught her, sending shockwaves through her body at the touch. When she looked up, she was surprised to see Jaxon holding her. He didn't look happy though, far from it.

Jaxon sat Destiny down on the chair, and then refocused on the vampire standing behind him.

"And who is this little beauty?" William asked as he reached out to shake Destiny's hand, however before he made contact Jaxon moved in front of Destiny blocking his way. "Ah, she is yours then."

Jaxon nodded, then without making eye contact he spoke to Edna. "Edna take Destiny upstairs." Jaxon waited until the women had disappeared from sight before continuing. "We agreed you wouldn't turn up here with strangers William, it unsettles the pack."

"I'm only here on business Jaxon, to warn you." William replied.

"Warn me?" Jaxon let out a low growl, showing his displeasure.

"Calm down, we are friends Jaxon, we have fought side by side. If I didn't value our friendship I wouldn't be here." William pointed to a seat. "May I?"

Jaxon nodded and then sat facing him. "Okay…. so, what do you wanna warn me about?"

"I have reports of a couple of rouge vamps, feeding on super naturals, at first I didn't believe it, but then as each report came in, I went to check the bodies, they were all drained dry and mummified."

"So, we hunt them down and kill them." Jaxon replied dryly, he couldn't see what all the fuss was about.

"You don't understand my friend, when a vampire feeds on a human, it gives him power, fresh blood, the elixir of life and all that. When I vampire feeds on a supernatural it gives him ten times the power because obviously the blood is more powerful, put that together with the mummification, we are looking at vampires with some sort of magic."

It suddenly hit Jaxon just how bad this could be, if more vamps joined them, they could quite easily wipe out the wolves, and Destiny, he had to protect Destiny, after all she's supernatural. "Why aren't the Vampire council taking care of this?"

"They sent an army of six to find them only one came back. They let him go with a message to the elders of the council, 'if you come for us, we will come for you' that was carved into the vampires stomach. It wouldn't heal.... he died a couple of days later. So now we have a vampire council that will not lift a finger because they are scared and if they are scared my friend then you know how bad the situation is."

"How long has this been happening?" Jaxon looked up to the ceiling, he knew Destiny was listening in.

"We think the first killing was all hallows eve."

"And you're only just telling me now because?" Jaxon's temper started to rise, bawling his fists he jumped up and started to pace the room.

"We couldn't make sense of what was happening, like I said the vampire council thought they could deal with it, but now it's way out of hand, that's why I'm here, we need to work together Jaxon. Something bad is coming, I can feel it, and I think it's coming here." William rubbed his neck, a sure sign he was worried.

Jaxon watched closely; he could sense the worry radiating from the vampire. "Have you been tracking them?"

"Yes, but that's not the only reason I think they're coming here, well not now anyway, when I drove into town I could sense a great power, I can't pinpoint it but it's definitely here and its definitely close and it's definitely old." This time William rubbed his temple. "If they get hold of this power then all of humanity is finished, human and supernatural."

"And the Vampire Council knows this?" Jaxon knew the elders were weak, their only power they had was the red tape they used to confuse people with.

"They won't listen, they have shut themselves away in the vaults underneath the Kremlin, like the cowards they are. Hiding. Hoping someone else will sort their problems." William shrugged his shoulders but had the good manners to look ashamed, not for himself but for the vampires that ruled.

"Okay, we need to find the source of the ancient power and neutralise that, hopefully that will stop whatever plans they have and then find them and kill them." At the same time as Jaxon was talking, he could only think of saving one person.... Destiny.

"I think we should also call Anubis and Hera." William added.

"I think we should hold off for now. Let's find out what we can first." Jaxon replied.

"Agreed, right Jaxon, I'll be off now, I'm staying in a motel about a fifteen-minute drive down the freeway, you have my number, when I get an update, I will let you know."

"Okay…. And William, thanks for the warning."

William bowed his head slightly and left the coffee shop.

"You can come down now." Jaxon turned to watch Destiny walk down the stairs. "Do you always listen into other people's conversations?"

"It's not my fault if you talk so loud, try whispering or better still don't have it in a public coffee shop." Destiny folded her arms and stood defiant.

Jaxon felt his heckles rise yet again. "You do know I'm the Alpha, you do know that means you show me respect, you shouldn't even be making eye contact, never mind talking to me like that."

"Are you for real?" Destiny laughed. "Of all the self-conceited arseholes about, I have to meet the BIGGEST!"

Edna tried to intervene. "Destiny please don't shout at the Alpha."

"Aunt Edna, keep out of this, this is between me and Mr shit bag here."

"I suggest you stop acting like a spoilt brat, no wonder your dads a drunk, poor blokes trying to blot out the memory of you." as soon as Jaxon said it, he regretted it.

"I think you should go Jaxon." Destiny could feel her eyes misting up, she didn't want to cry, she had cried enough when her mum had died, she didn't want this jerk having the satisfaction of seeing her hurt feelings. "Before you go dog, who is Anubis and Hera."

"You just can't help yourself, can you? I tell you what, as you know everything you tell me." Jaxon turned on his heels and marched out of the door. He paused as heard Edna speak.

"Destiny, you can't keep talking to the Alpha like that, he has a position to consider." Edna pulled out a chair and nodded for Destiny to sit on it. "I'll make some fresh tea."

"He started it." Destiny squeezed her eyes together to stop the tears, but it didn't work, they started as small sobs and then the flood gates opened.

Jaxon listened as his chest tightened. He opened the door and sat down next to Destiny, then handed her a tissue. When she opened her eyes they were red and blotchy. He had done that to her, he had done that to his mate. "I'm sorry Destiny, I should never have said that about your dad, it was wrong of me."

Destiny nodded between sods. "I...I.... shouldn't have called you a dog, I'm .... sorry."

"Shhh, please don't cry, I feel so bad for upsetting you." Jaxon wiped Destiny's eyes for her, glad that the tears were starting to stop.

"It's not just what you said, I mean, it was a bit, but I lost my mum and stepdad, last Halloween, in a car accident, I've been sad since then." Destiny blew her nose and looked at Jaxon. "What's wrong?"

"I lost my parents on the same night." Jaxon wondered if everything was linked, he knew it was a long shot but what were the odds of both of them losing their parents on the same night in the same way. "We need to speak to Magnus. EDNA!'"

"What's wrong Alpha?" Edna asked as she rushed back from the kitchen.

"We need to speak to Magnus; do you know where he is?"

"I think he's living in the woods, I'm not sure where, he had a little camp last time he let me see him, but he moves it around and puts a cloaking spell on it so no one see's it." Edna thought for a minute and then smiled. "Destiny, I'm sure if you call, he will answer, you may have to travel around the forest but I'm sure Alpha will go with you."

Destiny glared at her aunt. "And why can't you come with me?"

"What's the matter cupcake, scared?" Jaxon asked, grinning.

"No and stop calling me cupcake. I'll go on my own. I certainly don't need a babysitter." Destiny stood up and threw Jaxon's tissue back at him.

Jaxon caught her hand and pulled her closer to him. "You do realise how big the forest is, you'd be lost in an hour and then the town would have to send a search party."

"I'll take a map and a compass." Destiny's reply even had her aunt laughing.

"A map and a compass? You've got this covered. Just be careful of the wolves that live out there, they don't like strangers and it's been a tough winter, they may be hungry." Jaxon walked towards the door he knew she would call him back, as he grabbed the handle, he heard her annoyingly cute, sexy voice.

"Wait! Fine, you can come, but don't be bossing me around." Destiny didn't normally backdown but the thought of being eaten by a wild animal was enough to persuade her.

"Go get changed, wear Jeans and sneakers, I'll meet you back outside here in 20 minutes." Jaxon continued to open the door but stopped when he heard her.

"Which bit of don't boss me about didn't you get?" Destiny whispered under her breath, not realising he would hear her.

"The bit that says I'm the Alpha." Jaxon shut the door behind him and sighed. He knew it was important to see Magnus, he just wished it were with anyone else rather than the witch. She annoyed him, the way she spoke back. The way she ignored his orders. Why couldn't his life be simple. Jaxon wished his father were here, he was the wisest man he had ever known, if only he could ask him now, should he take her as his mate or should he reject her. Just that one thought gave Jaxon a physical pain in his heart, he felt his wolf inside getting angry, he knew his wolf wanted her. His wolf roared and pruned himself at the mere thought of being with Destiny. Jaxon shook his head and went to see Carlton before embarking on his search, more confused than ever.

CHAPTER 9

Destiny reluctantly changed from her dress to a pair of jeans and found her trainers or as Jaxon called them, sneakers, at the bottom of her case. Normally at home she wore jeans all the time, but here for some reason she felt like dressing up; she had no idea why. Making her way back to the coffee shop she noticed Jaxon talking to a woman with long blue hair, she was beautiful, her body was lean, and she was wearing very little clothing. How did she not feel cold? Destiny felt her annoyance rising along with her jealousy. As the woman looked over to Destiny, she scowled and gave her the filthiest look possible, bearing her teeth, before walking away.

"Good you're ready, we'll drive to the edge of town, come on." Jaxon opened the door of his truck and waited for Destiny to climb in.

"Who was that women you were talking to?" Destiny asked.

"Why…. you jealous?" Jaxon grinned.

"Oh please…. I've never seen hair that colour, she's beautiful." Destiny turned to look out of the window, berating herself for asking in the first place.

"Yeah, she certainly is." Jaxon replied.

"Can we just get this over with, we've no need to talk." Destiny attempted to pull the seat belt out, but it was jammed, the harder she pulled the more her frustration grew.

"Hey, stop, let me before you break it." Jaxon lent across Destiny and reached for the seatbelt, slowly pulling it out, he could feel her breath on his cheek, and desperately wanted to turn his head and kiss her. "There, gently does it." Clipping in the seatbelt he then attempted to start the engine, attempt being the right word.

"Maybe if you worked for a living, you could afford a decent motor, you know one that worked." Destiny smirked.

Suddenly the engine sprang to life and Jaxon roared off. "You know you're right, we've no need to talk." After ten minutes of driving Jaxon came to a halt at the pack house. "Do you see all those cars, the Porsche, the Lamborghini, the brand-new SUV, and those over there?"

Destiny nodded but didn't reply.

"Well they are all mine. I own every single one of them. How, do I hear you ask, well that's a good question. I own them because I work for a living, now is there anything else you wanna know, anymore insults you wanna throw at me, because believe me Destiny, your attitude stinks." With that Jaxon roared past the pack house and up a dirt track. "We are in this because it's the best motor for the job."

Destiny felt the same feeling of shame wash over her. Yep the best idea was to not talk, that way she couldn't upset anyone. Instead she leant her head back against the seat and refocused on the view out of the side window. Destiny sat forward when she spotted a dear. The dear jumped and sprinted away through the trees. She turned to tell Jaxon but then remembered the no talking policy. It was then Destiny realised how lonely she was, how lonely she would always be. Weeks, months, or years would never make a difference, her mum was gone, and she would always be alone.

Jaxon watched from the corner of his eye, he could sense the mood change, he could even feel her sadness. "You're not alone cupcake." He told her softly.

Destiny focused on the front windscreen. "Yes, I am."

They continued in silence until Jaxon pulled up just off the track. "We can start from here." jumping out of the truck, Jaxon started to strip.

"What on earth are you doing, this is no time to get naked." Destiny's eyes almost popped out of her head when Jaxon pulled his T-shirt over his head.

Jaxon shook his head in disbelief. "Seriously, we have a job to do. I'm gonna shift and you're gonna get on my back, we'll cover the area a lot faster." Jaxon continued pulling his jeans down.

Destiny turned around trying to put the view out of her mind, but her briefs were already damp.

Jaxon smiled as he smelt her arousal, she had the same effect on him, he could feel himself getting hard, as he slapped himself down, he reminded himself that she's a witch. He started to shift. He padded in front of Destiny like a show horse, standing tall, showing his mate he could protect her. He then crouched and waited for destiny to climb on. As she slipped her arms around his neck, they both felt the electricity course through them, it was a feeling neither of them had felt before, and it was a feeling they both wanted more of.

Jaxon wished he could mind link with her, he would have to shift back if he needed to talk, but then on second thoughts it was probably better they didn't talk, especially after there last conversation.

It was just after seven when they returned back to the truck, Jaxon felt his legs burning after spending the day running, there had been no sign of Magnus, not even with Destiny calling him.

"I think we should drive further up the hill and then make camp." Jaxon said as he pulled on his T-shirt.

"What? Why can't we go back?" Destiny's first thought was about the wild wolves that would eat her and then how cold it was getting; would she freeze to death?

"Look we need to get an early start. I've got some food in the back, and there's a couple of bottles of water. You'll be fine."

"But it's cold." Destiny watched as her breath turned white.

"Get in the truck you'll be warm in no time." Jaxon grabbed the bag of food and the water and climbed in behind the wheel, taking his jacket off he passed it to Destiny. "Put that over you, it will help you warm up quicker. I'll drive to the next spot then we can eat."

Destiny gratefully took the jacket but looking at Jaxon just in his T-shirt made her feel colder. "Look take that back, I don't need you freezing to death, I'll be stranded out here on my own, then the wolves will eat me."

"Why can't you just admit you're worried about me, you don't like the thought of me being cold?" Jaxon turned and looked at Destiny, the more time he spent with her the more he wanted her. "Because that's how I feel about you, I can't stand the thought of you being cold...... or sad, or lonely, or with another man." Jaxon closed his eyes. He had said to much.

Destiny looked down at her hands. "Okay, I don't like the thought of you being cold, now we should get going, it's getting late."

Jaxon opened his mouth to say more but then thought better of it, baby steps he decided, as argumentative as she was, at least she had admitted she was worried about him, yeah, baby steps.

After an hour of driving, listening to the radio, Jaxon pulled off of the track and into another clearing. It was pitch black, and the trees were much thicker here. He jumped out and stretched his legs while walking round to Destiny's door, opening it he reached for her hand.

"What are you doing? you're letting all the warm air out." Destiny shuddered as the cold air hit her.

"Get out and stretch your legs or you'll get cramp, hurry up so we can eat." Jaxon grabbed her hand and pulled her out, lifting her down onto the ground, he kept his arms around her, looking at her beautiful face.

"I'm scared, I want to get back in the truck." Destiny went to turn but Jaxon stopped her.

"Why are you scared, don't you think I would protect you? My wolf would die before he would let anything happen to you."

"But I'm not standing here with your wolf, I'm standing here with you." Destiny shivered as the wind picked up.

"I am the wolf cupcake, now stretch your legs, then we can eat."

Destiny was glad to get back in the truck, it was so cold she had goosebumps in places she never knew existed. "So what's for dinner then?"

"Let's have a look…... we got bread, cheese and ham, chip's and some biscuits and your aunt gave us some cakes." Jaxon laid the food out.

"Wont the chips be cold?" Destiny looked for them but couldn't see them.

"You have hot chips in England?" Jaxon always knew the English were eccentric, but seriously, who would eat hot chips. He picked up a pack of ready salted chips and passed them to Destiny, "We eat them cold here."

"They're not chips, they're crisps." Destiny scrunched her nose up causing Jaxon to laugh.

"No, they're chips, wait do you mean what we would have with steak?"

"Yeah, steak and chips, egg and chips, ham and chips, you get the picture." Destiny sat back and stared at his perfect face.

"We call them French fries." Jaxon took a huge mouthful of ham. "I'm more of a meat eater myself." he mumbled with his mouthful.

It was Destiny's turn to laugh. "Well I can see you're enjoying that."

WHEN THEY HAD FINISHED and cleared away, they both settled down to get some sleep, although they both knew they wouldn't sleep, they couldn't, the air around them was electric.

"Let me just check your door, make sure its locked cupcake." Jaxon said as he slid over and hit the lock button with his right hand while his left rested on Destiny's seat, behind her head. "There, all locked up and safe, just don't rest against the window."

"What? Why? Jaxon, what's out there?" Destiny slid closer to him when she thought she saw movement outside.

Jaxon put his arms around her and pulled her closer to him. "It's okay, you're with me. I won't let anything hurt you." Jaxon pulled her chin up and brushed his lip's against hers.

Destiny shook as their lip's locked, this was her first kiss, her nerves evaporated as she felt Jaxon's tongue probing her mouth. She wanted more, she wanted all of him, everything he had to offer. The whole world melted away as the electricity seeped out around them. It was a feeling Jaxon had never felt before, not with anyone else and he had certainly had a fair few. That one kiss took his breath away, and then it hit him, this was what it was to be mated. This was the first time Jaxon King had ever been in love.

Destiny sat back. "Well, that was…" she stopped, she didn't know how to describe it.

"Fantastic!" Jaxon finished,

"Shh, I heard a noise outside." Destiny pushed Jaxon away, but he held her firmly.

"It's just your imagination, come on, let's have another go." He moved in one more time feeling her lips against his, until a loud bang stopped them.

"GET OFF OF MY DAUGHTER!"

CHAPTER 10

Magnus banged against the window causing both of them to jump. Jaxon let out a low growl, showing his teeth. His eyes started to change, as his wolf fought to come out. How dare this piece of garbage come between him and his mate. Jaxon pushed his wolf away, as much as he wanted to rip Magnus apart, he knew he couldn't, but he could still let Magnus know how he felt.

"Magnus?" Destiny asked as she unlocked the door, but before she could get out Jaxon was standing in front of her. "Jaxon, what are you doing? we came here for answers, remember?"

"Fine but were picking that straight back up after." He turned and faced Magnus. "You're a hard man to find."

"Not really, my daughter found me…. Destiny look at you, all grown up." Magnus took a step nearer to his daughter, but Jaxon moved blocking his way again.

"Seriously will you two stop this. Magnus, we need you to come back with us, we need to speak to you about recent events." Destiny looked at both men, waiting to see which one played up first, sure enough it was Jaxon.

"He can make his own way back. He's not coming with us."

Jaxon folded his arms and stood guard over not only Destiny but also his truck.

Magnus ignored Jaxon and continued to stare at his daughter, he could briefly sense her last night in the bar, but he was so drunk he couldn't focus on her face, especially as at the time, he was face down on the floor. He could see a resemblance to her mother, the beauty was there, the eyes were her double, that same amazing green colour with flecks of silver running through them, like beautiful emeralds, shimmering on a summers day. Magnus wanted to pinch himself, just to make sure this moment was real, he was certain he would never see her again, and yet here she stood, larger than life, right in front of him.

"Magnus?" Destiny looked at the man that was her father, he was taller than she remembered from last night, although to be fair he went from stool to floor in 0.5 seconds, so she didn't really have time to tell. His eyes were a dark brown, virtually the same colour as his hair. He had a strong jaw line, not as strong as Jaxon's but still well defined. His hair was long and looked in desperate need of a wash along with the rest of him.

"MAGNUS!" Jaxon shouted, annoyed that he hadn't answered Destiny.

Magnus winced; his head was still suffering from the after effects of the alcohol he had consumed last night. In fact, he needed another, just to get him through the day. "Jesus Jaxon, quit shouting." Magnus rubbed his forehead, but it didn't help. "Destiny, it's cold out here, come to my place, it's warm and there's food, you can stay the night…… in separate rooms." Magnus looked pointedly at Jaxon, there was no way he was gonna let him pick up where he had left off. Magnus could see where his hands were heading, and there would be none of that, not on his watch.

Jaxon was about to say no, they would stay at the pack house, when Destiny beat him to it with a yes.

"Yes, that's really kind of you Magnus, isn't it Jaxon?" Destiny looked at Jaxon and caught him scowling at her father. "I said isn't it Jaxon?"

"Yeah, really kind, thanks…. Maggot…nus." Jaxon grinned at

the jibe he had given until he saw Destiny's face, her eyebrows were raised in a questioning stare and her mouth was set in a straight line.

Magnus smiled, she was sticking up for her dad, this was the second time in his life that he felt like a father. The first was when Destiny was born, it was a feeling like no other, the feeling of pure love coursing through his body. Then she was taken, and that feeling was stolen from him and replaced by longing. That's why he drank, to take the emptiness away. But here she is, standing only a few feet away from him, agreeing to stay the night at his, and putting the mut in his place.

"That's great, it's only a ten-minute drive." Magnus looked at Jaxon, he knew this was killing him.

"Okay, shall we go then?" Destiny glanced between Magnus and Jaxon, waiting for Jaxon to answer. "Unless you'd rather we walk Jaxon?"

"Fine. Get in." Jaxon opened the door for Destiny and watched her arse as she climbed up the step and into the truck, which was one view he would never get tired of. He turned and glared at Magnus as he walked round to the driver's side and jumped in.

The atmosphere in the cab was strained, to say the least, and they were all pleased when Magus told them they were there. Jaxon marched to the passenger door and yanked it open, he stood back and waited for Magnus to exit the vehicle before barging him out of the way so he could help his mate out safely. After all, no maggot will ever come between him and his mate. Jaxon lifted Destiny down, and placed her on the ground, breathing in her scent of wild honey suckle and cupcakes. All he wanted to do was whisk her away to the pack house and his bed, that's where she belonged. Not here, not with Magnus.

"Ok sweetheart, welcome home." Magnus beamed to Destiny, pointing to a clump of trees, and thickly grown undergrowth.

Looking at Jaxon, to see if he could see the same as her, he looked just as puzzled as she did. "You live in a tree?" Destiny asked.

"Oh." Magnus laughed. "Silly me." He waved his hands, and, in a flash, a little cottage appeared where the trees had once been.

Destiny and Jaxon looked at each other, both amazed. Jaxon knew Magnus was a once powerful warlock, his father had told him stories of the magnificent things he had done for the pack, it was only when he had lost Destiny his powers had faded, or so everyone had thought. Was Destiny as powerful as her father, he wondered. That would be a bonus to the pack, not that it would make any difference, he had already made his mind up, witch or not, she was his.

Magnus led the way to the front door, turning to face Destiny as he pushed it open. "Welcome home Destiny. This is where you were born."

"I thought Aunt Edna said I was born on the edge of the forest, near town?" Destiny asked, confused. Her mother had also told her she was born in the UK.

"Follow me." Magnus led them into a long hallway, where there were stairs to the left and a door to the right, and directly in front of them a long passageway with another door at the end marked town. Heading straight down the passageway, Magnus stopped, and turned to his daughter. "Open the door, Destiny."

Jaxon pulled Destiny back and grabbed the handle himself, he wasn't letting his mate open a door that could lead to danger.

"Jaxon, what…" Before Destiny had finished Jaxon had already pulled the door open, and there just outside almost opposite was the bar, in all its glory, they could all hear the jukebox playing and the chatter of the people drinking inside.

"How is this possible?" Destiny turned to her father. "We drove for nearly two hours through the forest looking for you, how can we be back at town?"

"It's magic Destiny, magic of which you are capable. I could feel your power when you walked into the bar." Magnus smiled; he could see she was impressed.

"I'm surprised you could feel anything after falling on the floor, drunk." Jaxon reminded him.

Destiny stepped in when she felt the tension heighten between them once again. "Okay, maybe we should have that chat, it's late and I'm tired."

Magnus led them back through to a cosy lounge, it had an open fire that was burning brightly, a comfy sofa with two matching chairs and a desk tucked in the corner, piled high with books. On closer examination, Destiny realised they were spell books. Sitting back on the sofa, and kicking off her sneakers, Destiny frowned when Jaxon sat next to her, his leg touching hers, sending shockwaves through her body again. "Jaxon move up a little, please, I can't concentrate."

Jaxon grinned, glad that he affected her the same way she did him, and moved up a centimetre, then frowned, when he didn't like the distance.

"Right. I'll put the kettle on, and then we can get down to business." Magnus walked through another door into a tiny kitchen, then returned a second later with three cups of steaming hot tea.

Jaxon eyed the tea carefully, it looked normal, but he knew far too well, anything made with magic wasn't made to eat or drink. "Why don't we go to the pub?"

"Oh perfect, best place to go to talk to an alcoholic." Destiny glared at Jaxon. "Besides, I thought this was private."

"Well you're here, so it isn't that private, is it?" Jaxon countered.

"Do you want me to leave then?" Destiny stood up abruptly. "Because I think I've spent more than enough time in your company."

Magnus watched the exchange between the two, his head was still throbbing, and the thought of his daughter leaving was too much to take. "SILENCE." He bellowed, at the top of his voice, as the sound echoed around the room, everything started to shake. Books fell from the tables and shelves, and the light fittings swung from side to side. "Now Destiny, please, sit down. And Alpha, there's a bottle of Jack Daniels over there in the cabinet, help yourself…... Now I suggest you get to the point of your visit, as it's quite clear this isn't a family reunion."

Destiny noticed the sadness flicker across Magnus's face and was immediately consumed with guilt. "I'm sorry Magnus, of course I want to get to know you, you're my dad. But this is important, so can we sort business out first….. Please?"

Jaxon slumped back down on the sofa with his glass of Whisky and placed the bottle on the table. "She's right, this is important, so I would be grateful of any help you can give me."

Magnus eyed the whisky bottle, but didn't reach for it, if the Alpha had come to him for help, he knew it was serious. "Okay, I'm all ears."

"I had a visit today from William, there's rogue vampires killing supernatural's. They don't just drain their blood though. The corpses end up mummified. William recons its some kind of magic, have you heard of anything like this before?" Jaxon drained his glass and refilled it.

Magnus walked to a bookshelf and run his hand alone it, until he came to a large green book. Pulling it off the shelf he studied it thoughtfully before sitting down and opening it. "Is there anything else you can tell me?" Magus continued turning the pages and running his finger down, almost reading as he went. "Aha, here. Mummification, for any supernatural to be able to do this they would be under a spell from a Demon, hmm that doesn't sound good."

Destiny joined in. "The vampire also said he thinks they are heading here. He said there's something old here, something really powerful, do you know what that could be?" Destiny noticed Jaxon look at her, as he shook his head. "What?"

"Just how much of the conversation did you eavesdrop on?" Jaxon looked back at Magnus; he already knew the answer.

"All of it." Destiny smiled, smugly, no man, sorry, no dog was telling her what to do.

"I've felt it too, the last few days it seems to be getting stronger, it is worrying. Look I can go through my books and see if I can find anything. I have a room of ancient scrolls too. I'll start looking there first." Magus closed the green book and refocused on Destiny. "What a time to turn up, just as the world looks like it's going to end. Maybe we could have dinner first?"

CHAPTER 11

Destany sat on the edge of her bed, trying to get her temper under control. She was still fuming at Jaxon for shouting at Magnus for suggesting dinner. What was wrong with that, you have to eat, even if the world is going to end. And then the way he stormed off, saying he couldn't trust a witch, and something about rejection was the answer. Destiny flopped back and stared at the ceiling, annoyed with herself for spending so much time thinking about him, a war was coming, and she needed to pack. It wasn't her war after all.

"Yes, it is, and you need to be ready." The voice came from the mirror.

Destiny looked closer and saw Mrs Richards looking back at her. "How did you get in there?"

"Never mind that, get dressed, we need to prepare you." All of a sudden there was a loud pop and Mrs Richards was standing in front of Destiny. "Hurry up, time is running out."

"What do you mean, you don't expect me to fight, do you?" Destiny walked to the edge of the room and picked up her case, as soon as she had hold of it, it disappeared. "What the hell. Where is it. Give it back, this isn't my fight, and you can't make me stay."

"Destiny, it's because of you this is coming. Sit down deary." Mrs Richards pointed to the bed. "Let me start at the beginning…. When you were taken it upset the balance of nature for the supernatural world."

"Hang on, that doesn't make sense, supernatural's live among us humans, that's what you said."

"Destiny. You are a supernatural, a witch. You most definitely are not human." Mrs Richards sighed. "Are you willing to let everyone here die, Magnus, Edna, Jaxon, do they mean nothing to you?"

"Of course I don't want them to die, but can I remind you that until a couple of months ago I thought I was human, and now you tell me I'm a witch and you want me to save the world. I'm still the same now as I was before, so tell me, how am I supposed to do it?"

"I don't expect you to save the world, I expect you to play your part and for that you need to come with me and practice. You deary are a very powerful witch, and when they find out who you are, they are going to take you."

Destiny jumped back up in panic. "Who's going to take me?"

"The demons, you are the ancient power, that's who the vampire spoke off, you child." Mrs Richards watched as Destiny paced the room.

"You've made a mistake Mrs Richards. I'm 17, that's not ancient. Now if you don't mind, I really need to pack."

"Destiny, look at me." Once Mrs Richards had Destiny's attention, she led her to the mirror. "Look in there. What do you see?"

Destiny shrunk back as she watched the scene, trembling slightly. "Fire, I see fire, every where's burning. People are burning." Pulling away, Destiny placed her head in her hands and started to cry. "Is this the future?"

"It's one possible outcome, there are three altogether, this one is the one where you flee. Now you have a choice, you can run." Mrs Richards snapped her fingers and Destiny's case appeared in front of her. "Or you can stay and play your part, the choice is yours. If however you do want to stay, I will wait for you in there." Walking to the mirror, Mrs Richards turned and smiled. "I have faith in you Destiny, that's why I returned."

"Wait." But Mrs Richards had already gone. Destiny stood in front of the mirror but could only see her own reflection. "Returned from where?" Walking over to the window, Destiny watched as the town people went about their daily lives, unknowing of the battle to come. Jaxon pulled up down the street, and Destiny felt a stab of jealousy when he held the blue haired girls hand. They were laughing together. Stepping back quickly when Jaxon glanced up, Destiny cursed herself for not controlling her feelings. It was pretty clear he was a player. Destiny grabbed her case and placed it into the bed, then started throwing her things into it, until it bulged before she sat on it and zipped it up. "I'm not a hero Mrs Richards, I'm sorry." Destiny remained on her case and thought about Magnus, she didn't know him, but he was still her dad. And then there was Aunt Edna, who had given her a job and a home. How could she leave them to die. Reaching for her magic bag, once she was dressed, Destiny stood in front of the mirror. "I'm only seventeen, I can't do this. I'm sorry Mrs Richards."

As Destiny uttered the last word, two sets of hands reached out of the mirror and pulled her in. "WHAT THE HELL!" She screamed as the feeling of lightness hit her, followed by a light sensation of pins and needles. Within seconds she floated through the mirror into the land of fae.

The colours were so much more vibrant, the grass was a deep green, but the trees were different colours. Pinks, blues, purples, reds, in fact every colour of which you could think. Destiny turned when she heard giggling behind her. There floating just above the grass were two fae, just hovering, like it was no big deal.

"Is that her?" One giggled.

"Dunno, I'll ask her." The faery floated towards Destiny and landed in front of her. "Are you her?"

"I Don't know." Destiny took a step back as the other Fae joined them.

"She doesn't know who she is." Giggling once more the two fae held their tummy's while Destiny watched.

"What's your name?" The other asked.

As Destiny opened her mouth, she quickly closed it again, remembering the warning in the book. If they know your name, they will hold power over you and possibly complete control. "Where's Mr's Richards?"

"Who?" The two fae asked in unison.

"The other witch that came through the mirror?" Destiny's temper was starting to fray. Mrs Richards said she would be waiting for her, so where was she?

"Oh we don't know any Mr's Richards, you should go to the palace, it's that way, no hang on maybe it's that way, do you want me to take you?"

"No, I'll find it, thanks anyway." Destiny looked around to find the highest point, if she climbed it, she may be able to get her bearings.

"Good luck your highness." The two fae flew away back into the trees, still giggling, leaving Destiny alone.

"Highness?" Destiny shook her head and followed a path up the hill, she wondered what Magnus was doing. If only she could have told him where she was going, before being pulled through the mirror. What if she got trapped here, what would happen to him and Aunt Edna, and of course that pig, Jaxon.

As she approached the top of the hill, Destiny stopped and looked out across a city, with a palace smack bang in the middle of it. "Well that was easier to find than I thought."

A male voice came from next to her. "You haven't crossed the river yet, so don't build your hopes up."

Turning, Destiny came face to face with a man who had pointy ears, "Who are you?"

"Sir Gideon, your highness." Bowing he smiled. "I am at your service."

"I am not royal Mr, just a regular 17-year-old witch." Turning back, Destiny spotted the river. "Where can I get a boat from?"

Gideon laughed. "There are no boats your highness, sorry, witch."

"Then how do people cross?" Destiny frowned at the man. "It looks pretty wide. Can you help?"

"Magic! This is a magical kingdom. We don't need boats or cars like the human world. I thought you would know that being the chosen one." Gideon walked towards the river, ignoring Destiny's plea for help.

"What do you mean chosen one?" Watching as Gideon walked away, Destiny sighed. "Looks like I'm on my own then."

An hour later Destiny stood at the bank of the river. It was wider than she first thought, and the current was fast flowing. Definitely too fast to swim. Looking at her bag, she decided to ask for help. "Show me how to get across the river." Plunging her hand in, she pulled out a pair of arm bands. "Funny! So you have a sense of humour…. Look, I need help so help!" Pushing the arm bands back in she pulled out the book of magic. As she frantically scanned the pages she came to a teleportation spell. Reading down she noticed this spell would take a lot of practice before perfecting. She didn't have time for that. She needed to find Mr's Richards, so she could get back to Valley Fall's, grab her case and run. Maybe she could convince Magnus and Aunt Edna to run with her. Destiny sighed; they didn't seem the type to run. She placed the book back into her bag. "This is great, just bloody great." Pulling her knees up she hugged them tightly, as she tried her best to think. Broken from her thoughts when the earth beneath her started vibrating, accompanied by a loud thumping, she jumped up. "What the hell?" As she scanned the horizon she spotted the troll. A 10-foot, grey skinned troll, and he was heading straight towards her. Picking up her bag she decided to run for it, but as she turned, she heard a sad voice.

"Wait…. Please…. Don't leave me." The troll cried out in a desperate plea.

Destiny thought back to the book. 'Trolls are clumsy, which gives them a bad name' Holding her breath as the giant troll approached, she closed her eyes and waited to get squashed.

"Are you sleeping human?" The troll asked, he didn't know humans could sleep standing up.

Destiny opened her eyes and shook her head. "No. And I'm not a human."

"What are you then? Cos you look like a human." Sitting down with another tremble of the ground, the troll looked at Destiny with a curious smile.

"I'm a witch." Destiny flinched as the troll wrapped his arms around his head.

"Please don't hurt me."

Taken aback by the sentence, Destiny sat down next to him. "I'm not going to hurt you. Why would I?"

"You said you're a witch, witches do magic, magic is bad." Putting his arms down, the troll eyed Destiny, suspiciously.

"Well I'm not a bad witch. My names Destiny, what's yours?" Destiny held her hand out ready to shake his.

"My names Raymond." The smile returned to his face as he reached down to Destiny's hand.

"Ouch. Gently Raymond…. Anyway, why did you say don't leave me?" Squeezing her hand shut, Destiny waited for the feeling to come back. Raymond had quite a grip.

"I'm lonely. Do you want to play?" Raymond asked hopefully. "Cos we are friends now."

"Yes we are friends, but I have to get across the river to the palace. I'm sorry, it's important." Destiny watched Raymond's face drop. He looked like he was about to cry. "It's important Raymond, otherwise I would."

"Can I come with you?" Raymond stood, looking down at Destiny as he towered over her.

"Yes, you can…. Raymond?"

"Yes Destiny."

"Could you carry me across the river, to the other side?" Destiny looked up hopefully, noticing the smile spread across Raymond's face.

Clapping his large hands together Raymond nodded. "You will have to climb onto my shoulders and hold on very tight."

"Okay, let's go." Destiny waited for Raymond to bend down then allowed him to lift her onto his shoulders. The smell hit her at once, it was the most unpleasant smell she had encountered. Hoping the river would take the smell away, the pair continued into the water.

CHAPTER 12

Magnus threw the last ancient scroll across the room in temper. He had spent the whole night going through everything he had and had come up with nothing. There were no warnings of a prophecy or no mention an ancient power. His head was still thumping and his hands shaking from the alcohol withdrawal, which made the task more difficult. Thinking back to the previous night Magus allowed himself a wry smile. Destiny and Jaxon had argued and then Jaxon had stormed out. There would definitely not be any mating between those two. Destiny had stuck up for Magnus, calling Jaxon a petulant child. It was the highlight of the evening, especially when Jaxon declared rejection was the answer.

Magnus returned to his tiny kitchen and looked out of the window. He wanted to check on Destiny, make sure she was okay after the previous night's antics. Walking through to the hall, he checked himself out in the mirror. He wasn't happy with the stranger staring back at him. When did his hair get that long? And as for the overgrown stubble on his chin. He hung his head in shame. No wonder people laughed at him, drunk all the time, and looking like a down and out. "Right Magnus. Time for change." With a click of his fingers, Magnus's hair was immediately short, and the stubble was gone. Next he headed to the shower. He would make sure he was worthy for his daughters attention.

Magnus walked out of his front door and took a deep lungful or the crisp winter air. Life was good. He turned right and made his way to his sister Edna's coffee shop. As he passed the towns resident he greeted them with a smile and a good afternoon. The surprised looks on the town folks faces made his smile broaden. When he reached the coffee shop, he took another deep breath, then let himself in. "Good afternoon Edna, beautiful day."

Edna squeezed her eyes shut and then opened them, just to make sure she wasn't dreaming. Sure enough, Magnus stood in front of her, like the magnificent warlock he had once been. "Magnus, what a wonderful surprise. I must say you're looking like your old self."

"Thank you Edna, now where is my daughter?"

"She hasn't been in today Magnus." Edna walked to the counter and placed her cup down.

"What do you mean, she hasn't been in today. She's staying here!"

"Destiny hasn't moved in yet.... I thought she was at yours?" Edna watched as Magnus started to pace the floor.

"Where is she staying then?" Magnus stomped to the window and looked outside. There was Jaxon, heading towards the shop. Unable to stop himself, he grabbed the door and yanked it open, then he came face to face with the alpha. "Where's my daughter?"

Jaxon growled at the sudden ambush, his temper immediately turning to worry for Destiny. "She stayed at yours last night, have you lost her already?"

"She decided to go home. Now where's home?" Magnus looked anxiously between Edna and Jaxon.

"You mean you don't know where she's staying?" Jaxon started pacing the floor just like Magnus had done. "I thought it weird that I couldn't pick up her scent. Let's start at the last place we both saw her. Magnus, come on."

The two men walked back to Magnus's and made their way into

the lounge. Magnus was the first to speak. "Can you pick up her scent?"

"Shhh." Jaxon frowned as he took a huge breath, he could just about smell Destiny, but it was faint. He then headed to the front door, turned right, and headed down the sidewalk.

Magnus followed, eager to find his daughter. She had been here two nights, and no one knew where she was staying. He found that odd. Magnus was forced to stop when he crashed into Jaxon's back. "Why are you stopping here?"

Jaxon turned and scowled at Magnus. "Because the scent end's here."

Both men looked at the burnt out remains of the old bed and breakfast. Everything was charcoaled. Part of the roof was missing, and you could see through to the upstairs where the floorboards had burnt away.

"She couldn't be staying here, it's unsafe not to mention the smell." Magnus took a careful step closer to the burnt-out building.

"Well as the scent ends here I think we should check it out. Wait here if you're chicken." Jaxon grinned as he made the insult then walked through the burnt-out doorway into, what was once a reception room.

Jaxon looked around at the fire damage, everywhere was blackened by the smoke damage and fire. Why would Destiny stay here? It didn't make sense. Was this some kind of magic or was she under a spell. Jaxon turned around when he heard Magnus's footsteps approach. "I'm gonna check upstairs, you look around down here." Jaxon continued up the stairs cautiously. Watching each step as he made his way up. When he reached the top he looked at the four doors leading to the bedrooms.

The first door he tried, had a large hole in the floor, where the fire had burnt its way up. The second door as he pushed it open, crashed to the floor causing ash and soot to fill the air. After a succession of sneezes, Jaxon tried the third door. There on a neatly made bed was Destiny's case. "MAGNUS, UP HERE!"

Magnus ran into the room and stopped dead. "This room looks like it's been untouched by the fire, but how's that possible?"

Shaking his head he made his way to the bed. There on top of the case was a note. He snatched it up and unfolded the piece of paper, his hands shook as he began to read aloud.

To Magnus and Jaxon.
Gone through the mirror, to the land of Fae.
Working on my powers, ready for the battle.
Will be back in a couple of days.
Destiny X

Both men looked at each other, before Jaxon spoke. "What does she mean through the mirror?"

"It's how you get into the fae world. Not every mirror has the ability to transport you. They have been strategically placed around the world for the fae that live in the human world." Magnus took a step closer to the mirror when Jaxon grabbed his arm.

"Is it even safe there? Could she be in danger?" Jaxon asked without waiting for an answer. "We need to go and get her, come on."

Before Jaxon stepped into the mirror and vanished, Magnus grabbed his arm. "Theres something you need to know before we go."

CHAPTER 13

Destiny scrambled from Raymond's shoulders onto the riverbank. It had taken longer than she had thought to get across. The current had pushed Raymond downriver about quarter of a mile. As she dried off her shoes on the long grass, Destiny watched Raymond from the corner of her eye. He was smelling the meadow flowers and then picking them, one by one.

He walked towards Destiny with his hand outstretched, smiling. "These are for you. I picked the best ones; they smell nice like you."

Destiny took the flowers and smiled back. "You're the first man.... Troll....to have ever given me flowers Raymond. I love them, thank you."

Watching as Raymond's cheeks coloured Destiny laughed. "Okay, we really need to get going. Come on." Destiny stood placing the flowers into her bag and made her way back along the riverbank with Raymond following.

After a fifteen-minute walk, Destiny noticed Sir Gideon standing in the distance. As they approached him, he turned to face them.

"I must say, it took you longer to get across the river than I thought, but well done. You made it in the end." Gideon glanced at Raymond and smiled. "Shall we go?"

Destiny glared at Gideon. "So you want to help now?"

"It's your quest Destiny, I'm only here to observe. Now, I believe it's this way." Gideon set off without waiting for a reply.

Walking along a winding path, the trio headed into a forest. As the foliage thickened, the natural light seemed to fade, making it difficult to see.

The hairs on Destiny's arms stood up as an uneasy feeling came over her. "Hey guys!" She whispered, "I think we're being watched."

Gideon laughed. "Of course we are being watched. This is Snodlin territory."

"What the hell is a Snodlin. Are they dangerous?" Destiny moved closer to Raymond, despite his smell, she hoped he would save her.

Gideon watched as Destiny's eyes darted around the trees. "They are perfectly friendly to those they like, but if you upset one, they turn into a big spikey ball and throw themselves at you.... So don't upset them."

After walking a few more feet Destiny heard a low humming, it was a beautiful sound. The harmonies were pitch perfect and as the noise grew louder, Destiny felt herself entranced by the melody. Without realising it, she had wandered off, following the direction, from which it came.

As Destiny approached a clearing in the trees, she peeked through and watched as a group of Snodlin's sat in a circle singing. They were only about three foot tall. And although they had a human appearance, they had fur covering their bodies. As one spotted her she ducked back, closing her eye's, and wished she were invisible.

"STRANGER!" One of the tiny Snodlin's called as they pointed in her direction. All the Snodlin's jumped up and ran towards her, but as they stood in front of Destiny, they couldn't see her.

"Where is it?" One asked.

Opening her eye's, Destiny watched as the Snodlin's looked around. They were even staring straight at her, but they couldn't see her. Waiting until the Snodlin's returned to the clearing, Destiny slowly backed away then made her way back to the path and headed off to catch Gideon and Raymond up.

After jogging for five minutes she spotted them up ahead. "Hey. Wait for me."

Gideon and Raymond stopped as Destiny caught them up, Raymond scratched his head, puzzled. "Where is she?"

"I'm right here!" Destiny waved her arms about in front of the pair, while they scanned the area. "HERE!"

Gideon looked at where Destiny's voice was coming from. "So you can do magic!"

"What?" Destiny stepped back in surprise. "What are you talking about?"

"You're invisible Destiny." Raymond pointed out.

Destiny looked down at her body, her heart rate had increased, and a film of sweat had gathered on her brow. She could see herself, why couldn't they? "How do I make myself not invisible?"

"How did you make yourself invisible in the first place?" Gideon shook his head in despair. "Just reverse it."

"I don't know how I did it, one minute I was spying on the Snodlin's, then the next they spotted me, and I closed my eyes, wishing they couldn't see me." Destiny sat on an old tree stump. "What am I going to do?"

"Close your eyes and wish you are visible again. It might not work but it's worth a try." Gideon stood back and waited. "Well, are you trying?"

"Of course I'm trying. Nothing's happening." Dropping her head in her hands, Destiny felt the first wave of anger. "I never wanted to be a witch. I never wanted to come here, and I certainly don't want to fight in a war. I'm 17, I should be looking forward to my future. Shopping, making friends…" Destiny trailed off as Raymond's face fell.

"But we are your friends." Plonking himself onto the ground Raymond's lip quivered.

Before he started crying, Destiny jumped up and walked towards him, placing her hand on his shoulder. "You are my friend

Raymond. I didn't mean to upset you. I'm sorry. Let me try again." Destiny closed her eyes and wished she could be seen.

Raymond jumped up cheering. "I can see you. I can see you." Clapping his hands together, he did a little dance while Gideon rolled his eyes.

"Okay enough. We need to get going, you shouldn't keep the queen waiting." Continuing on his way he ignored Destiny's questions.

"What do you mean the queen, I'm meeting Mrs Richards. Gideon.... Gideon, wait." Running to keep up Destiny tripped on a tree root and fell forwards, towards the ground. As she reached out to stop herself, she wished she weren't falling. Suddenly Destiny found herself upright once more. As she looked up, she noticed Gideon and Raymond didn't witness that little mishap, for which she was grateful, although she did wonder how she managed to not fall. Could this really be her magic? Was it that easy, Just wish something and it happens? She decided to ask Mrs Richards, after all, she would know.

THE TRIO MADE their way out of the forest and into glorious sunshine, Destiny looked around at all the beautiful flowers lining the path up towards a tall wall that surrounded the city. On further scrutiny she noticed the path stopped at the wall. There was no door, or archway. In fact there was no way of getting in. "Gideon?"

Gideon stopped and turned to face her, tapping his foot impatiently. "What now Destiny?"

Destiny pointed to the end of the path. "How do we get in, there's no door?"

"That's for you to figure out. This is as far as we go, you must continue on your own. We will meet again soon. Come on Raymond." Gideon and Raymond strolled off towards the side of the wall, leaving Destiny standing with her mouth open, staring after them.

"WAIT! CAN'T YOU GIVE ME A CLUE?" She hollowed after them, but it was too late, they were gone.

Destiny made her way to the end of the path and looked up at the giant wall, it was at least thirty feet tall. There was absolutely no chance of her climbing it. She didn't like heights after all, even if she could have. Her first decision was to reach out. If she felt the large stones maybe she could connect with it, even find a weakness. Destiny sighed. She closed her eyes and wished she were the other side of the wall, when she opened them however she was still in the same place. "Of course it wouldn't be that simple." Destiny was tired, tired, hungry and lonely. She sat down and leant back on the wall. If she couldn't get into the grounds she wouldn't get to Mrs Richards and then how would she get back to Magnus and Jaxon. What good was magic if she couldn't use it? "I wish you were here mum?" Destiny felt the loneliness consume her as the tears started to fall.

When Destiny had no more tears left, she wiped her eyes on the back of her hand and stood up. Then she turned to face the wall, she felt the sadness leave, replaced instead with anger. She had come too far to let a wall stop her. Taking a step back, she focused on the wall and held her hands out in front of her. "Right. Damn you wall. I am Destiny Black and I demand you to let me in." She stood and watched as nothing happened. Destiny's temper grew deeper. "I SAID, I AM DESTINY BLACK AND I DEMAND YOU TO LET ME IN." Jumping back as the large stones started to move, she watched on in ore as the stones moved into the shape of an archway. She was cautious when she made her way through, Destiny watched as all the people bustled about on their daily business, paying no heed to her or the magnificent archway she had conjured. As she walked on through the tiny streets she came to a signpost, pointing out the direction of the palace. At last feeling like she was getting somewhere, she carried on with a newfound strength. As she approached the main street, she headed towards a large fountain that sat proudly in the centre of a crossroads. Taking a seat on the edge, she listened to the water trickling out of a large urn, held by a figure of a woman wearing flowing robes. Destiny wondered who the woman was, maybe it was a famous fae. As Destiny sat daydreaming she was interrupted by a familiar voice.

"What are you doing now?" Gideon asked as he munched on an apple. Raymond stood beside him holding a giant bunch of bananas, pulling one off he tossed it into his mouth, Skin, and all.

Shaking her head Destiny turned from Raymond and focused on Gideon. "I'm having a rest. Where did you get the food?" Watching Gideon point to a market stall, she followed his gaze and noticed all of the goodies, piled high. "Have you got any money?"

Raymond screwed his face up as he answered. "What's money, and why do you need it?"

"To pay for something to eat. I'm hungry too." Destiny climbed off the fountain wall, then made her way over to the stall with Gideon and Raymond following. "Can I have a piece of that cake please."

"Destiny watched as the woman cut a large chunk of cake and placed it on a serviette. "That'll be 1 gold coin Miss."

Taking the cake Destiny took a large bite, closing her eyes as her tastebuds tingled. After swallowing it down she looked at Gideon. "Pay then."

"I don't have any gold coins." He then turned to Raymond and shook his head. "I doubt he has either."

The woman looked at Destiny and pointed. "You owe me for the cake. Pay up or I'll call the queens guards."

"But I haven't got any gold coins." Destiny jumped in horror as the woman started shouting for the Queens guard's, shortly followed by the stampede of feet as they approached.

"Arrest her, she's a thief!" The woman folded her arms and watched as Destiny was apprehended then lead away.

"Shouldn't we help her?" Raymond questioned.

"No Raymond. She needs to learn how to use her magic." Shaking his head Gideon sighed. "If she can't save herself then there's no chance of her saving the rest of us."

CHAPTER 14

Destiny sat on the cold stone floor of the dungeon and looked around. The place was damp, she could feel it creeping into her bones. She rubbed her arms to warm them up, but stopped when she heard footsteps approaching. As she looked up, the door opened. Destiny was amazed to see Mrs Richards standing there. "Mrs Richards, boy am I glad to see you. I thought I'd never get out."

Mrs Richards put her hand up to stop Destiny. "I'm not here to let you out deary."

Destiny's smile faded. "Then why are you here?"

"To remind you who you are…. You are a powerful witch. You should never have let yourself get into this position. Now it is only you who can get yourself out." As soon as Mrs Richards had spoken she turned and left.

Destiny watched as the door slammed shut, jumping at the sudden action. "BUT THEY'VE TAKEN MY MAGIC BAG!" No answer came, so despondent, she slumped back down onto the floor. Destiny closed her eyes to blot out the tears. There was no time for crying. "Think Destiny think…. I made myself invisible. I stopped myself from falling. I conjured an arch…. What's the common link?" She opened her eyes she smiled. "Emotion!" Destiny looked at the heavy Iron door and held her hands out in front of her. "Right Destiny, let's go get your bag and get out of this dump." She focused on the door and imagined the door opening. "OPEN!" But nothing happened. "Shit." She took a deep breath as her temper grew, she threw her hands out in front of her and screamed louder. "OPEN." The door flew off its hinges and crashed to the ground. Destiny didn't allow herself to feel pleased, she needed to keep her anger. Instead she marched her way up a narrow staircase and approached a closed door at the top. Once again she threw her hands out and shouted "OPEN." Again the door flew off crashing to the ground. As Destiny's determination grew, she made her way down a long corridor. She could feel her heart as it pounded in her chest. She felt no fear, only anger. As she neared the end she could hear people chatting and laughing. Mrs Richards cackle filled Destiny's head. This enraged her more. She was left in a damp dreary dungeon, and Mrs Richards was having the time of her life. Without thinking Destiny threw her hands out and without speaking the door flew off its hinges and crashed to the floor. Everyone stopped what they were doing and turned to look at Destiny as she stormed through the doorway. Destiny's anger was soon replaced with shock when she spotted Raymond and Gideon standing with the queen. As she looked behind them she saw two cages. One held Magnus and the other held Jaxon. Her temper began to build as she walked towards the queen, ready to tear apart anyone that stopped her. As the queens guards surrounded Destiny she threw her hands out and watched as they flew to the side of the room. Each man was knocked out cold.

Destiny stopped when she stood in front of the queen. "I want my bag. Now."

The queen smiled as she looked upon Destiny. "My, you are beautiful Destiny, just like your mother."

"You knew my mother. How?" Destiny looked closer at the queens features; she looked familiar.

"I'm your mothers younger sister. You know Destiny, she would have been queen, but she choose to give up her status to marry that thing." Pointing at Magnus, the queen shook her head. "My parents really weren't happy with her choice."

"That's my dad you're talking about, be careful what you say." Destiny's temper started to build to the point of no return. "And while we are on the subject, you can release them, they will be coming with me."

"All in good time child." The queen clicked her fingers and refreshments were brought in. "Sit and eat, you will need to keep your strength up." A long table that was in the centre of the room was soon filled with refreshments; the queen pointed to a chair as she looked at Destiny. "I said sit."

Begrudgingly Destiny pulled out a chair and sat, keeping her eye closely on the queen. "What do you want?"

"The queen popped a grape into her mouth and chewed slowly before answering. "I want you to succeed. Now you have finally started to conquer your magic, your abilities should grow. But remember Destiny, you have fae blood in you too. Fae blood is a very powerful healer, and it can be used in spells, so never give it to anyone."

"Okay, can you let Magnus and Jaxon go now?" Destiny looked over to the cages. Both men staring back at her.

"Ah yes, that brings me to the wolf. Destiny you really cannot mate with that thing. Your children would be an abomination. Can you imagine, Fae, Witch, and Wolf. It's unheard of in the supernatural world.

"Listen your majesty. Aunt or whatever you are. I will mate, marry, whatever, whoever I please. And rest assured it will only be for love. Now I'm going to ask one last time. Let Magnus and Jaxon go, before I really lose my shit." Destiny stood abruptly, causing her chair to tip backwards. "And while we are at it, I want my bag."

"If you want them released then carry on, but you will not be getting the bag back. That now belongs to me." The queen stood and walked away, leaving through a door the other side of the room.

Destiny walked to the cages and threw her hands out. "OPEN!" As the two cage doors flew open, Magus and Jaxon walked out.

Jaxon grabbed Destiny and checked her for signs of injury. "Are you hurt?"

Destiny smiled at his worried expression. "I'm fine. How did you get here?"

Magnus held the note out in front of him. "We didn't want you to be on your own, so we followed you through the mirror."

Snatching the note Destiny read the few lines. "But I never wrote this. I was pulled into the mirror by a couple of annoying fae."

"Well who did then?" Jaxon asked as he rubbed his neck. "Look we can sort that later; we really need to get back. Who knows what's happening at home."

As Jaxon grabbed Destiny's hand to lead her to safety she pulled away. "I'm not going anywhere without my bag. Wait here, I won't be long."

Magnus stood in front of Destiny. "We are going with you. Lead the way."

Destiny continued to the door the queen had left through. She threw her hands out in front of her and watched as it crashed to the ground. The three companions marched over it.

"Wow impressive." Jaxon walked over the door and stood next to Destiny. "When did you learn to do that?"

"When they locked me in the dungeon. Come on this way." They continued along another corridor, until Destiny slowed. "I'm not sure which way to go."

Magnus grabbed her arm and pulled her around to face him. "You need to picture it in your mind. Forget everything else and just concentrate on the bag."

Destiny gave Magnus a curt nod and then closed her eyes. She visualised the bag. Her mothers bag that was now hers. No one was going to take it. She smiled as her eyes opened. "This way." They continued from room to room until Destiny stopped outside a door. "It's in here. Stand back." Throwing her arms out in temper, they all watched the door as it flew to the other side of the room and shattered as it hit the wall.

"You're getting good at this." Magnus smiled proudly. "Right, where is it?"

Destiny followed Jaxon into the room and scanned the area. "There. It's in there." There standing proud was an old antique chest that matched the one she had first found the bag in, in her mother's loft. The carving on top was the same woman standing with the wolf. "I don't understand. This looks the same as the one from home."

The queens voice came from behind her. "It is the same chest child. It goes to wherever the book is. Now all you have to do is open it and this part of your training will be complete."

"What? What do you mean this part of my training. This was a test?" Destiny threw the queen a filthy look. "You do realise I spent 2 hours in a damp, dark, dungeon." Destiny held out her hand towards the chest. "GIVE ME MY BAG." The lid slowly opened and out flew the bag into Destiny's open hand.

The queen smiled. "Right, follow me please." Leading the group back to the main hall, Destiny was surprised to see Gideon and Raymond still there. Also next to them were the two fae, Willow and Magnolia, only now the fae were full size, just like a human. Destiny took a double take as she spotted the Snodlin who had shouted stranger.

The queen took a seat on her throne, then took a deep breath before she began. "Right Destiny. You took a little while to master your craft, you now need to learn how to use it without letting emotion get in the way." She turned to Magnus and Pointed. "That will be your job Magnus. Teach her everything you know. And you Jaxon." The queen moved her finger in Jaxon's direction before she continued. "You are to guard her with your life, after all, you are true mates." The queen paused and smiled at Destiny. "You are not alone child, when the final battle starts, Sir Gideon, will be there to fight alongside you, he is the elves top archer and swordsman. Raymond will be there to protect you. His skin cannot be penetrated by bullet, arrow, or tooth. He will shield you when you are in need. Willow and Marigold will be there to assist you with their magic, you may not always see them so just call out if you need their help. Finally, the Snodlin's will come when you need safety. They can spike themselves together to form a defence as well as launch themselves at an enemy. Now any questions?"

Destiny took a step forward before she spoke. "I was told they would come for me. Why?"

"Because you hold the ancient power. As soon as you found the book, it belonged to you Destiny. Pardon the pun, but this is your Destiny." The queen rose and walked towards the unlikely army. "You all have a role to play, but I'm afraid Destiny, you have the biggest part."

"What if I leave the book here. They won't come for me then, right?" Destiny held the bag out to the queen and motioned for her to take it.

The queen pushed Destiny's hand away. "I'm sorry child, this was always going to be your burden. The only way it can be passed to another is by death."

"Great." Destiny swallowed down her sadness. She was going to die; she was sure of it. For a second she looked around at all the faces staring back at her. How could she let them down. Didn't they know she was a fraud and not some all-powerful witch.

Jaxon walked forward and grabbed her hand. He could sense her mood. "I am with you cupcake, we all are." He smiled.

"Okay. I guess we had better get back. I don't suppose you have a shortcut back to Valley Falls?" Destiny asked as she turned towards the queen.

"That I can help with, but first I have two gifts for you." The queen pulled a large emerald ring from her finger, then slipped it onto Destiny's. "If you need help, call into the ring and help will come." Next she reached behind her and pulled out a sword. "And this is for when all magic fails. It will protect you well. Now go. Prepare for battle, for the days grow dark." As the queen finished speaking a large sash dropped from the wall, showing a giant mirror. "Your way home Destiny. I hope we meet again one day."

"Wait." Destiny called to the Queen. "Where is Mr's Richards?"

"Who?"

"Mrs Richards, I was supposed to meet her here." Destiny frowned when the queen shook her head.

"I don't know any Mrs Richards child. Now go."

As Destiny, Magnus and Jaxon stood in front of the mirror, the Queen called out one last time. "Destiny, keep in the shadows."

"Keep in the shadows, what's that supposed to mean?" Destiny looked at her case on the bed. She wanted to run now more than ever.

"Wolves use the shadows to hunt, maybe that's what she meant." Jaxon grabbed the case, lifting it off the bed.

"What are you doing?" She reached out to snatch it back, but Jaxon placed it behind his back.

"It's not safe for you here. One. The buildings about to fall down and two. I need to protect you, so you will be staying at the pack house."

Before Destiny could protest, Magnus replied. "He's right Destiny. It's not safe here. I will be staying at the packhouse too."

"I don't remember inviting you." Jaxon glared at Magnus. "The queen said it's my job to protect her."

"And the queen instructed me to teach her how to use her magic. Plus she's my daughter." Magnus glared back.

"Well she's my mate." Jaxon shot back.

"Will you two stop arguing. You're worse than kids. It's getting late, so if I have to stay at the pack house can we go." Walking out of the room, Destiny ignored their stares. As she walked down the stairs, she noticed, for the first time, the fire damage. Had this happened while she was in the land of fae? The main reception room shocked her the most, she took in the burnt and charcoaled furniture. The blackened walls and the smell. The smell reminded her of Mrs Richards. When she exited the bed and breakfast she turned to look at the building. It looked little more than a shell.

As Jaxon stood beside her, he slipped his arm around her waist. "You're lucky the floor didn't cave in while you were sleeping."

"When did this happen?" Destiny felt her blood run cold. "Because it wasn't like this when I arrived 2 days ago."

Magnus looked at his daughter and then back at the building. "It happened four years ago. It was an inferno, the owner perished in the fire too. Despite all attempts to rescue her. They recon she was using dark magic."

"What was her name?" Destiny already knew the answer before she heard it leave Jaxon's mouth.

"Beverly Richards. She's buried out in the woods. They wouldn't allow her body in the cemetery. The priest recons anyone who uses dark magic can soil consecrated ground." Jaxon grabbed Destiny's hand. "Come on, let's get you home."

As Destiny walked towards Jaxon's car she had the strangest feeling like she was being watched. She pulled back and turned her head to the upstairs window of the burnt-out bed and breakfast. There staring back at her was Mrs Richards. She wasn't smiling she was just staring, with dead, black, eyes.

CHAPTER 15

Jaxon opened the door to the pack house and ushered Destiny inside. Magus followed behind the pair. Destiny's eyes darted around the large entrance hall. To the right there was a large kitchen and to the left there was a large lounge. There seemed to be people everywhere.

Carlton walked towards Jaxon, stopping when he spotted Destiny and Magnus. "What's going on, why are they here?"

"They need to stay, Destiny is under pack protection, which means we all watch out for her. I'll address the pack after I've got her settled. Destiny. This way. Carlton find Magnus a spare room." Jaxon grabbed Destiny's hand and lead her up two flights of stairs. Stopping at the first bedroom door along the landing, Jaxon opened it and pushed Destiny in. He dumped the case down onto the bed and grinned. "This is where the action happens princess."

"As long as you don't expect any action with me, we'll get on fine. Where will you be sleeping?" Destiny watched as Jaxon's smile dropped. Replaced with an annoyed look. "I'll be sleeping in the bed with you, how do you expect me to protect you if I'm not with you. Unpack and we can eat before I tell everyone what's going on."

"I'll sleep on the floor, just to be on the safe side." She told him as she grabbed her case. She unzipped it and started to get her things out.

"What's the matter, scared you won't be able to control yourself?" Jaxon pulled open the sliding door to his walk-in closet. "There's plenty of room in here for your clothes."

"I'm perfectly capable of controlling myself." Destinys heart was beating a little faster and she found herself feeling flustered. She grabbed an armful of clothes and hung them next to Jaxon's. His scent was strong causing Destiny's concentration to waver.

When she had finished the pair made their way back down the two flights of stairs and into the kitchen. Destiny noticed straight away the blue haired girl, who sat glaring at her. Destiny did her best to ignore her, but she was making it increasingly difficult when she spoke.

"Jax baby, this is a pack house, it's not a place for second rate witches." Gene smiled as she flicked her hair back. She could see Destiny was getting wound up. "I think we should vote on whether she stays or not."

"Firstly Gene, you will address me as Alpha, and secondly, I decide if she's staying or not. If you don't like it go and stay at your parents." Jaxon sensed the atmosphere was frosty, not just from Gene but also other pack members. "Round up everyone and get them out front, I'll be addressing everyone in five minutes." Jaxon glanced at Destiny but before he had chance to reassure her Magnus walked in.

"What did I miss?" Magnus could feel the tension in the air as the pack members made their way outside. "Destiny, are you okay?"

"I think we made a mistake coming here." Destiny sat down at the table and folded her arms.

"If you want to stay at mine we can leave now?" Magnus sat next to his daughter. He hated seeing her upset.

"No one's going anywhere. We all have a job to do and that's the end of it." Jaxon pointed to the door. "Shall we?"

Magnus and Destiny followed Jaxon outside and stood on the porch next to him. They watched the crowd as they stood in silence waiting for their Alpha to speak. Carlton joined them and nodded to Jaxon.

"Listen carefully everyone. I'm not going to repeat myself twice. As you are aware there are rogue vampires that are not only killing supernatural's, but they are also draining every drop of blood, leaving the corpse's mummified. These vampires are under some sort of spell…" Jaxon was interrupted by Gene cutting in.

"Then why doesn't your witch friend cast a spell and put a stop to it. How is it our problem?"

"Because they are killing our kind too, and if you interrupt once more, I will rip your throat out. Now shut up and listen." Jaxon bared his teeth and watched as Gene hung her head. "A war is coming, and we will all have a part to play. I want everyone training, morning and afternoon. No exceptions. In the meantime, Destiny and Magnus will be staying here. Destiny is under my protection; anyone attempts to harm her they will have me to deal with. Understand?"

"Why are you protecting a witch, surely she can protect herself?" Gene made her way to the front of the crowd. "You're putting us all in danger Alpha."

"Because she is the key to winning this war, now enough talking. Omegas start preparing food." Jaxon turned to Destiny. "See, it's all going to be okay."

Destany watched as the crowd made their way back in, the atmosphere was still frosty, but she did get the odd greeting. As Gene approached, Destiny held her breath.

"The Alpha's mine witch. Touch him and I will kill you." Gene smiled and continued through the door to the kitchen, content that she had made her point.

Magnus pulled on Destiny's arm. "Come on, let's go in."

"No. I want you to start training me." Destiny walked down to the front lawn and looked out. The place was breath taking. In front of the packhouse there was a garden area that stretched out two hundred feet, and at the end of that there was a large lake, with an island made of rocks in the middle. Behind the lake in the distance, for as far as the eye could see was forest. The place felt safe and secluded. Destiny turned to Magnus. "We need to be prepared."

"Wait Destiny. Now there is no shortcut with magic, however I know a way you can master spells quicker." Magus motioned to his daughter. "Follow me."

After making her excuses to Jaxon, Destiny climbed the stairs and grabbed her bag, then followed Magnus to his room. "So what do I do?"

"Firstly I want you to read the first spell."

Destiny opened the book and read down the first paragraph. unimpressed, she looked at Magnus. "Why do I need to learn how to tidy my room? I can do that without magic."

"You need to learn everything, so we will try this one first. Now place your index finger from your right hand onto the spell." Magnus watched as his daughter did as he said. "Perfect. Now breath in the words with your finger."

Destiny burst out laughing. "You do realise you can't breathe with your finger."

"Destiny! Concentrate. Please. Now visualise it. Take a deep breath. You should feel slightly dizzy if it works." Magnus studied Destiny as she took a deep breath and crossed his fingers. "Well, do you feel it?"

Destiny clicked her fingers and watched as Magnus's jacket hung itself up. "OMG. That's bloody brilliant. Right next one."

"Hang on young lady. Not so fast. Taking in too many will jumble your brain, it can lead to strokes and heart attacks. So one more for tonight and that's it. Now next spell."

"Can I learn fire?" Destiny scanned the pages looking for the right spell."

"No, they are written in order for a reason. Now what one's next?" Magnus knew his daughter was inpatient. She took after him after all. But patience is a virtue and with magic it is also a must.

JAXON LISTENED from outside the room. His jealousy had got the better of him. Unable to contain himself a minute longer he grabbed the handle and barged in. "Time to get some rest. Destiny follow me."

"It's customary to knock, not barge in." Destiny remarked as she picked up the magic book and placed it in her bag.

Jaxon ignored the dig, instead he stood filling the doorway and tapped his foot impatiently. Destiny had a way of getting under his skin and to be honest he didn't like it.

Destiny pushed past him, immediately feeling the electric sensation shoot through her as their body's touched. Briefly stunned by the sensation her steps faltered until she contained her composure.

Jaxon grinned as he watched her, glad that she felt it too. "I said follow me." Jumping over the banister rail, Jaxon landed in front of Destiny, stopping her in her tracks. "I have a job to do, remember. So let me do it."

Leading Destiny back to his room, he locked the door behind her and pointed to the ensuite. "You can get changed in there."

Destiny grabbed her pyjamas and walked into the ensuite, shutting the door firmly behind her. Her fingers searched for a lock unsuccessfully, she sighed. "Of course there's no lock."

Jaxon laughed. "I don't need a lock. This is my room, remember. Now get changed, I'm not gonna barge in without knocking."

Destiny closed her eyes, of course he heard her, he's a wolf after all. She got ready for bed and brushed her teeth, before returning to the bedroom. "Where am I sleeping?"

"In the bed." Jaxon made his way to the ensuite and started to strip.

"Where are you gonna sleep?" Destiny pulled the covers back and slid in. The bed was comfortable, but it smelt of Jaxon. How on earth was she supposed to sleep with his scent filling her nose.

"I'm gonna shift. My wolf will guard you better, my senses will be more alert. Now get some sleep." Jaxon started to shift. The sound of cracking bones filled the tiny ensuite.

Destiny's eyes went wide when the huge black wolf came padding into the bedroom. It was smiling at her. As she flopped back on the pillow, Destiny closed her eyes. This whole scenario was a nightmare. How was she supposed to sleep with a wolf in her room. Well his room. Destiny let out a scream as the wolf landed on the bed next to her. "Omg, you better not molt all over the bed." Huffing she turned her back and pulled the covers up to her chin.

Jaxon's wolf nudged closer to Destiny, she was his mate and he wanted to be as close as possible. With one ear turned toward the window, the wolf watched Destiny as she slept. He could sense what was coming.

CHAPTER 16

Destiny opened her eyes and let out a piercing scream. There inches from her face was Jaxon's wolf. He was just staring at her, with that same daft grin on its face. "What the hell…. Back up Jaxon." Swinging her legs to the side of the bed, Destiny made her way to the ensuite. Her heart rate was returning to normal after the shock she had just encountered. Listening through the door she could hear the sound of Jaxon's bones cracking as he returned to his human form. "I'm getting in the shower." She informed him, hoping he wouldn't come in.

Ten minutes later Destiny walked back into the bedroom, wearing nothing but a towel. She noticed Jaxon watching her, his eyes traveling up and down her body. She ignored him and continued to the closet. Destiny studied the rail; she wanted something comfortable to wear while she was perfecting her magic. She spotted a pair of jeans and a t-shirt, grabbed them then proceeded to get dressed while Jaxon was in the shower.

Destiny made her way down to the kitchen and was pleased to see Magnus sitting at the long table all by himself. "Morning. I don't think we are very well liked around here."

"Good morning Destiny. Wolves are strange creatures. They are suspicious of magic. Although their transformation is somewhat magic. Still let's not worry about them, we are here to do a job. Do you want a coffee?" Magus walked to the worktop and grabbed the coffee jug, refilling his cup he reached for another.

"No thanks. Is there any tea?" Destiny joined Magnus and searched the cupboards.

"What are doing? Get out of those cupboards." Gene walked in and slammed the cupboard door shut. "This is a pack house not a witches coven. Don't touch what doesn't belong to you."

"What's going on?" Jaxon looked between Gene and Destiny; he could feel the tension in the air.

"I wanted to make a cup of tea. It's okay, I'll go to town to get one, after all, I wouldn't want to touch anything that doesn't belong to me. Magnus, are you coming?" Destiny stopped talking when Jaxon banged his fist on the table.

"STOP." He directed his anger at Gene. "I told you last night if you have a problem then leave. Destiny is my guest and as I own everything she can help herself to whatever she likes. Now get out of my sight." Jaxon turned to Destiny and took a deep breath before continuing. "You are here so I can protect you, so you won't be going anywhere without me. Understand?"

Destiny nodded then turned to Magnus. "I suppose we should start training."

"I'll go and prepare. Join me outside when you are ready." Magnus gave a short sharp nod to Jaxon. "Alpha."

Destiny went to follow Magnus but felt Jaxon's hand on her arm. That same feeling of electricity filled her whole body. "I need to go Jaxon."

"Not so fast." Jaxon pulled out a chair. "Sit. You need to eat. You didn't eat last night. I'll make some eggs and bacon."

Destiny watched as Jaxon prepared breakfast, placing a cup of fresh tea in front of her he then continued to butter toast and placed it on the table.

"Here dig in." He handed her a knife and fork and then sat ready to eat his own.

Destiny pushed the food around the plate. Her stomach was in knots at the thought of what was to come, made worse by her present situation. She looked up at Jaxon. "No one wants me here."

"They are scared of you. Magic normally brings trouble. It's not personal Destiny and besides, this is where you need to be. They will come around, just give them time." Jaxon replied before stuffing a forkful of bacon into his mouth.

"But we don't have time Jaxon. Do we?" Destiny placed her knife and fork down and pushed the uneaten breakfast away.

Jaxon pushed it straight back towards her then picked up the fork. "If you won't feed yourself then I will feed you. Your choice?" Jaxon laughed as Destiny grabbed the fork and started feeding herself.

"OKAY DESTINY the next spell is appearance. Rather handy if you want a change of clothes. Now hold your finger on the chapter and breath the magic in.

Doing as Magnus said, she got the feeling of tiny pins pricking her body, it sounded more uncomfortable than it actually was. As she breathed out she could feel the magic course through her body. "Okay. Let's try it." Looking down at her jeans she visualised a black skirt with long leather boots.

"Marvellous!" Magnus exclaimed as he clapped his hands together."

Destiny felt her skirt, it was real. The boots were real. She would never be stuck for something to wear again.

"Okay, let's take a break. I need a drink." Magnus made his way back into the pack house, while Destiny made her way to the edge of the large lawn that spanned the back. This was at least five hundred feet long and again surrounded by forest. She watched the scene in front of her with wide eyes. Taking it all in. She had never seen anything like it. The pack all stood in neat lines copying the moves that Jaxon showed them. Then they broke off into pairs and started training.

Magus joined her by her side minutes later and smiled. "Impressive bunch aren't they?"

Destiny nodded and then turned. "I suppose we should continue my training." They returned to the front of the house, Destiny looked out over the large lake that stood at the front, surrounded at the back by a thick forest of pine trees. "It's beautiful here. And peaceful. You would never know a war was about to start."

Magnus noticed the far-off look in her eyes, he knew she was thinking of her mother. "You're not on your own Destiny. I will be with you every step of the way. Now let's try something different, as we have a lake here, let's start with the water element, there are four you know. Fire. Water. Earth and Air. A witch can only conquer one, so let's find out what your one is."

Destiny pulled the book from her bag and proceeded to scan the pages. "Here it is." Placing her finger on the chapter, she breathed in, soaking up the knowledge. As she let out her breath the feeling of falling through time hit her, her vision faded, and she slumped backwards. When she opened her eyes she was in Jaxon's arms. "What happened?"

"Shh it's okay, you fainted.... Magnus I'm gonna take Destiny up to her room. She needs to rest." Jaxon lifted Destiny up and carried her back to the bedroom. Laying her gently on the bed, he watched as she closed her eyes again. "I don't want you doing this, it's not safe."

"I have to, you heard the queen, we all have a part to play. I'll be fine, I just breathed the spell in too quickly." Pushing herself up Destiny looked up at Jaxon and smiled. "I'll be fine."

"Look, rest for a bit. I'll go and get you a drink." Jaxon left the room, closing the door as he did.

Destiny could still feel the magic coursing through her body, the power felt amazing. All her senses were still tingling. Standing up she made her way to the window and looked out over the lake. She smiled as the water rippled. She now had the knowledge and as the saying goes knowledge is power.

"I thought I told you to rest!" Jaxon place the glass on the bedside table and pointed to the bed.

"You know you are extremely bossy." Crawling back onto the

bed Destiny lay back. "What are you doing?" The bed shook as Jaxon jumped next to her.

"I'm guarding you. To make sure you do as you're told. Now rest." Jaxon grinned as he folded his arms behind his head. The grin soon fell when he had the urge to kiss Destiny. He had to remind himself she was a witch, and this was purely business. Feeling his pulse quicken he turned to look out of the window. "She's a witch." He said out loud.

"Who are you talking too?" Destiny sat up and looked around the room. "Are you seeing people? Cos I can assure you there's no one here but us. And for the record, I know I'm a witch."

Jaxon jumped up and stormed out of the bedroom, as he made his way down the stairs, he cursed himself. He couldn't be that close to her; it was making him confused. He had a job to do, a Luna to choose and a battle to win. As he hit the porch he started to shift. A run was what he needed to clear his head.

Destiny watched from the window as Jaxon took off at great speed. She had to give it to him, his wolf was magnificent. But why were things so strained between them. One minute he couldn't bear to be away from her the next he couldn't bear to be near her. Just what was going on with him. As movement caught Destiny's eye, she looked across to a group of women. They were standing at the edge of the lake. There in the centre was Gene, pointing up at the window. They were all laughing at her. In a rage Destiny looked at the lake and visioned a wave that would drench them. Lifting her hand, the water rose up at the same time, then pulling her hand towards herself, the water came forward in a wave and splashed over the group. The women screamed and ran towards the pack house. Destiny burst out laughing. As a soaking wet Gene looked up at Destiny, Destiny smiled back. "You're right Jaxon, I am a witch and it's time I started acting like one."

As she made her way down the stairs she came face to face with Gene. "Has it been raining?" Destiny asked sweetly.

"I know you did this and when Jaxon finds out he will kick you out of the pack house, just you see." Barging past, Gene ran up the stairs, into her bedroom and slammed the door.

When Destiny got to the porch, Magnus was sitting on the top step, holding her bag. He looked despondent. Not his usual chirpy self. "Magnus what's wrong?"

"Destiny! Are you okay?" Magnus jumped up and pulled her into his arms. "I was so worried about you. I should never have tried to jump the spells."

"I'm fine. It had to be done. Now come on, let's work on the next one, pass my bag." Destiny grabbed the bag and pulled out the book. "Okay, shall we try an easier one." As Destiny scanned the next page she felt the hairs on her arms stand up. The last time she felt like that it was when the Snodlin's had been watching her in the land of fae. Walking towards the tree line to the right of the packhouse, Destiny scanned the area.

"Destiny. What is it?" Magnus stood watching as Destiny took a step back.

There in amongst the trees stood Mrs Richards. The same Mrs Richards that she saw in the window of the bed and breakfast. Destiny realised that her eyes weren't black but missing. Mrs Richards opened her mouth; a high-pitched scream filled the air. Destiny placed her hands over her ears and fell to the ground.

"Destiny?" Magnus grabbed his daughter and helped her up. "What's wrong?"

"Didn't you hear that?" Destiny looked back at the trees; Mrs Richards had gone.

"Hear what? I think that spell you soaked up earlier did more damage than we thought. You're shaking. Let's get you back inside." Magnus guided Destiny back to the pack house.

Before they turned out of sight, Destiny took one last look at the forest and scanned the area, she could still feel a dark presence. "I know you're out there." She whispered.

CHAPTER 17

"Where's Jaxon, he should have been back by now. It's getting dark." Destiny continued to scan the area out of the kitchen window. She could feel something was wrong. "I'm gonna go look outside."

"No. I'll go." Carlton got up from the table and made his way to the door. He was worried too, although he wouldn't say anything to the others. Tempers were already frayed what with a witch and a warlock staying there.

"I'm coming with you." Destiny grabbed her bag and went to follow.

"No. I said I'll go. Now wait here." Carlton pulled his clothes off and shifted as he got to the grass. He could smell Jaxon, he was near. Sprinting off he followed the scent.

Destiny watched as he ran out of sight and into the trees. "I've got a bad feeling Magnus."

Magnus could also sense the danger in the air. He didn't want Destiny to worry though, so changed the subject. "Don't you think it's time you started calling me dad?"

Destiny's head snapped around and she starred at him in disbelief. "What?"

"Oh come on Destiny, I'm your dad. Surely I deserve that title?" Magnus smiled. "I remember when you were born. You were such a dainty little thing, until you cried. Goodness you were loud enough to wake the dead." Magnus sighed. "And then you were gone."

As Destiny opened her mouth to reply a scream came up from outside. Running out as the rest of the pack house made their way out too, she got caught up in the crowd. Fighting her way to the front Destiny stopped dead when she saw Carlton holding Jaxon's limp body.

"GET THE HEALER!" Carlton shouted as he lay Jaxon onto the grass. Destiny knelt next to him.

"What's happened?" Watching Jaxon's chest she noticed the large gash running down the centre. It was filled with black blood. The blood was also spreading along his veins. He looked so pale, the colour from his face had drained away.

As the healer came to tend to Jaxon, Carlton pulled Destiny away. "She needs room to work."

Destiny watched as the woman shook her head. "This is some kind of dark magic. I can't help him. I'm sorry."

Destiny thought of the words the fae queen had said. Fae blood heals, never give it away. She pushed Carlton away and knelt at Jaxon's side. "Get me a knife, and hurry, he's dying."

"Here." Carlton passed Destiny his knife and stood watching as she held her hand up.

She then used the knife to slice through the palm of her hand, it stung, more than she thought it would, but she needed to at least try to save Jaxon. She squeezed her blood into his wound. The blood trickled out covering it completely. Destiny felt herself weaken as the blood continued to trickle from her hand. She felt Magnus grab her and wrap her hand in something soft. As she looked down at Jaxon, she watched the black veins recede until they disappeared altogether. "Take him to his room Carlton. He should be fine by morning."

"How did you do that?" Carlton starred at Destiny in disbelief. "I mean I'm grateful that you did but how?"

Destiny turned without answering, she felt weak and needed to lie down.

Magnus grabbed his daughter as she started to wobble and guided her into the pack house. "That was a good thing you did, saving the Alpha. Stupid but good. Don't ever tell anyone how though. You don't need anyone coming after your blood."

DESTINY WATCHED AS JAXON SLEPT. His wound had been bandaged and the colour had returned to his cheeks. She lay down next to him, wondering what could have caused his wound. The healer was right, it was some kind of dark magic. Destiny sat back up. There must be something in the spell book, something that would give her answers. She gently climbed out of bed, careful not to wake Jaxon and grabbed the bag. She pulled out the book and took a seat on the floor. Frantically she scanned the pages, looking for an answer, one by one until she came to a cloaking spell. "That should help." She whispered as she placed her finger on the paragraph and breathed in. Once content she read down further. The next spell that caught her eye was a shield spell, an invisible shield that could be put in place to keep everyone safe. Again she placed her finger on the paragraph and breathed in. Content, Destiny replaced the book into her bag and made her way to the kitchen, surprised to see most of the pack in there. Before she had a chance to turn around, Carlton saw her.

"Hey Destiny, I want to thank you for what you did tonight." He pulled out a chair and motioned for Destiny to sit down. "Are you hungry?"

"Yeah, I am a bit." She took a seat and noticed all the smiling faces staring at her.

"Get Destiny some food. What do you like? We got Lasagne in the fridge, or we can make something fresh." Carlton asked as he pointed to the fridge.

The woman that did the cooking smiled down at Destiny as she waited for an answer.

"That'll be fine thanks.... Carlton I need to speak with you. Have you ever seen a wound like that before. The black stuff, do you know what it is?" Destiny took the plate and smiled at the woman. "Thanks."

"Nope, never seen anything like that before. So you have no idea what could have done it Destiny?" Carton looked at Destiny's lasagne as his stomach grumbled. "Can I have a plate too." He called to the woman, who nodded in return.

"No, I'm pretty new to this whole witch thing, until a few months ago I thought I was an average 17-year-old. That's why Magnus.... my dad is training me. I've got a spell I can put around the pack house. It's an invisible shield. It will keep everything out and I can also cloak it to make it invisible, but I need to talk to Jaxon first. Find out what happened." Finishing the last mouthful of lasagne, Destiny called to the cook. "That was lovely, thank you. What's your name?"

"Rose, Miss Destiny." Rose's cheeks flushed as she took in the complement. "I'm glad you enjoyed it. I'll be off to bed now. Do either of you need anything?"

"No Rose. I think the rest of you should get some sleep too." Carlton ordered everyone to bed. "Destiny, you must need rest, I'll come and see Jaxon in the morning. Goodnight."

Destiny nodded and left to climb the stairs, as she entered the bedroom she looked at Jaxon. He was sleeping peacefully. *You are handsome even when you sleep*, she thought.

"You think I'm handsome?" Jaxon opened his eyes and grinned.

"What?" Destiny felt her cheeks colour, thanking god she hadn't turned the light on.

"You said I'm handsome, even when I sleep." Propping himself up against the headboard he reached for the light. As soon as the room was illuminated she was met with a grinning Jaxon.

"I didn't say anything." Placing her hands on her hips Destiny sighed. "You can hear my thoughts?"

"Yep cupcake. I've got your blood in my body. I can hear every last one of them." Jaxon reached out and grabbed Destiny's hand. Pulling her closer to the bed.

"Get off. Jaxon, You need to rest and so do I." She slapped his hand away and noticed his face drop.

"Get in the bed then."

"I am. Now stop it." Destiny climbed in next to him and noticed the heat radiating from his body. "You seem very hot?"

"Thanks, so do you."

"What…. No, not that type of hot. Hot. Hot…. Like boiling hot. Are you sure you're alright? Destiny felt his forehead, it was hot but there was no fever. "Maybe I should go and get the healer."

"Destiny. You know I'm a werewolf right?" Jaxon asked, amused.

"Yeah, I know." Destiny rolled her eyes, as if she didn't know. That's all this lot talk about.

"Our body temperatures a lot higher than humans. It's perfectly normal, and it's not all we talk about."

"Will you stop listening to my thoughts." Annoyed Destiny turned over. She didn't have to look at his smug face.

"I'm not smug…. Okay, well maybe a little bit." Jaxon laughed.

"Why can't I hear your thoughts?" Destiny rolled over and looked at Jaxon. "Because it seems a little unfair."

"Because you haven't got any of my blood. You need to bite me. Fancy having a go?" Jaxon winked.

"I won't be biting you anytime soon and I don't need to be a mind reader to know what you are thinking." Destiny grabbed the quilt and pulled it up to her chin, then moved to the edge of the bed. "Goodnight."

DESTINY WOKE to the sound of birds singing. She stretched her arms over her head and yawned loudly. She glanced next to her and noticed Jaxon was already up. Destiny pushed the covers off and trudged to the ensuite. She turned on the shower, it was more than a little welcome to feel the water washing away the tiredness.

After she scrubbed herself clean, she dried, dressed, and headed down to breakfast. She could hear Jaxon shouting his orders outside. Obviously training the troops already. "Morning Rose."

"Morning Miss Destiny, what do you fancy today?" Rose pulled out a large plate full of sausages, bacon, and pork chops from the fridge and started to lay them on a large gribble. "I'm making pancakes too, and eggs. How do you like them, scrambled, over easy?"

"Can you call me Destiny. Drop the Miss, it doesn't sound right, and I'll have whatever you're cooking."

"Something smell's good." Jaxon walked to the stove and grabbed a slice of bacon, then shoved it in his mouth.

Destany watched as her eyes slid down to his bum, his jeans fitted perfectly. As she looked back up Jaxon turned around and grinned.

"You've got a nice bum to, cupcake."

"I'll be back in a minute Rose; I just need to do something." Running from the room, Destiny darted up the stairs and into her bedroom. Pushing the door firmly shut behind her. She pulled her spell book from her bag and scanned the pages for a blocking spell. She wouldn't have him listening to her thoughts. Finally she spotted what she wanted and placed her finger on the paragraph. As Jaxon barged through the door, she breathed in quickly and the mind link was broken.

Jaxon stood in front of her. "Why did you do that?"

Destiny noticed the sad tinge to his voice and was consumed with guilt, but she didn't know why. "Because it wasn't fair. We have a battle to fight, and I can't concentrate if I'm worried about you hearing my thoughts."

"Fine, but remember this, one day you might just wish I could." Jaxon stormed from the room and left Destiny alone.

CHAPTER 18

It had been three weeks since Destiny had started her training. Jaxon spent no time in her company anymore. Since she had put the invisible shield around the pack house and grounds he told her she didn't need him. He wouldn't even look at her. If she walked into a room, he walked out. Destiny had now made her way through a quarter of the spell book and her magic abilities were remarkable for someone of such a young age. She could magic up a feast when she was hungry. No longer did she mix with any of the pack members. She was an outsider. She needed to remember that.

Destiny watched from the window as Jaxon messed around with Gene on the grass. They were supposed to be training but all she could hear were Genes giggles. She wondered if that's where he had been sleeping, in Genes bed. Destiny shook her head as jealousy started creeping in. He didn't want her, so she wouldn't allow herself to want him.

Destiny's attention was drawn to the noise of a car, she watched as it stopped at the edge of the shield. She recognised it as William the vampire's. Destiny made her way out of the packhouse and to the car just as Jaxon did.

He stepped in front of her and glared at the vampire. "William.

I take it this is important as you've come to the pack house." Jaxon growled.

Destiny moved to the side and smiled at William as she raised her hands to open a door in the shield. "Come through William. We can talk by the lake."

Jaxon grabbed Destiny's arm and pulled her to one side. "What the hell do you think you are doing. It's my job to keep you safe and you invite a vampire in here."

"That's interesting Jaxon. How do you propose to keep me safe from Genes bed?" Shrugging his hand off, Destiny called to William. "Follow me please."

Before Jaxon could reply, Destiny and William had walked away. Begrudgingly he followed. This was his home, his land and he would call the shots, not some kid of a witch. As the pair sat on the grass, Jaxon stormed over. "As I'm the alpha perhaps you could run this past me, or are you now the alpha Destiny?"

"I would have run it past you, but you don't talk to me anymore and I certainly wasn't going to interrupt your playtime with Gene." Destiny turned and addressed William. "We need to get the timeline of events in order. Starting from the beginning. I can feel whatever 's out there is getting closer. My dad, Magnus has gone to look at his scrolls again. Whatever is going to hit will hit on the summer solstice, that's one off the most powerful nights of the year. So on that note, it only gives us a month to finish preparing."

"Anubis and Hera have been called, unfortunately they have another battle going on in the underworld. One that needs their full attention. So we are on our own, I'm afraid." William looked at Jaxon's surly expression. "We need to work together Jaxon. For all our sakes."

"Fine. Everyone here's ready. We need a plan. Hang on." Jaxon mind linked with Carlton. 'Bring out the bourbon and join us. Williams here.' Looking at Destiny he noticed she looked sad. Had he done that? "Okay, let's get started."

"Hang on my dad's back." Destiny jumped up and ran towards the edge of the shield, raising her arms as she did so.

William watched as Destiny opened the shield. "She is very

powerful Jaxon. I wouldn't have thought she had it in her. She is also very beautiful."

Annoyed Jaxon growled. "She is also mine. So keep away."

"Does she know that, because from where I'm sitting she doesn't think she belongs anywhere or to anyone." William stopped as Magnus and Destiny joined them.

"Okay so what did you find out?" Destiny looked a little more hopeful than she felt.

"The mating ritual needs to happen as soon as possible. Alpha you need to choose your Luna. Shall we say Saturday?" Magnus didn't notice the sad look in Destiny's eyes as he spoke. "The Alpha once mated with the Luna will give the pack double the strength. At all cost this must happen."

"Dad did you inform the towns people like I asked?" Destiny butted in. She didn't want to hear about Jaxon and Gene.

"Yes they are packing now and will start arriving tomorrow. Edna will be here later tonight. She can't wait to see you Destiny." Magnus stopped when Jaxon cut in.

"What do you mean they will arrive tomorrow?" Jaxon looked between Destiny and Magnus. "Well?"

"We can't leave them out there to fend for themselves Jaxon. They would be slaughtered." Destiny glared. "I know you only think of yourself, but I can't."

"Well I'm not having them here. They will have to find somewhere else to go. You had better go and tell them Magnus." Jaxon stood up and pointed down at Destiny. "You are to blame for all this. Not me. You."

Destiny looked at the faces staring at her. Her dad and William were full of pity, while Jaxon and Carlton were full of blame. She felt her heart break, just a little, like a little piece had fallen off. She held back the sob that was building in her throat and jumped up. She wouldn't cry in front of them. As she ran, as fast as she could to the pack house, unable to stop the tears as she reached the door, she sobbed all the way to the bedroom, slamming the door behind her. Destiny threw herself onto the bed, and replayed Jaxon's words over and over again. He was right. It was her fault. She wiped the tears away and took a deep breath before standing. "Then I need to fix it." With one click of her fingers her case was packed and laying on the bed in front of her. Placing her bag over her shoulder, she grabbed her case and disappeared.

Destiny reappeared in the burnt-out bed and breakfast, right in front of the mirror. She turned and looked at the room. It was black and charcoaled. How hadn't she seen it? She had spent two nights here. Sighing, she stood and waited for Mrs Richards. She knew she was the only one to give her answers, even if she didn't like what she heard. "I know you're here. Show yourself."

"Hello deary."

The voice came from behind her. Destiny turned and looked at the distorted figure. "Mrs Richards, I must say you're looking rough today. Forget to slap your face cream on?"

Mrs Richards put her hand to her face and pulled off a large lump of hanging flesh, leaving her jawbone on display. "Is that better deary?"

"Much. Now I haven't got time to waste on idle chit chat. So why don't we get down to facts. Firstly You said you found me after my mum died but that's not true, someone killed my mum, so who was it. You?"

Mrs Richards let out a long cackle. "Yes deary it was me. Did you like the rain. You know your mother knew it was unnatural. But by then it was too late, she was as good as dead. Did you know we saved you in that crash. Although I must admit you've caused us a lot of problems. But that doesn't matter now, your time is near."

"Who's us?" Destiny watched as Mrs Richards tone changed.

"Always so nosey. Keep your nose out!" Mrs Richards snapped.

"No need to get angry. Shall we try an easier question. What do you hope to achieve?"

"We are going to open a doorway." Mrs Richards cackled once more. "A darkness will cover the world, all of humanity will perish."

"Why did you bring me here?" Destiny watched as the shell of the old lady started pacing the room.

"Because we needed to keep an eye on you. You have something we want and the only way to get it was to bring you here, so you could discover your birth right."

"My birth right? You told me I was a witch, why couldn't you have left me there, out of this shitshow."

"No deary, you had to be here. We couldn't have you ruining our plans."

"There you go with that 'WE' again. Who's we?" Destiny ducked as a lump of wood flew at her head. "That's not very nice, I'm a guest here Mrs Richards, or can I call you by your real name. Galdreola."

Destiny stood her ground as Mrs Richards body started to convulse; her head bent backwards as a new head emerged. A large green scaley face, appeared with glowing red eyes. It had human features although instead of having hair it had spikes. As the body split in two, six arms appeared followed by a serpents body.

Galdreola rose to her full height, hitting the ceiling. Looking down at Destiny the giant monster smiled, showing four rows of razor-sharp teeth. "It's good to be free. Destiny, you are a clever girl. How did you know my name?"

Destiny smiled. "Not only am I a witch, but also I follow clues. When you came to the fae castle, your form was distorted. I didn't pick up on it at first but then I got thinking. No one else ever saw you, even in the bar that first night. As I walked away I heard them muttering, 'who was she talking to' I realised I had to open my mind. When you stared at me from this window, your real reflection showed in the glass. It was faint, but I could just make out your real face. So after that I spent my spare time studying my magic book. And there you were. Did you know it describes you as a human snake? Not very flattering for something that believes its all-powerful." Destiny laughed. "Anyway let's get back to business. Mrs Richards answered most of my questions, but I have one more. "Why did you kill the alpha and his wife?"

Galdreola snaked her way around the room then stopped suddenly. "I think I'll let you work that one out. Or shall I kill you now."

Destiny rolled her eyes. "You can't kill me. You're not really here are you. You are stuck in between this world and the underworld, waiting to be released. If those rogue vamps don't manage it, you'll be stuck there forever. In between worlds. So as great as it's been chatting, I really must go and read up on my magic."

"Yes you should, learn it all. It will be your only chance of winning." Galdreola weaved her way to the window. "Now leave."

Destiny frowned, there had to be a reason for the demon to want her to learn all the magic from the book. Making her way out, Destiny turned. "Oh and just a word of advice, you've got something stuck in your teeth." Destiny marched out of the bed and breakfast smiling. At last she knew what to do.

CHAPTER 19

Magnus paced the kitchen, his temper hanging by a thread. "This is all your fault Jaxon. If anything happens to my daughter I will hold you personally responsible."

"Carlton have you searched the grounds?" Jaxon asked hopefully. "Any sign of her?"

Carlton shook his head. "We've checked everywhere. She isn't here Jax."

Cursing himself Jaxon jumped up. "I'm gonna head to town, see if I can pick up her scent. Magnus. Isn't there a location spell you can do?"

"Don't you think I've tried that!" Magnus stopped pacing. "I'm coming with you."

Before Jaxon could answer Alex came running in. "Jaxon, you're gonna want to see this."

Marching out to the porch, Jaxon watched as a long procession of vehicles approached the pack house boundary. There at the front was Destiny with Edna. "I'm going to kill your daughter Magnus." Taking off to meet the oncoming line, Jaxon cursed under his breath.

Destiny smiled as Jaxon's angry face came into view. "Good afternoon Alpha. What a beautiful day."

"We need to talk Destiny. In private." Dragging Destiny away from the gathering crowd, Jaxon stopped when he couldn't be overheard. "I told you they can't stay here."

"And I told you they haven't got anywhere else to go.... Look Jaxon, you can play the hero, you and your new Luna, Gene. I told them you wanted them here. To protect them. What's it going to look like if you turn them away?" Destiny pleaded as she pointed to the waiting crowd.

"The pack house can't hold that many people, where are they supposed to sleep and let's not forget about food. Where's that supposed to come from?" Jaxon rubbed his temple; he could feel a headache coming on.

"They have tents and all the food from town is now in those trucks. Please Jaxon." Destiny sighed. "I can't protect everyone if they are spread out."

"It's my job to protect everyone, not yours." Jaxon realised what he had said. As he watched the smile spread on Destiny's face he shook his head. "They do not come into the pack house. Understood?"

"Perfectly." Destiny threw her arms around him and laughed. "I knew you would do the right thing."

Two HOURS later everyone was in the grounds and setting up their tents. Carlton and Alex ran around giving orders while the rest of the pack assisted those that needed it.

"Have you gone soft Jaxon?" Gene asked as she watched the spectacle unfolding. "Only the Alpha I knew wouldn't have done something so stupid. You are supposed to look after the pack. Not the town."

"Not now Gene." Jaxon watched Destiny as she went from family to family checking they were okay and giving them assistance. Without the use of magic.

Following Jaxon's eyeline Gene glared. "When I'm Luna this won't be allowed. Remember that. And she has to go." Pointing to Destiny, Gene wished she could get rid of her. As an idea popped into her head she smiled.

"Who said you're gonna be Luna?" Jaxon walked away leaving Gene open mouthed.

DESTINY ARRANGED a large fire pit in the middle of the ground, She dug it out by hand and placed large stones around it. Then went in search for something iron to hang over the middle so the town people could cook.

"What are you doing witch?" Gene stood with one hand on her hip and the other pointing at the hole in the ground. "Did you ask me for permission?"

"Gene, what a pleasant surprise, have you come to help?" Destiny turned to walk away, but Gene grabbed her arm.

"I said what are you doing. Answer me or I'll have Jaxon banish you." Glaring at Destiny, she stopped. "That is if he makes it back."

"What do you mean if he makes it back. Back from where?" Destiny felt the hairs on her arms stand up as the worry edged into her mind.

"He went for a run in the woods because you landed all this shit at his door. He's been gone a while now." Gene looked off into the distance. "If anything happens to him…."

"I'll find him. Tell Magnus where I've gone." Destiny walked to her case that was leant against a shed and searched for her sword. Once she had it in her hand she walked to the edge of the shield and waved her arms, opening a door. Once through it she raised her hands once more and shut it.

Taking off through the forest Destiny tried to locate Jaxon with a spell, but there was no sign of him, she couldn't pick up anything. As she continued on her way she noticed the sky growing darker. It was a beautiful May day. The sun had been shining with not a cloud in the sky. Destiny sensed the evil; she could almost taste it. Whoever cast this spell was an expert in dark magic. The further she went into the forest, the darker it grew. As she walked she noticed there were no sounds. The birds had stopped singing and there were no signs of the usual wildlife. The leaves on the trees were brown and crinkled and the bark was grey. The trees had been sucked dry of all life. Further in she spotted the rotting corpse of a rabbit, followed by the corpse of a hedgehog. Suddenly she heard her own voice, it was in her head. 'Use your magic. Save the forest.' Destiny didn't answer, instead she stopped and looked around. Everything was dead. The darkness grew and she had trouble seeing. She closed her eyes and listened, there had to be something, some sign of Jaxon. Shaking her head she continued on slowly. This had turned into a nightmare.

"HAS ANYONE SEEN DESTINY?" Edna walked from tent to tent, anxiously asking every occupant.

"Haven't seen her since 3pm. Maybe she went to get wood for the firepit?" The elderly man replied.

Edna turned and made her way to the front of the packhouse. There sitting on the porch was Magnus speaking with Carlton. "Magnus! I can't find Destiny anywhere. Have you seen her?"

"Not for the last hour, I thought she was with you." Magnus stood as Jaxon and Gene walked out of the packhouse.

Jaxon noticed Edna's worried expression straight away. "What's going on?"

"Alpha, I can't find Destiny. One of the town folk thinks she may have gone into the forest to collect wood for the campfire." Edna noticed Gene's smug look, and knew she was somehow involved. "Where is she Gene?"

"Why are you asking me." Holding on to Jaxon's arm she attempted to pull him back into the packhouse. "I don't associate with witches, now if you don't mind, the Alpha and I have much to discuss."

Jaxon shook Genes hand away and turned to face her. "What have you done?"

"Jaxon are you really going to listen to her?" Gene pointed towards Edna and scoffed. "I thought you would have had a little more faith in your future Luna."

"I have plenty of faith in my future Luna Gene.... If you've done anything to jeopardise this pack, I will personally tear you apart myself. Now one last time. What have you done?" Jaxon's eyes started to change colour as his temper flared.

"I couldn't find you, so I asked her to look for you. I don't know where she is." Gene turned and made her way back into the packhouse. She would keep out of the way until Destiny's body was found. There was no way she would survive out there alone. Witch or not, these rogue vampires would be on her before she could sense them.

Destiny sat on an old fallen tree. It was now pitch black and her vision was almost zero. The thought of Jaxon being out here alone scared her more than she was scared for herself, and she was really scared. Without using her magic she couldn't see a way out of this mess. But she couldn't use magic. Galdreola had told her to learn all the magic she could from the book. There had to be a reason for that. Destiny snapped out of her thoughts when she heard a twig snap from behind her. She Jumped up and spun around, her pulse beating in her ears. There were two red glowing eyes coming towards her. Stumbling back in a state of panic, Destiny tripped and ended up on her back, winded. Without thinking she raised her hands and let out a bolt of energy, throwing the vampire back a few feet. As she scramble up right she noticed the vampire stand and head back towards her faster than before. She grabbed her sword without thinking and swung with all her might right through the vampires neck. The body fell to the ground, but it didn't disappear. Instead it oozed the black blood that Jaxon had been poisoned with. Destiny rested against a tree; her legs felt weak. The blast had used a lot of her energy. She looked at the vampire's head and decided to take it with her. She took off her top and used it to wrap the vampires head in then threw it over her shoulder before making her way back. The air was already sweeter, and the leaves had started to turn green once more. As she neared the packhouse the familiar sound of birds tweeting filled her ears.

"Are you telling me we are stuck in here Magnus. What if Destiny is in trouble. How the hell am I supposed to save her." Jaxon punched the shield and immediately regretted it. He looked down at his throbbing fist and cursed Gene. He knew she was jealous of Destiny, but he didn't think she would go this far.

"Calm down Alpha, I'll see if I can open a door." Magnus raised his hands, but nothing happened. "This is strong magic; it might take me a while."

"Alpha." Carlton pointed to the other side of the grounds as Destiny appeared.

Without waiting, Jaxon ran towards Destiny in temper. "What the fuck do you think you were doing, taking off like that without telling anyone?"

"It's nice to see you too Alpha." Destiny smiled as Magnus joined them.

"Why are you half-dressed Destiny?" Magnus looked at his daughter who was wearing a bra.

Jaxon immediately took off his t-shirt and placed it over Destiny's head. "I'm asking the questions here. Why didn't you tell anyone where you were going?"

"I asked Gene to let Magnus know. She sent me looking for you, because you went for a run in the forest because and I quote 'I landed all this shit at your door. So if you want to shout at anyone, go and shout at your soon to be Luna."

"We can't get through the shield, so exactly how did you think Jaxon went for a run?" Magnus watched as Destiny frowned.

"I thought Jaxon was in danger, I didn't think about the shield. Look I'm sorry okay. I didn't mean to worry anyone." Destiny finished putting on Jaxon's t-shirt, then motioned to her top, she was still holding. "We need to get William over here. I came across this out in the woods." As she threw her top on the floor, everyone watched as the dismembered head rolled out and landed at Jaxon's feet.

"What the hell. Where did you find that?" Jaxon asked as he pushed it over with his foot.

Destiny smiled at the shocked looks on Jaxon's and Magnus's faces. "I found it attached to the rest of its body."

CHAPTER 20

"I forbid you from leaving the packhouse. In future you stay with me." Jaxon ordered.

Magnus nodded. "The Alphas right Destiny. You shouldn't have gone out there on your own."

"Well it's just as well I did; the final piece of the puzzle has been revealed. If you would care to listen." Destiny watched as both men sighed.

"You could have been killed. Or doesn't that bother you?" Jaxon folded his arms in a sign of irritation.

"Destiny." Magnus tried to choose his words carefully. "You may think you are a powerful witch but there's still plenty you haven't learned yet."

"If you would both shut up and let me explain, then you both might learn something." Destiny glared between both men, daring them to speak.

"Okay, we'll humour you. Continue." Jaxon grinned as the irritation flashed across Destiny's face. It was short lived though.

As Destiny replied, it was her turn to grin. "Why thank you mighty Alpha, who couldn't get through the shield…. Now I went to see Mr's Richards earlier."

"The ghost?" Magnus asked.

"Technically she's not a ghost and she's not Mrs Richards either. The shell was used to mask who she really was. When you came to get me from the bed and breakfast, as we left, I turned and saw Mrs Richards staring out of the window. She had no eyes. It was creepy. Then I saw her reflection in the window pain, it showed her true form. It's a demon called Galdreola."

"Again I say you shouldn't have gone there on your own. Do you ever think of the consequences?" Jaxon tried to keep his temper in check by taking a deep breath.

"Will you let me finish Jaxon?" Destiny sighed. "It's just as well I did. I questioned her, found out she was the one that killed my mum. She said they spared me because they needed me to discover my birth right. So they have been leading all the events up until this moment. Now I couldn't understand at first, Mrs Richards was great, heling me with a few simple spells. Giving me confidence to learn more. So none of it made any sense when I found out who she really was. It's all to do with the magic book. Galdreola wants the magic it contains."

"Then why doesn't she just take the book?" Jaxon turned to Magnus who then began to explain.

"The only person that can see the writing is the owner of the book, which is Destiny. She inherited it from her mother when she passed away." Magnus's voice had a sad tinge to it. He had loved Vanessa, part of him still did. "I think they thought Destiny wouldn't be as strong or as clever as she is, so she would have been an easier target than her mother."

"True, but there is another way she can get the contents of the book. If I learn everything in the book, then all she has to do is kill me in some sort of ritual, eat my body and voila. She will have all the power the book holds." Destiny looked seriously at Jaxon. "Before she can take me, I need you to promise to kill me."

"I'm not going to kill you. I'm also not going to let her take you." Jaxon paced in front of Destiny before facing her. "Stay inside the shield, you'll be safe that way. We have Magnus, he can use his magic to help."

"That's another thing, magic cannot be used. It gives them more power. When the rogue vampire attacked I used magic to blast it away. As it came back it was faster, more powerful. So this fight needs to be done the old-fashioned way. And that brings me to the next thing, Jaxon I need you to train me to fight. I was lucky this time, but luck doesn't last forever."

"I've just told you to stay in the shield. You are not fighting!" Jaxon looked at Magnus. "Will you tell your daughter?"

"Destiny." Magnus jumped when Destiny pulled out her sword.

"Why won't you listen to me. Magic cannot be used. That means the shield will have to come down. I'll be a sitting duck. Now will you teach me to fight, or do I have to ask someone else?" Pointing the sword out in front of her, Destiny lunged forward. "It can't be that hard after all."

Before Jaxon could reply, Carlton came running over. "William's coming over." Carlton eyed Destiny who was still lunging with the sword. "What is she doing?"

Jaxon rolled his eyes. "Learning to fight apparently. Come on Zorro, let's see William." Picking up the dismembered head with Destiny's t-shirt, Jaxon marched away.

"Magnus who's Zorro?" Destiny whispered as she followed.

Jaxon smirked as he turned around. "A famous swordsman, so you don't know everything after all."

Ignoring his comment, Destiny walked towards William.

"Jaxon. To what do I owe the pleasure of the summons, I was trying to contact the others?" William smiled at Destiny. "Nice t-shirt, a little big though."

Destiny blushed as William looked down her body, she didn't need a mind link to know what he was thinking.

Jaxon growled he could sense it too. "She's wearing my t-shirt. Now if you don't mind can we get down to business." Dropping the head onto the ground Jaxon watched the smile leave William's face. "Is this one of the rogue vamp's you were talking about?"

William nodded slowly. "You killed one Jaxon. I'm impressed."

Destiny stepped forward. "Actually I killed it. I need to know how many of them there are and where's the rest of them?"

"I'm even more impressed Destiny. Did you use magic?" William bent down and studied the head. He could sense the evil, despite it being dead.

"You can't use magic on these things. It only makes them stronger. Now please, how many, and where are they?" Destiny bent down and wrapped the head once more in her top as she looked up at Jaxon. "This will need burning, outside the shield though, in case it contaminates the air with dark magic." Standing once more she watched William as he rubbed the back of his neck. "What aren't you telling us William?"

"There's been no sightings recently. I sent a couple of scouts out and they never returned. I suspect they are now rogues too." William looked at Destiny. "If you've killed one here then they must be close by. Can't you sense them?"

"I didn't see it coming, it was only because a twig snapped I noticed. They will need numbers, surely. I mean Wolves would tear them apart in a battle, unless…" Destiny closed her eyes.

"What?" Jaxon grabbed Destiny by the arms. "Destiny?"

Destiny shook Jaxon's hands away. "Is it possible they can turn wolves? I mean this is powerful dark magic."

"No, impossible." Jaxon said hesitantly.

"But if they did, you wouldn't be able to fight them, they would be more powerful than a normal wolf." Destiny felt her eyes mist up as she put her head down. "They could be here within the next few days…. You'll have to do the Luna ceremony tonight. There's no other way. You should go and tell Gene to prepare." Destiny turned and walked away. She could feel her heart breaking as the tears trickled down her cheeks.

Jaxon watched Destiny walk away. He could feel her sadness. Carlton stood watching his face. "Don't you think you should tell her?"

"Tell her what?" Jaxon strolled back to the packhouse with Carlton hot on his heels.

"Tell her you've been staying in my room. Come on Jax, I see the way you look at her, she's your true mate." Carlton stopped abruptly as Jaxon swung around.

"I'm the alpha, the pack has to come first, besides, I don't know if Destiny would survive the bite. Gene will make a good Luna; she knows our ways." Jaxon stormed up the stairs and into his bedroom.

Carlton knocked and then entered without waiting for permission. "Gene will be a good Luna. Do you really believe that? Look Jax, I love you like a brother. I want you to be happy and I will stand by you, whatever you decide. But. Remember Destiny is the one you will have pups with. Not Gene, and Gene is not going to like that."

WILLIAM WALKED OVER TOWARDS DESTINY. "Hey, you need to let me out." Stopping when he noticed her tears he sat on the grass next to her. "So you're not okay with the Luna ceremony. So why suggest it?" William handed Destiny his handkerchief.

Drying her eyes, Destiny looked out towards the forest. "It's the only chance the pack have got, it will double their strength."

"I'm not an expert but surely mating with their true mate would give the pack the best chance?" William asked.

Destiny shook her head as she handed the hanky back to William.

"Keep it, looks like you're gonna need it more than me."

"I'm a witch, wolves and witches don't mix. Well not in the mating way. Besides, when this is over I'm heading back to the UK." Blowing her nose Destiny let out a sob. "If this is love you can keep it."

William put his arm around Destiny and held her as she cried into his shoulder. "Let all out. You'll feel better after."

But Destiny knew better than that, this feeling would stay with her forever.

MAGNUS LOOKED at the small island in the middle of the lake. That was where Jaxon would take his new Luna. After a short ceremony they would bite each other on the collar bone and that would be that. Joined together until death. A night of partying would follow the ceremony, enjoyed by the whole pack. His thoughts turned to Destiny. She had been practicing with her sword all afternoon, totally ignoring all the party plans. She looked sad. He hated that she was hurting, and he found himself hurting too. He didn't know how to make this better, in fact he couldn't. Turning around Magnus watched Gene laughing with other pack members. They were combing her hair and telling her how great she was going to be as Luna. Magnus almost burst out laughing. He hadn't forgotten what she did to Destiny, sending her into the forest to die. He would even that score eventually.

"Magnus is Destiny okay?" Edna walked towards Magnus with a concerned look on her face.

"I don't know. Maybe you should go and speak with her. I would but I'm not good with girly stuff, and Edna, let me know what she says." Magnus watched Edna make her way towards Destiny. As Destiny looked up he turned and looked out over the lake again. Jaxon had asked him to look something up, but he wasn't sure that he wanted to. If the answer to the Alphas question was yes, it would change all their lives.

Destiny stopped swinging the sword as Edna approached. "Did Magnus send you?"

"No.... Yes.... He's worried about you, so am I." Edna put her arm around Destiny's shoulders. "Shall we go for a little walk?"

"I need to practice Aunt Edna, there's not much time." As Destiny tried to shrug Edna off, Edna held on tighter.

"Ten minutes won't hurt. Now come on." Smiling, Edna led Destiny around the edge of the pack grounds. "Sometimes a walk helps you clear your head."

"I don't think a bomb would clear mine." Destiny smiled at the towns people as she passed their tents. They all greeted her like she was some great hero, when in fact she felt like an imposter. "All these people are counting on me. I'm seventeen years old and I'm responsible for their safety. Have you any idea what that feels like?"

"No Destiny I haven't.... But can I point out that you got them here, where they are safe. You did that, you made Jaxon see sense." Edna watched Destiny's face drop.

"Look I really need to get back to training. Thanks for the little pep talk. It's helped." Destiny looked up just as Jaxon was making his way towards her.

Edna beamed as he walked closer. "Alpha, I'm so glad to see you. Destiny needs some help, I'm sure she's holding the sword all wrong. Could you be so kind as to give her some pointers?"

"Aunt Edna!" Destiny threw her aunt a filthy look. "I'm managing just fine." Storming away, Destiny cursed under her breath. Jaxon was the last person she would ever ask help from again.

Jogging behind her to catch her up Jaxon grinned as he watched Destiny's bum sashay from side to side, with each step she took. "Wait. Look if you need help I'm here. It's for the good of the pack after all."

Destiny stopped dead and spun around. "I'm not here for the good of the pack. I'm here to keep Magnus and Edna safe, and the towns people. As you've made it perfectly clear the packs your domain, you look after them. Now if you don't mind I've got things to do."

Destiny watched as Jaxon walked away, but she needed to hurt him like he had hurt her. "And by the way, make sure you reject me before you take up with your new Luna."

Jaxon felt like he had been stabbed through the heart. The mere thought of rejecting her caused a physical pain deep inside. As the anger inside him built, he turned to look at her. "Destiny Black. I reject you."

CHAPTER 21

Destiny had been laying on the grass for an hour, holding her heart as she sobbed. The physical pain was too much to take. This was the worst pain she had been in, and she didn't know if it would ever stop.

"Destiny."

Sitting up, Destiny looked around. "Who's there?" She couldn't see anyone, but the voice had come from near her.

"Destiny. Look at your ring."

Holding her hand up Destiny saw the Queens face staring back at her. "What's going on?"

"What's going on, your majesty." The queen replied sharply.

"What's going on your majesty." Destiny sarcastically answered. "Is this like a telephone call wishing me good luck as I go into battle?"

"I need you to come here for the last of your training. Now hold the ring out and you should see a green glow. Walk into it." The queen commanded.

Holding her hand out in front of her, Destiny watched as a green glow illuminated off of the ring. "Are you sure it's safe?"

"It's quite safe now hurry up, you've not much time." The queen watched as Destiny appeared. Standing a few feet from her. "At last. Now, Sir Gideon is here to teach you the art of the bow and sword. If you follow him into the royal grounds you can begin." Destiny bowed slightly and walked away, following Gideon. "And Destiny." The queen called after her. "Everything will be as it should, if you win."

Destiny frowned as she walked out into the palace grounds. What did the queen mean, everything will be as it should. Nothings as it should be, she had just been rejected by the man she loved. Or should that be wolf? But the pain had stopped, that must mean it's over, but why did she still long for him?

"Destiny I need you to concentrate." Gideon stood holding a bow with a quiver full of arrows, thrown over his shoulder. "Come now."

Destiny stood next to him and took the bow. "Okay. Now what?"

"Now watch and you shall learn." Taking his own bow, Gideon pulled out an arrow and placed it into the bow. "You hold it like this." Then he pulled it back and let it fly through the air when he released it.

Trying the same, Destiny sighed when her arrow landed three feet in front of her. "This is going to take a while."

JAXON LAY on his bed trying to control the pain. Why did he have to bite, he knew what she was doing, pushing him away because he had treated her so badly. He stumbled of the bed and to the door, as he grabbed the door he bellowed. "MAGNUS."

Minutes later Magnus appeared. "Alpha, you look awful." Helping Jaxon back to his bed he stood and watched him. "You've rejected Destiny."

"Yes.... Look I need you to reverse it, I can't fight like this." Jaxon held his stomach. "Please Magnus."

"Have you any idea of the pain this will cause her? I need to find her." Magnus turned as Jaxon bellowed again.

"MAGNUS. REVERSE IT. NOW!" Jaxon growled his eyes flashed amber.

"I don't know if I can. I've never heard of a rejection being reversed. Let me look at my books." Magnus left Jaxon on the bed in agony while he ran to his room.

"What did he want?" Gene walked in and sat on the edge of the bed looking at Jaxon as she did so. "What's wrong with you. You better not be trying to get out of the mating tonight." Folding her arms she studied his face. "You're really in pain."

"Gene get out." Jaxon rolled over and closed his eyes.

"Did that witch do this to you, I'm going to kill her." Leaning over Jaxon's body, Gene kissed his cheek. "I'll deal with this."

Jaxon swung around and grabbed Gene by the face, slowly he pulled her towards him. "I said get out. I don't love you Gene, I don't even like you. There will be no mating ceremony tonight. Now get out of my sight, because the next time I see you, I'll rip you apart."

Gene ran from the room as Magnus walked back in. "What's up with her. She had a face like thunder."

"Can we stick to the point. Can you reverse it or not?" Jaxon swung his legs around and perched on the edge of the bed, still holding his chest.

"I've found something but be warned I'm not sure it will work. Now I need some of your hair and some of Destiny's. Let me find her hairbrush." While Magnus left Jaxon alone, he grabbed his hair and pulled a few strands out and placed them on the side.

"Here we are, now place them in this pot with yours. Ah, oh dear." Magnus read the spell ingredients and sighed. "I need blood from both of you Sorry, looks like it won't work."

"Wait. I have Destiny's blood in me. Remember when she healed me?" Jaxon reached for a knife and cut his palm, allowing the blood to drip into the pot.

"Might work, on the other hand you might end up mating with yourself." Magnus laughed until he saw Jaxon's scowl. "Okay, just pop these herbs in and give it a stir. Now a flame of passion." Magnus pointed his finger, as Jaxon watched in amazement. There at the tip of Magnus's finger was a flame. Igniting the ingredients in the pot Magnus then placed a lid on it. "Let the mating spell begin. Let the two hearts beat within. Let them bond and mate as one. Let their love forever come." Taking the lid off, Magnus looked inside the pot. "How do you feel?"

"I feel fine. Actually I feel better than fine." Jaxon stood up and laughed. "Magnus, you're a genius." Running out, Jaxon made his way down the two flights of stairs in seconds. "How's the prep going for tonight?"

"Nearly done Jax. Gene didn't look very happy when I saw her just now. You two had a row?" Carlton finished placing down the box of beers he had brought up from the cellar.

"I do not want to discuss Gene, not now, not ever. And Carlton I want everything to be perfect tonight. It's going to be a night to remember." Jaxon laughed then grabbed Carlton in a bear hug and spun him around. "I need to find Destiny."

"Bravo Destiny. Bravo." The queen clapped as she watched Destiny shoot her arrow straight at the bullseye.

Taking a bow, Destiny laughed. She felt good. This un-mating lark was the best thing that had happened to her these last few months. "Now watch me with my sword. Gideon."

Gideon stood facing Destiny and raised his sword. "Are you ready for an arse whipping?"

"Bring it on, goldilocks." Destiny took a step forward as she swung her sword.

After what seemed like hours Destiny stood over Gideon as he lay on the ground. "Fancy another go old man?"

"I don't think you need any more practice Destiny. Help Gideon up." The queen walked over to them and smiled. "You've taught her well Gideon. Thank you. And as for you Destiny, I'm pleased you've picked it up so quickly. You are a natural with a sword and bow. All you need now is something decent to fight in. Come with me."

Destiny followed the queen into a large dressing room. She had never seen a room so big; it had every kind of garment of which you could think. She watched as the queen pulled out a leather pair of pants and a leather top with jacket.

"Put these on. They will protect you from sharp objects." Handing them to Destiny, she watched as she slowly stripped. "My dear child, use your magic."

"Sorry, I forgot." With a click of her fingers Destiny was changed into the leather outfit.

"Perfect. Now it's time to go back. Time is running out. When this is over I hope you will come back and see me. After all, I am your aunty."

"I'd like that. Okay. So how do I get back?" Destiny looked at the ring. "Does it work to get home to?"

"Just point it Destiny. And if you need to come here, use it. Now come along Gideon, there's things to do. Oh and Destiny, Raymond said he can't wait to see you again. He would have been here today, but he had to go somewhere with his parents. Cheerio now."

"I'll see you soon." Destiny pointed the ring and started to walk through the green light but heard the queens voice drift through. "This isn't the final battle, so it won't be soon child."

Destiny landed straight back at the pack grounds. What did she mean this isn't the final battle? Looking at the ring Destiny screamed at it. "Hello. Hello. What did you mean?" Flopping down on the grass, Destiny felt the despair take hold. As music caught her ears Destiny looked over at the pack house. It was starting to get dark, and all the lights were blazing from the windows. She could hear laughing and shouting coming from the other side.

Standing up she put her bow and quiver on her back and grabbed her sword. She may as well wish the happy couple her congratulations. As Destiny walked around the corner she came face to face with Jaxon.

"Where have you been? I've been looking for you everywhere." Jaxon looked down at what Destiny was wearing. Feeling himself get aroused, he looked away. "I need a word with you." Leading Destiny around the corner of the packhouse, he didn't make eye contact. "I had to undo the rejection. Now don't blow your top. I had to do it because I couldn't function, but I've been thinking...."

Destiny cut him off. "So you're going to take Gene as your Luna even though you're connected with me? Wow Jaxon, that's unbelievably selfish of you. I don't want to be your mate; I don't want the mate bond and I certainly don't want you. So here goes. I REJECT YOU!" Destiny stood waiting for the pain to hit. When nothing happened, she tried again. "I REJECT YOU!" Looking up at Jaxon she narrowed her eyes. "Why isn't it working?"

"I don't know. Look I've got things to do. Go ask your dad, he cast the spell." Jaxon turned, deciding to let Destiny calm down before he broke the news to her.

Destiny stormed around the corner and looked for Magnus. When she spotted him talking to some of the towns people she made her way to him. "Magnus. Can I have a word please. In private."

"Destiny. You look erm, different." Magnus watched as Destiny's eyes sparkled with anger. "Okay, let's go to my room."

"No. I'm never setting foot in there again. Come over here." Leading him around the back of the packhouse, Destiny poked her finger in his chest. "What have you done? More to the point why? Do I mean nothing to you?" Destiny felt her anger growing by the second. "I told him to reject me. You had no right."

"Destiny it's not what you think." Magnus grabbed Destiny's hand. "And I would be grateful if you would stop poking me. It hurts."

Destiny snatched her hand away. "You've reversed the rejection. I don't want to be his mate. I don't even want to be anywhere near him. He disgusts me.... I thought you was on my side." Destiny looked away; tears of anger were pricking her eyes.

"I didn't reverse the mating spell, I made it that you both had free will. That way if you end up together it would have been meant to be. I am on your side Destiny, but I had to do something to make you both better. This battle is just the beginning." Magnus looked at the bow on her shoulder. "Where did you get that from?"

"The queen. I've been training. Obviously, my mother's sister cares about me." Destiny saw the hurt on Magnus's face. It didn't make her feel any better though.

"Save that anger for what's to come Destiny and know one thing. I will be at your side because I love and care for you. Now let's get something to eat." Magnus grabbed Destiny's hand and led her to the food table. There was a smoky smell wafting in the air from a BBQ and a hog roast was being turned on a large spit, over a fire.

Destiny watched all the people standing around chatting. Jaxon was in his room getting ready and Gene was no doubt doing the same. It was hard trying to smile when all she felt like doing was screaming. It was unfair. Life was unfair. Why couldn't she still be at home with her mother. Baking cakes and listening to music. Why did she have to come here. Just why?

"Penny for them?" Carlton smiled as Destiny looked up.

She returned his smile before replying. "They're not worth a penny."

"Would you like a beer?" Carlton handed a cold bottle to Destiny and then burst out laughing as she tried to prise the top off. "Here let me." Carlton put it between his teeth and levered the top off. "There."

Destiny stared at Carltons mouth. "Didn't that hurt?"

"No. I'm a big strong wolf. Remember?" Clinking his bottle against Destiny's, he took a long swig. "So, are you enjoying the party?"

"I'm not staying, I'm going to patrol the boarder of the shield. I've got a bad feeling." Destiny looked out into the darkness, she had an unnerving sensation, like something was watching her.

"Come on, you need to let your hair down once in a while. We're wolves, we will sense something long before it gets here." Carlton grabbed Destiny's hand and lead her to the edge of the lake.

"Why are we here?" Destiny looked up just as Jaxon came out of the packhouse. He was wearing a suit. She wouldn't allow herself to think how handsome he looked. Her eyes darted to find Gene, but she was nowhere to be seen.

"It's about to start." Carlton whispered. "You'll get used to all our traditions once you give the Alpha a son."

"What?" Destiny's mouth dropped open.

"You have to mate with Jaxon to give him a son, you knew that right?" Carlton saw the startled look in Destiny's eyes and mentally kicked himself. "Jeez, I thought you knew. Gene isn't Jaxon's true mate. So for him to have a child he needs to mate with his true mate, which is you, or a witch that's been promised, which funnily enough, is also you. It's your Destiny."

Destiny threw the beer down and marched to the shield. There was no way she would ever have intermate relations with that pig. "Of all the god damn cheek." Destiny turned and watched as Jaxon stood staring at her.

Sighing Destiny turned away; she didn't want to see this. Looking out into the darkness Destiny grabbed her sword, she could sense whatever was out there wasn't here to pay it's respects. She took one last peek at Jaxon, then Destiny started to raise her hands when an almighty crack of thunder bounced off of the shield, followed by lightning. As the lightning illuminated the area, Destiny could see the rogue vampires lining up around the shield. There were many more than she had thought, maybe two hundred. Destiny looked back and saw the pack running towards her, with Jaxon in the front. "STOP!" She shouted as she raised her hand.

"Destiny get in the packhouse, we'll take care of this." Jaxon grabbed her arm and attempted to pull her away.

"No. You need to finish the ceremony before you all fight. There's at least two hundred of those things, you'll be slaughtered." Destiny pushed Jaxon back. "Go, I'll hold them off."

"You are not going out there on your own." Jaxon puled Destiny away.

"ALPHA." Magnus ran through the crowd.

"Did you find it?" Jaxon asked, still holding on to Destiny.

"Yes." Magnus drew in breath. "She will survive the bite."

Destiny looked between Magnus and Jaxon. "What are you talking about. Who will survive the bite."

Jaxon threw Destiny over his shoulder and marched back to the lake. "You will. Now shut up and do as you're told." Jaxon placed Destiny in the boat and made his way to the island.

"Jaxon. What are you doing. Where's Gene?" Destiny looked around but she couldn't spot her.

Jaxon didn't reply, he pulled the boat up and then picked Destiny up and carried her to the sacred rock. "I don't want Gene. Now will you be my Luna, my one true mate. In life and in death. In this world and the next? This is where you say yes."

Destiny stared in disbelief. "Have you gone mad?" Another crack of thunder rang out followed with a flash of lightning.

"We haven't got much time. Destiny say yes." Jaxon pulled his jacket and tie off and started undoing his shirt.

"This is no time to get naked Jaxon."

"Just answer the damn question." Jaxon threw his shirt down and grabbed Destiny around the waist.

"Yes, okay. Now what?" Destiny watched as Jaxon's teeth bared. "Now we bite each other." Sinking his teeth into Destiny's skin, he felt her tremble as he sucked at the wound. Destiny looked at his collar bone, and then bit down as hard as she could. The warm metallic liquid seeped into her mouth. Swallowing down, she felt a power course threw her veins. She felt different. Stronger. Looking up at Jaxon she smiled. "Do you feel that?"

"Yes." Jaxon smiled back. "Now we kiss." Jaxon's mouth crashed into Destiny's with a passion neither of them had ever felt before. Pulling away Jaxon looked at the bite mark on Destiny's shoulder, it was turning into the Luna ring. He wanted to drag her to his bed, but he knew that would have to wait until later. "We need to go, are you ready to take the shield down?" He asked.

Destiny nodded. "I guess so."

CHAPTER 22

Destiny and Jaxon stood at the edge of the shield. The towns people and elderly wolves had been sent to the packhouse. Swords had been given to every eligible fighter, including Magnus and William. Jaxon had his army spaced around the outside. Looking at Destiny he felt the urge to protect her. "I wish you would go into the packhouse where it's safe."

"This is my war too…. Now remember, you can't shift. Are you ready?" Destiny raised her hands and waited for Jaxon's reply.

"SWORDS READY." Jaxon waited for everyone to raise their weapons then looked at Destiny and nodded. "Stay behind me." As the words left his lips another crack of thunder rumbled, and the lightning struck the shield once more.

Destiny noticed some of the wolves step back as the rogue vampires lit up. They were all gathering against the shield wall, ready to charge. Their eyes red, their mouths open, snarling.

"HOLD THE LINE." Jaxon shouted. "AND DON'T SHIFT."

"I'm going to bring the shield down gradually, starting here at the front. It may give us a better chance. If the magic effects the rogues though, I will have to take it all down." Destiny waved her hands and brought the front half of the shield down, her eyes widening as the rogues approached. The pack leapt forward to meet them head on, swords swinging from side to side. The rogues speed was remarkable, within seconds they were upon the wolves. Destiny raised her sword and started swinging taking the rogues down one by one.

Jaxon felt the power in him building as he made his way through the rogues. With each one he killed he felt stronger. Out of the corner of his eye he spotted Gene heading towards Destiny, her sword raised. Jumping back he leapt in front of her with his own sword ready. As Gene lunged towards Destiny with the tip of the sword inches from her body, Jaxon swung out and cut her arm off. The sword dropped to the ground with her dismembered arm. Jaxon looked at Gene, her face was a mixture of pain and love. Love for him.

Gene swooped down and picked up the sword with her remaining hand. "If I can't have you Jaxon, neither will she." Turning towards Destiny one last time she raised her sword ready to strike. Jaxon swung his sword and plunged it into Genes chest. He watched as she fell to the ground. Before he had time to think a rogue had hold of Destiny's arms. His mouth open and his fangs glistening in the moon light. Destiny tried to shrug him off, but his grip was strong. As his mouth neared her neck, Jaxon carefully swung his sword, taking the rogues head off.

"You saved me." Destiny smiled. "Thank you."

"I will always save you, you're…" Before Jaxon had finished a loud shriek went up from somewhere around the grounds. "Now what?"

Destiny looked over towards the pack members to the right, one by one they were starting to shift.. "Jaxon. Stop them!"

"DON'T SHIFT. STOP." Running over to the first wolf he ordered him to shift back. "Destiny we need to protect them. Magnus, William, over here."

"If they get bitten you will have to kill them Jaxon." Magnus warned him.

"I know." Shaking his head, Jaxon lunged at a rogue before he had a chance to bite the wolf. "Shift back now!" He ordered.

Turning his head as a rogue grabbed one of the other wolves, Jaxon watched as William chopped the wolfs head off. Before he swung around another rogue had grabbed him and sunk his teeth into his neck. Before he had started to drain the body, Destiny swung her sword taking off the rogues head. The black blood spattered across the grass, covering William as he sank to his knees.

"Jaxon we need William." Destiny motioned to Carlton. "Can we tie him up and put him into the dungeon?"

"It's too dangerous. What happens when he turns? Look Destiny I can't allow it." Jaxon shook his head. "We need to kill him."

"NO!" Destiny stood in front of Jaxon, blocking his path. "I think I may be able to communicate with him. If I can find out what they plan next, it will help us in the final battle."

"What final battle, I thought this was it?" Jaxon looked at William then back at Destiny. "Will he be able to get out?"

"No. The cells are solid stone with 8-inch steel bars. No one would be able to escape from there. I can put a holding spell on him too if it makes you feel happier. If it doesn't work you kill him." Destiny replied.

"Okay. Carlton get Magnus to help you. If he starts turning into one of those things, kill him immediately." Jaxon looked at the bodies mounting up. There were casualties from both sides. "Destiny, will you be able to heal those of the pack, which have been injured?"

"I should be able to. But again, I would put them in the dungeons, just in case." Destiny pointed to the other side of the shield before she continued. "I won't need to open that half, looks like they have all come around here. We need to go out and check Jaxon. There can't be any of them left roaming otherwise they will just multiply again."

"Wait for Carlton and Magnus…. Don't you find it odd that all the dead are outside the pack boundary?" Jaxon asked as he scratched his head.

"It might be to do with the salt." Destiny replied, thinking Jaxon knew what she meant.

Jaxon stared blankly at Destiny. "What?"

"Oh, I forgot to say. Earlier I sprinkled salt around the edge of the shield, I didn't think it would work without magic, but I got the priest to bless it just in case. Maybe it helped after all." Destiny watched Magnus and Carlton as they walked back to them.

"He's secure, we chained him up, just to be on the safe side." Carlton stopped when he noticed the piles of bodies at the pack boundary. "I guess we need to burn that lot."

"You get a fire going, I need to go and make sure there's no more of those things out there. Destiny, can you start healing the wounded?" Jaxon saw the concern in her eyes. "Look, we need the pack to be strong, especially if another battle is coming. I'll be fine."

"I'll go with him." Magnus announced. "Jaxon's right. We will need the pack at its fittest. And it would be a good idea to teach the towns people how to fight."

Destiny agreed reluctantly. "But don't shift, and if you get in trouble call me. Please Jaxon."

"Okay. If it makes you feel any happier I will, but don't forget I'll have the mighty Magnus with me." Jaxon rolled his eyes. As if Magnus thought he could take Destiny's place. "Come on, the sooner we get this done the sooner I can relax with my Luna." Jaxon winked at Destiny then mind linked with her. 'You're all mine tonight' Jaxon grinned as Destiny blushed.

Magnus jumped in; he didn't need to be a mind reader to know what Jaxon was planning. "About that alpha. I'm afraid the final part of the mating ceremony cannot take place until the summer solstice."

"WHAT!" Jaxon's temper flared. He only started to calm down when Destiny placed a calming hand on his chest.

"That will be something to look forward to Alpha. Won't it." Destiny smiled. "Now go…. And be careful."

Destiny watched Jaxon and Magnus make their way through the pile of bodies and heads before turning and making her way to the packhouse. As she headed down to the dungeon she was greeted by the townsfolk, who looked pleased to see her.

"Can we go out now Destiny? It's a bit cramped in here." One elderly woman asked.

"I need you all to stay here for now, apart from the men who can help throw the rogue vampire bodies onto the fire. Those that are fit enough please make your way out to the entrance. Carlton will give you orders." Turning she continued down the stairs. Alex met her at the bottom.

"We've had to put a couple to a cell. There's seven casualties down here and of course William. He hasn't come around yet." Alex informed her.

"Okay, I'll start healing, who's the worst effected?" Destiny watched Alex point to the middle cell. He walked to the door and unlocked it. "The black stuff inside them is spreading, do you think you can help?"

Kneeling next to the first bed, Destiny looked up and shrugged. "I don't know but I'll do my best." Using her sword to cut the top away she watched at the black blood spread through the veins of the man lying there. Taking the sword she sliced through her palm and let the blood seep into the wound. Slowly the blackness started to recede. Moving to the next bed, she repeated the process. "These two can be bandaged up but keep them locked in here over night and I will check on them in the morning."

Jaxon and Magnus combed the area around the packhouse grounds. They couldn't find any trace of anymore rogues.

"We may as well make our way back Magnus, there's nothing out here." Jaxon turned to walk back.

"Okay Jaxon, spit it out." Magnus calmly fell in step with the Alpha. "I know you want to say something."

"Fine. Why have I got to wait until the summer solstice to finish mating with Destiny?" Jaxon glared at Magnus. "Is this another ploy to keep us apart?"

"Jaxon, you know I never wanted Destiny mating with you, but I've come to terms with it because I can see she loves you. We don't get to choose who we fall in love with and it's no one else's business. The reason you can't finishing mating with Destiny is because of your own ritual practices. It has nothing to do with me. The only thing I will say is, if you hurt her there will be a price to pay."

"You wouldn't be threatening me Magnus. I never had you down as being that stupid." Jaxon stopped as his eyes flashed amber.

"No Alpha, I am not threatening, I am promising." Magnus watched Jaxon's face change from anger to worry. "What's wrong?"

"It's Destiny, she's in danger." Before Magnus replied, Jaxon shifted and ran straight back to the pack house. As he entered the dungeon he shifted back. "Where's Destiny?"

Alex came out of a cell carrying Destiny. "She's passed out. I think she's used too much of her blood healing the pack."

Taking Destiny off of Alex, Jaxon made his way up to the bedroom. Lying her on the bed, he undid her top just as Magnus entered the room.

"What's happened?" Kneeling next to the bed Magnus noticed the pale complexion. "She need's blood Jaxon."

"Then she shall have mine." Pulling a knife from the side, Jaxon made a small incision in his wrist. Holding her head back so her mouth opened he let the blood drip in.

After a few minutes Destiny coughed as the deep red liquid filled her throat. Swallowing down she opened her eyes. "What…"

"Shhh it's okay, you fainted. You used too much blood healing, now you need to rest. Stay here I'll be back soon…. Magnus stay with her." Kissing Destiny gently on the lip's, Jaxon left to make sure all the rogues had been burnt.

"I need to put the shield back up." Trying to lift herself up, Destiny crashed back to the bed.

"Not so fast young lady. You're too weak to get up, never mind restoring the shield. We have half the shield; I'll get guards put out there for tonight. You should feel much better by the morning. Now do as Jaxon said, and rest." Magnus ordered.

"We did okay, didn't we?" Destiny closed her eyes but carried on talking. "Where's Jaxon, I need him."

"I'm here." Jaxon marched into the room and sat on the edge of the bed. "I'll be staying with Destiny now; you can go Magnus."

"Very well. I'm going to ask for guards to watch the boundary where the shield is down." Magnus stood to leave.

"I've already taken care of it. You should rest too Magnus. Who knows what we will face tomorrow." Jaxon took his shoes off and lay back on the bed with Destiny. "You worried me there for a moment."

"I worried myself." Destiny turned to face him. "I'm fine now you're here."

Placing his arm beneath Destiny's head he cuddled up to her. "And I'm fine now I'm here with you. Now sleep."

CARLTON STOOD GUARDING the pack grounds with his brother Alex and two of the fighters Hudson and Lucas. These four where the best of the fighters, other than Jaxon. Jaxon being the Alpha had more power than any other wolf. Now he had his Luna, no one would match him for speed or strength.

The four men watched as the rogue bodies burned, in three separate fires. All lighting up the road and forest as they did. Carlton kept his eyes on the shadows. If there was to be another attack it would come from there.

"Looks like it's gonna be a long night. Anyone fancy a drink?" Alex asked the others.

"We can't leave out post." Carlton replied. "I don't know if I made a mistake counting but I'm sure one of the heads was missing when we burned the body's."

"Shouldn't you have told the Alpha?" Hudson turned and faced Carlton. "I mean a head can't do any damage but even so, you should have told him?"

"The Alpha is with our Luna. He asked me to take care of things. I'll let him know in the morning, but for now keep your eyes peeled." Carlton sighed. "We don't want any more surprises."

Lucas laughed. "Our Luna. Isn't she the cause of all this?" Lucas pointed to the burning bodies. "Forgive me for talking out of turn but surely taking a witch for our Luna, Jaxon has put us all in danger?"

Alex was the first to reply to Lucas. "If the Alpha hears what you've been saying he will rip your tongue out. Now shut up and concentrate."

"Fine, but I'm only saying what everyone else is thinking." Lucas shrugged and walked towards the boundary. He had a feeling they were in for a lot more trouble with a witch in the pack.

Carlton turned and looked at the packhouse. The lights were shining out from the kitchen. He could see people moving about, he could even smell the food. "I'm starving. I'll get the cook to bring us some food out. Lucas?" Turning when he got no reply, Carlton scanned the area for his friend. "Lucas stop pissing about. Do you want something to eat or not?"

"Where the fuck did he go?" Alex went to walk to the boundary, but Carlton pulled him back.

"Stay here, you too Hudson." Carlton scanned the shadows, the hairs on his body were standing up. "Shh…. There's something out there."

Lucas walked towards the pack, dropping to his knees before falling to the floor.

Alex starred in disbelief. "Where's his head?"

CHAPTER 23

Jaxon paced around Lucas's headless body. "Tell me again how this happened when you were supposed to be all together.

"He walked to the boundary, we were talking about getting some food and then he was gone. The next thing we knew he came walking back, then fell to the floor. Minus his head." Carlton shifted from foot to foot, he could tell Jaxon was about to lose his temper.

"Jaxon. What's going on?" Destiny walked towards Jaxon; her face showed her concern.

"Destiny will you please go back to bed. You're supposed to be resting. I'll be back in a bit." Jaxon stood in front of the body shielding Destiny from the gruesome sight.

"Jaxon. I know what you're doing, please let me see." Destiny walked around Jaxon and bent down, studying the neck wound.

"Can you please not get so close, it's not safe." Kneeling down next to her, Jaxon jumped as the headless body sat up and pointed towards Destiny's ring. Jaxon immediately grabbed Destiny and pulled her away.

"Wait he's trying to tell me something." Destiny watched closely, moving her eyes down his body for signs of dark magic. "Have you noticed he's still beathing?"

Jaxon watched Lucas's chest rise and fall. "Your right, but how can this be possible?"

"It must be the rogues, there's no other explanation." Carlton announced. "When I was burning the body's, I thought I miss counted. There may have been a head missing."

"And you're only telling me this now because?" Jaxon growled. "So now we have two heads missing. Why didn't Lucas turn into a rogue though?"

Destiny stood up and addressed the men. "Because this has nothing to do with the rogues. This is something entirely different." Raising her hands, she closed the shield. "There. We're safe for now. I need to consult my book. Jaxon we need to let Magnus know."

"Jaxon what are we going to do with the body?" Carlton pointed at Lucas. "He's not dead so we can't burn him."

Jaxon rubbed his face with both hands. "I guess it's another one for the dungeon…. Jeez at this rate we're gonna need a bigger one."

Jaxon grabbed Destiny's hand and marched back to the packhouse. "Is it too much to ask for one night with my mate." Before Destiny could answer Jaxon continued. "Apparently yes it is, because I'm surrounded by idiots."

Laughing Destiny stopped and pulled him back. "I hope I'm not one of those idiots." Standing on her tiptoes she placed her lips against Jaxon's and kissed him. She felt the tension leave his body as all the blood rushed to his manhood. Pulling away she smiled. "I'm looking forward to the summer solstice when you can use that." She pointed to his groin and heard a low growl leave his lips. "Why Alpha, I do believe you're aroused."

"You keep doing that and I won't be waiting for any solstice." Jaxon pulled her back and just as he leant forward to kiss her; Magnus appeared. "Magnus. You seem to have a knack for turning up at the wrong time." Sighing Jaxon lead them up to the bedroom. His and his mates bedroom. He was starting to get fed up with all the intruders. "We have a headless body that's still breathing, Destiny is going to look through her book, but we wondered if you had any idea what could cause this?"

"I have heard of a type of Goblin that does such things,

although it's been many years since I've seen it." Magnus rubbed his chin. "I'll check my scroll's, although I must say, they normally only do bad things if someone insults them. I wonder what Lucas did?"

Jaxon snarled. "Why would you think Lucas did anything?"

"Calm down Alpha. Goblin's are creatures of habit. We can't even ask Lucas what happened." Magnus turned and left the room.

"I wish you would stay calm Jaxon. We asked Magnus for help; he was only telling us what he knows." Destiny grabbed her magic book and perched on the bed. "Come and sit with me." Destiny tapped the bed next to her.

Jaxon sat down and sighed. "Why is this all happening. I mean it's been one thing after another since my parents died. It's like their deaths have caused these events."

"You know you could be right. My mother dying has done the same, it's like everything is connected." Taking Jaxon's hand Destiny gripped it tightly. "We will get to the bottom of it all, but in the meantime we have each other." Destiny laughed. "Even if it was a rocky start."

"Made it more exciting though…. Your face when I picked you up and threw you over my shoulder." Jaxon burst out laughing. "I thought you were going to hit me."

"Yes I'm sure it amused you. I really thought you were going to mate with Gene. Talking of Gene, where is she, I haven't seen her?"

"She's gone…. Now concentrate on your book and see what you can find, then I want you to get some rest. I'll go and check on the pack." Jaxon pecked Destiny on the lips and then left.

"Right, let's see…. Goblin's. Goblin's….Ah. Here we go." Destiny read down the page.

'They are invisible but can manifest into small humans, looking about four years old. Most commonly the creatures are household spirits of ambivalent nature.' "What the hell does ambivalent mean?" Destiny shook her head then continued reading. 'While they sometimes perform domestic chores, they play malicious tricks if insulted or neglected.' "Chopping some body's head off is a bit more than malicious."

"Destiny. Who are you talking too?" Magnus entered the bedroom and looked around before focusing on Destiny.

"I was talking to myself. Anyway, what have you found out?" Destiny closed her book and placed it into her bag.

"There is a Goblin who has been known to collect heads. I didn't think he was around anymore. Still. You can summon him if you know his name. As he was so close to pack grounds, I would say someone here knows him. We need to find out who." Magnus smiled. "You are looking better, but don't you think you should get some more rest."

"I feel fine, it must be all that Alpha blood rushing through my veins. Anyway, I need to solve this and get Lucas's head back onto his body. He is one of the best fighters and the pack will need him. Shall we get some breakfast, I'm suddenly starving." Destiny stood and made her way down to the kitchen with Magnus following.

The smell of bacon was wafting up the stairs, making Destiny's stomach growl. She realised she hadn't eaten since the morning before, what with the argument with Jaxon, the un-mating, being summoned by the queen, the mating ceremony and then the battle. It had been quite a day. In fact it had been quite a few months of one thing after another. Jaxon was right. His parents being killed along with her mother had caused all these events. But what was the link?

Rose looked up from the griddle as Destiny entered. "Good morning Luna. What would you like to eat?"

Destiny returned her smile. "A cup of tea would be lovely to start with. Please feed the pack first, I can wait." As she glanced around the large kitchen, Destiny noticed it wasn't as tidy as normal. "Would you like me to help?"

"No Luna, it's not your job." Flustered, Rose wiped her hands on a tea towel and started making Destiny's tea.

Destiny noticed her hands were shaking as she tried to steady the cup. "Rose. My job is to assist the pack and you are one of the pack, correct?"

"Yes Luna, but only omega's do menial tasks. It would be

beneath you." Rose placed the cup of tea down in front of Destiny. "Everything is under control, now please, enjoy."

"I don't call cooking for the pack a menial task, it's a very important job. Without being fed the rest of the pack wouldn't be able to do their jobs." Destiny looked around at the faces staring back at her. "Rose. Take the rest of the day off."

"Luna...The Alpha will banish me, I have too much to do." Rose sniffed back the thought of not having a pack, not having a home. She may be a simple Omega, but this was still her family, even if they did treat her badly at times.

"I order you to take the rest of the day off. If the Alpha or anyone else has a problem they can deal with me. Now go." Destiny pointed to the door and watched as Rose slowly left.

Looking around the kitchen table, Destiny wanted to laugh at the shocked faces staring back. "Right you lot, make yourselves busy. This breakfast isn't going to cook itself. I'll wash up."

Jaxon walked in to find Destiny at the sink, her arms plunged into the water as she scrubbed the dirty pots. "What the hell is going on. Where's Rose?"

Destiny spun around and smiled. "I gave her the day off. She looked exhausted Jaxon. So we will all chip in. Now, take a seat we can eat together."

"Destiny. You can't give the only Omega of the pack, a day off. This is her responsibility, not yours or anyone else's. Go and call her back." Jaxon pulled out a chair and sat down as the pack stared between the two of them.

"No." Destiny folded her arms and glared at Jaxon. "Correct me if I'm wrong, but isn't it my job to assist the pack and help where needed?"

"EVERYONE OUT!" Jaxon stood up so quickly his chair tipped back causing a mass exodus of the kitchen. "You cannot speak to me like that in front of the pack. I'm the Alpha. You know the one that's in charge. The boss.... Why would you try to undermine me?"

"Jaxon. Alpha. Do you trust me?" Destiny walked towards Jaxon and placed her hand on his chest. "Well, do you?"

"Of course I do.... But you don't know our ways. Destiny, you can't change the order of things." Jaxon pulled Destiny closer. He loved the calming effect she had on him. "This is where we kiss."

Jaxon scowled as Destiny pushed him away and mind linked with him. 'I think the Goblin has been helping Rose. Look at the mess in here. She always has it spick and span. Now I'm hoping he will show up, but he won't if every ones in here. Rose looked sad this morning; her hands were shaking. She knows who he is. When I finish here, if he hasn't showed himself I will go and talk with her. Please Jaxon, let me do this my way.'

'Destiny, if she knows who the Goblin is she should have told us as soon as she realised. If what you are say is true, she will need to be punished.'

'Punished! Well there's your answer. Why would she tell you anything if she knows she will be punished?'

Jaxon growled. "You have an answer for everything." Jaxon sighed. "You have an hour. After that I will be questioning Rose."

"I love you Alpha." Destiny grinned; she had got her own way again. "Now we can kiss."

AFTER DESTINY HAD FINISHED CLEANING up the mess in the kitchen, she made her way up to Rose's room. She was surprised to find it was in the attic. Gently knocking on the door, Destiny stood back and waited for an answer.

"Luna. Do you need me in the kitchen?" Rose stood looking down at the floor.

"No Rose. Every things done for now. You know what I want to talk about. May I come in?" Destiny entered the tiny room as Rose stepped aside. It was so small it only had room for a single bed and a set of drawers. It was darker than the rest of the rooms and had a tiny round window that let the sun in at midday.

Rose watched Destiny, as her eyes flicked around the room. "I know it's not much but its mine." Rose sat on the edge of the bed and waited for Destiny to speak.

"Look Rose, I need to know your fiend's name. As you know

Lucas is missing a head. Now it's my job to find it and put it back where it belongs, on his shoulders. ...So I want to know who the Goblin is that's been helping you in the kitchen."

"I didn't know he was capable of bad things. He's only ever been nice to me." Rose looked at her hands, they were still shaking.

"I know you didn't." Destiny took a seat on the bed next to Rose and held her hand. "I'm going to make everything right, but I need his name."

"It's Grimly, but he's vanished since last night.... Does the Alpha know?" Rose looked up at Destiny. "He will banish me if he does."

"Yes he does, but no ones being banish, only the Goblin. Now why don't you go and get some fresh air and then you can start preparing lunch. I think every one's going to be starving as the breakfast wasn't as good as yours." Destiny stood ready to leave as Rose called out her name.

"Destiny. You are a good Luna; the Alpha is lucky to have found you."

"He is a good Alpha too Rose, I'm lucky to have found him." Destiny continued down the stairs to her bedroom and a waiting Jaxon.

Jaxon jumped up as soon as Destiny walked in. "Well?"

"It's a Goblin called Grimly. He's been helping Rose with the chores. Jaxon he's been good to her, she had no idea that he would do this." Destiny watched as Jaxon started pacing around the room.

"That's no excuse. She will have to go. We'll get a new Omega. One that can do the damn job." Jaxon changed direction and headed towards the door, only stopping when Destiny stood in his way. "Now what?"

"Jaxon King. Sit down please, we need to talk, or rather I need to talk, and you will listen." Destiny placed both hands on her hips and glared.

Jaxon sat as Destiny kneeled in front of him. "Make it quick, we have a head to find."

Rolling her eyes Destiny almost laughed as she watched Jaxon's face turn Purple with rage. "It will take as long as it takes. Now, listen. How long has Rose worked here?"

"Since I was pup. Her mom was the Omega before her, why?" Jaxon asked. He wasn't sure why Destiny wanted a history lesson.

"Okay. So I'm guessing she works every day?" Destiny waited for Jaxon to nod. "Right. Every day with no break, no days off, no holiday and she looks after 50 pack members. Cooking, cleaning, washing, oh the list just goes on and on and on."

Jaxon jumped up. "That's her job. She's an Omega. Destiny I've already told you not to interfere in our customs. This is how it is. This is how it's always been."

"I'm not interfering as you put it. Rose gets ignored, she has no friends and the only time anyone speaks to her is when they want feeding. Can you really blame her for wanting a friend, especially one that helps?" Destiny sighed." Jaxon, please don't banish her."

"Destiny it would have to be the packs choice, we all get a vote in these situations. I can't go against tradition. I'm sorry." Jaxon grabbed Destiny's hand and pulled her back onto the bed. Rolling on top of her he laughed as she tried to push him off.

"Jaxon no. You know we are not allowed to do this. Keep your hands to yourself."

"I'm the Alpha, no one tells me what to do. Now lay still, I want you now." Jaxon fiddled with Destiny's top, but he couldn't get it off.

"And I want a white wedding in a pretty dress, I guess we're both disappointed." Destiny watched Jaxon's face drop. "Hey, we have each other though. That's what's important, right?" She added.

"Right. Come on lets go and find this head." Jaxon walked from the room deep in thought. He never realised she wanted a human wedding. But then why would he, he was a wolf.

CHAPTER 24

Destiny made her way down to the dungeon, surprised to see Alex standing staring at Lucas. "What are you doing?"

"I can't believe he has no head. Will you be able to find it?" Alex asked hopefully.

"That's why I'm here, I need to talk to him. Can you open the door?" Destiny noticed the puzzled look spread across Alex's face.

Pointing at Lucas, Alex sighed. "He has no head, how are you going to talk to him?"

"Let me worry about that. Now open the door please." Destiny entered the cold cell and watched as Lucas's body twitched. He knew she was there. "Lucas, I'm going to ask you some questions. I want you to raise your left hand for yes and your right hand for no. Do you understand?"

Lucas raised his left hand and then dropped it again.

"Bloodyhell that's brilliant." Alex exclaimed.

Destiny continued ignoring Alex's outburst. "Do you know where your head is?" Again Lucas raised his left hand. "Is it in the fae world?"

"He's raising his left hand. You're a genius Luna." Alex almost gave Destiny a round of applause he was so excited.

"Okay Lucas, I'm going to find your head and bring it back. You need to rest, conserve your strength." Destiny turned and made her way back up the stairs just in time to hear shouting coming from the kitchen. "What's going on?"

Jaxon was standing at the head of the table. "They want Rose banished. I'm sorry Destiny but it has to go to the vote."

"They can't vote without us, and she needs a fair hearing. Can't this wait until we get back, after all, who is going to cook and clean if Rose goes. The shield can only be lifted by me and I'm not willing to send her out there until we know it's safe. Or I guess I could just take the shield down all together, leave you all to fend for yourselves. Shall we vote on that?" Destiny smirked as she watched the pack shake their heads. "No. I didn't think so. I'm going to find Lucas's head and bring it back. If anyone is horrible to Rose I will personally make those suffer. Do you all understand?" Destiny was met with a group of nodding heads. "Now this will be addressed by the Alpha when we return." Destiny turned to Jaxon. "Are you ready?"

Addressing the pack, Jaxon looked at each and every one of them. "Now as I had already said, this will be sorted when we are back. Carlton you're in charge. Luna, let's go?"

As they made their way outside Jaxon grabbed Destiny's hand. "Are you sure about this? I didn't get a very warm welcome last time I entered the fae world."

Holding her ring out, Destiny waited for the green glow to form. "You're my mate. We will both be fine. Come on."

JAXON LOOKED around the throne room as he emerged into the fae world. The last memory of this place wasn't at all good. The silver cage he had been shoved into was now gone, and in its place stood a large fountain, splashing water into a stone base. He snapped his head around when he heard the queens voice.

"Destiny, what a wonderful surprise, oh I see you've brought him with you." The queen turned her nose up and looked in the opposite direction.

"Your majesty, this is Jaxon. My mate. Your nephew now too. So now we know we are one big happy family, can we get down to business?" Destiny smiled sweetly as the queen almost choked. "We need to find a Goblin named Grimly. He has taken the head of one of our pack members and we are here to get it back."

The queen fanned herself with her hanky, she had become quite unwell at the thought of having a retched werewolf in the family. "What do you expect me to do about that. This doesn't concern the throne Destiny, I'm afraid you are on your own with this quest."

"Your majesty, I don't need you to find it for me, I'm more than capable." Destiny snapped back.

"Then why are you and that thing here child?" The queen grinned; she could see the Alpha was getting annoyed.

"Maybe we could stop playing games aunty." It was Destiny's turn to grin, she watched as the queen slid back into her throne and fluttered her eyes. "Now all I need to know is where abouts do the Goblins live in this realm, if that's not too difficult a question for you?"

"Sarcasm is the lowest for of wit Destiny. Maybe you need a little lesson in manners?" The queen called for her guards. "Put her into a cage."

Jaxon felt his temper ignite. As the guards came closer to Destiny he started to shift. Landing on four feet he stood in front of Destiny, guarding her. 'They are not going to touch you.' He informed Destiny through their mind link.

'I think it's a test Jaxon. She's testing you.' Destiny replied.

'A test for what?' Jaxon looked directly at the queen and snarled. 'Tell her to call them off or I'll rip them all to shreds.'

"Enough. Guards go. Well Jaxon, I'm pleased to see you would defend my niece. Despite what you think Destiny, you are very important to me. Now do you mind shifting back. Your fur is making my nose itch." The queen started rubbing her nose as Jaxon shifted back.

Before he had time to blink, Destiny had used her magic to replace his ripped clothes. "Are these real or am I really naked?"

Destiny giggled, "They are quite real, Alpha."

"The Goblin's live in the caves at the base of mount Grime. Named because it's a dirty smelly place. Now don't underestimate these little creatures. They can be quite nasty if you upset them, which I assume your friend did. Anyway you need to go, you only have 48 hours before the body will shut down." The queen rose, ready to leave.

Jaxon called out before she vanished from site. "Wait. What do you mean shut down?"

"Jaxon, he has no head. His body will run out of oxygen. I thought you knew that. Now one last piece of advice. To get the head back you will have to offer him something in return. It has to be something he wants. Right, Cheerio then."

"How far is this mountain?" Jaxon stared at Destiny's blank face. "You don't know where it is, do you?"

"No I don't. I've only been here twice. Maybe the ring can take us there. Hang on." Destiny held her hand out and closed her eyes. "Take us too Mount Grime." When she opened her eye's the green mist appeared. "Come on."

As Jaxon and Destiny walked through the green mist, they found themselves at the edge of a stream. The water was clear and trickled through the gemstones that lay at the bottom. ruby's, emeralds, onyx, diamonds, and Sapphires all sparkled as the sun hit them. "Wow Jaxon, it's so beautiful, look."

"Destiny, concentrate. Times running out, we need to find this mountain." Looking off into the distance Jaxon pointed. "Look, that's got to be the place. I'm going to shift, and I want you to get on my back, okay?"

Before Destiny replied, Jaxon was standing on four legs. He lowered his body as Destiny climbed on. 'Hold on tight.' He mind linked.

"You know I don't think I'll ever get used to hearing you in my head, it's strange…" Before Destiny had finished her sentence Jaxon dashed off towards the mountain, only grounding to a halt as they reached the bottom of the of the extremely large landmark.

'Can you smell that. It stinks.' Jaxon mind linked.

Destiny looked up at a huge mountain as she climbed down

from Jaxon's back. "Yes. Omg the smell, I think I'm going to be sick."

Jaxon shifted back and stepped in front of Destiny. "You stay behind me."

Jaxon took a deep breath as Destiny watched in horror. "What are you doing. You can't enjoy that stench?"

"I'm trying to pick up Lucas's scent. It's faint but I think I've got it. This way." Grabbing Destiny's hand, Jaxon lead her up the mountain path to an opening. "He's in here."

The cave was dark, a watery slime trickled down the walls making the floor dangerously slippery. Jaxon gripped Destiny's hand tighter as they walked further in. Destiny mind linked with Jaxon as the sound of talking came wafting along the walls. 'Can you hear that?'

'Yeah, there must be more than one. Stay here while I check it out.' Jaxon loosened his grip on Destiny's hand, but she clung on.

'I'm not staying here Jaxon. We go together or not at all.'

'Fine. Stay behind me.' Jaxon continued along the tunnel; it was getting smaller. The roof was so low now Jaxon needed to almost crawl, even Destiny had to crouch. The slime dripped from the cave roof, hitting their body's. That was where the foul smell was coming from, the slime. Thinking they may have to turn back; Jaxon breathed a sigh of relief when he saw a dim light up ahead. As they approached Jaxon pulled Destiny down with him. He placed his finger to his lips. 'Listen, I can only hear one voice.'

Destiny jumped as a loud roar came from somewhere behind her. As her heartbeat quickened, she clutched her chest trying to steady her breathing. Jaxon shifted and stood in front of her. Looking off into the distance he couldn't see anything, but he could sense it. Before Destiny blinked, Jaxon took off, leaving her on her own.

"What do you want?" The voice was sharp and full of spite, causing Destiny to spin around, almost losing her balance in the process.

After Destiny composed herself she crawled into the cave and starred at the tiny, wrinkled man that stood with a large skinning knife in his hand. It was covered in blood. "I Would like to speak with you please. My names Destiny…"

"I know who you are. You're the witch." As the Goblin came closer he smiled. "You can't curse me witch. Not in my cave."

"I don't want to curse you. I want to make a trade…. You have something I want." Destiny stepped back as the Goblin came closer. He smelt like the slime. It was a mix of stagnant water, rotten eggs, and a cess pit. Destiny tried to hold her breath, but it made her dizzy.

"What could I have that you want?" The Goblin turned around and picked up a dirty old rag and started cleaning the blood from his knife.

"You have a head of one of my pack members. Lucas. Please. I'll trade. Grimly." Destiny took a step back, hitting the cave wall as Grimly spun around.

"How do you know my name witch?" Grimly asked in his spiteful manner.

"Your friend Rose told me. I know you've been helping her. She likes you." Destiny explained. "She's been enjoying talking to you."

"That's because no one talks to her. Do this. Do that. Always orders. No friendship." Grimly snapped.

"I'm her friend. And I want to help her, but first, I need the head. So what can I give you for it?" Destiny took a step forward and wiped the slime from the back of her head.

"I want your head." Grimly grinned.

"You can't have my head." Destiny started to get fed up. This goblin was starting to grate on her. What with the smell, Jaxon taking off and now this, she had had just about enough. Placing her left hand on her hip, she pointed at Grimly. "You have no idea what you've done. Rose is in trouble because of you. I need to get the head back, save Lucas and then save Rose. Now if she's your friend, like you're making out, you will help me."

"Why is Rose in trouble?" Grimly paced the cave floor. "She is kind, not like the others."

"Because she knew you had taken the head, but she didn't tell anyone. That's what real friends do Grimly. They protect each other." Destiny knelt in front of Grimly and smiled. "Now it's your turn to protect her."

"There has to be a trade for the head. That's the rules. So what have you got that I want?" Grimly rubbed his hands together. "A head for a head, that's the price."

CHAPTER 25

Jaxon felt the sting of the bears claws as they ripped through his back. Jumping out of the way, he spun and lunged at the bears shoulder, digging his teeth in. He shook and pulled at the flesh ripping a mouthful away. Spitting it out he dived in for another bite until the bear swiped with his claws and knocked Jaxon back. With the wind knocked out of him, Jaxon lay motionless, as he struggled to breath. The bear approached and raised himself to his full height on his two hind legs, letting out an almighty roar at the same time. As he came crashing down towards Jaxon, Jaxon jumped up and grabbed the bears throat between his jaws. Shaking his head, he felt the warm blood drip from his chin. With the last of his strength Jaxon ripped away the bears throat. Moving back, he watched the bear crash to the ground. Jaxon lay down breathless, he felt his own blood oozing from the gash on his back. He needed to rest to heal, but he had no time. As he stood his legs gave way, and he lay motionless on the grass with his eyes closed.

'Jaxon. Can you hear me?' Destiny mind linked.

Jaxon opened his eyes, as the sound of Destiny's voice called to him. Was it a dream? Closing his eyes once more, Jaxon passed out.

"Grimly somethings wrong. I need to find Jaxon, but I will

come back." Taking off without an answer, Destiny made her way out of the cave. As she scanned the area, she caught site of the bear. Looking closer she saw Jaxon's wolf laying close by. "JAXON!" Rushing out into the grassland, Destiny stumble over a rock in her desperation to get to Jaxon. The cut on her knee stung and she cursed herself for being so clumsy as the blood seeped out. As she finally reached him, she grabbed his body and inspected the large gash. "Jaxon, wake up. Jaxon?" Destiny straddled Jaxon's body and raised her cut knee. The blood dripped slowly into the gash. Too slowly for Destiny. She didn't know if it would even work. This wasn't caused through magic. It was caused through battle.

As the blood dripped, Jaxon opened his eyes. Everything was hazy, but he could smell cupcakes and honeysuckle. 'Destiny.' His mind link was little more than a whisper in Destiny's head.

"Shh, rest." Destiny climbed off and lay beside him. "My handsome wolf." She stoked his fur and snuggled closer, giving him her strength.

The sound of cracking bones filled the air as Jaxon returned to human. "So you think my wolf's handsome?" Jaxon smiled.

"Yes just like you. Now let me see your back." Destiny watched as the wound closed slowly before her eyes. "You're gonna be fine." Kissing him on the lips Destiny enjoyed the feeling as much as Jaxon did. "I can't wait for the summer solstice. It's going to be the best night of my life."

"It's going to be everything you've ever wanted and more." Jaxon grinned; he had something very special planned for his mate. "Before we both get carried away we need to save Lucas."

"Ahh." Destiny grimaced.

Jaxon sighed. "Now what?"

"Grimly wants to trade. A head for a head." She watched as Jaxon smiled. "Do you have a spare head?"

"As a matter of fact I do." Jaxon pointed to the bear. "I don't recon you get many of those around here." Jaxon shifted and proceeded to Rip the bears head off with his teeth, making Destiny queasy at the sound of crunching bone. When he had finished,

Jaxon shifted back and proudly held the giant head up. "Come on, let's go get Lucas."

Crawling back into Grimlys cave, Jaxon threw the bears head onto the floor. "A head for a head."

Grimlys eyes popped out as the head rolled to his feet. "A bear? You've brought me a bear!"

Just as Jaxon was about to blow his top, Grimly started clapping and doing a little jig. "I always wanted a bear."

"Okay. So now we get our head. Where is it?" Destiny looked around the cave as she spoke. She couldn't see any passageways leading out of this main cave. Only the way they had come in.

Grimly clicked his fingers and there around the room appeared shelves, each packed full of heads. "Take your head and leave."

Jaxon scanned the shelves until he spotted Lucas. He grabbed the head, then turned to Destiny. "We better get a move on, times running out."

"Look." Destiny pointed to a shelf; it was holding the rogue vampires head. "Grimly, you need to be careful with that one, it's full of dark magic."

"It's not anymore. I've cleansed it." Grimly snapped.

"How?" Destiny asked in amazement.

"It's a secret." Grimly turned his attention back to the bear head.

Destiny smiled at Grimly. "Okay." She didn't want to make him angry. "Thank you…. Can I ask you something else?"

Grimly sat stroking the bears head, nodding he looked at Destiny.

"How long had you been at the packhouse?"

"Ever since Rose asked for help in her dreams. Four years." Grimly returned his attention to the bear.

"Why did you take Lucas's head?"

"Because he made Rose cry. He kicked her. Told her she was scum…. Now leave." Grimly picked up the head and walked to the corner of the cave.

"Grimly. Thank you for looking after Rose, but I will be looking after her from now on, so you don't need to come back. Understand." Destiny didn't smile. She starred menacingly at Grimly, and he understood the message.

Jaxon grabbed Destiny's hand. "Let's go home."

JAXON LOOKED at the headless body. "So now what?"

Destiny shrugged her shoulders. "I don't know. Try placing the head against his neck. I'll look at my book."

Magnus put his hand on Destiny's shoulder. "There's no need, stand back." Magnus waited for Jaxon and Destiny to move out of the way before holding his hands above the neck. He started reciting an incantation and closed his eyes.

Destiny leaned forward to hear better, but Jaxon pulled her back. He didn't like magic of any kind and even though Destiny was a witch, he preferred it when she didn't use her magic. 'Stay back' he mind linked.

'I want to hear what he's saying' She responded sharply, 'how else will I learn?'

'You don't need to learn everything' Jaxon shook his head as the neck healed back on to the head.

Lucas sat up and blinked, he rubbed the back of his neck and let out a long slow moan. "Jeez, I feel like I've been hit by a train."

"What do you remember?" Jaxon asked as he walked to the edge of the bed.

"I went to the boundary to check for movement, I thought I saw something.... Then everything went black. Why does my neck hurt so much?" Lucas flopped back down and closed his eyes.

"ALEX!" Jaxon shouted.

"Yes Alpha?" Alex looked between Jaxon and Lucas. "Is he alright?"

"He's fine but I want him moved to his room and get the healer to sit with him, if there's any change in him, come and get me." Jaxon looked over to Magnus as he interrupted.

"I think I should sit with him. I don't know what the side effects are to this magic. I would like to monitor it." Magnus smiled. "I might need to do some tweaking."

Jaxon sighed. "Fine. Now I have some things to sort out. Carry on."

Destiny watched them all leave and then turned her attention to Carlton, who had been sitting on the bottom step. "Any movement from William?"

Carlton shook his head. "No. Nothing." Carlton jumped up as Destiny stood in front of William's cell. "What are you doing?"

"I need to see if I can communicate with him." As Destiny reached for the door, Carlton grabbed her arm and pulled her away.

"Not without the Alpha's permission. I've been given strict instructions not to let anyone in."

"I'm not anyone. I'm the Luna." Destiny replied indignantly.

"The Alpha's words were, don't let anyone in, especially the Luna." Carlton laughed as Destiny huffed. Mind linking with Jaxon, Carlton pleaded for help. 'You were right. The Luna is here demanding to see William. Please come and sort her out, before she turns me into a frog.'

Destiny glared at Carlton. "The Alpha doesn't need to know!"

"The Alpha doesn't need to know what?" Jaxon jumped down the last few steps and landed in front of Destiny.

"I thought you had things to do?" Destiny realised Carlton had called him, looking around Jaxon she pointed at Carlton. "That was sneaky."

"Carlton leave us." Jaxon didn't take his eyes off of Destiny, As he listened to Carltons retreating footsteps. "Destiny, Carlton had orders for good reason. The first being, we don't know what he's turned into. The second being to keep everyone safe. The third and most important reason is to keep you safe. I knew you would try to see him alone. Now if you want to see him you do it with me. Understand?"

"Jaxon…" Destiny stopped as Jaxon cut in.

"I said understood."

"Perfectly."

"Good. Now let's go." Jaxon waited for Destiny to move, growling when she didn't.

"As you're here, we may as well get this over with." Destiny smiled sweetly, almost laughing as Jaxon's eyes flashed amber. "Call Carlton back and grab a sword."

"Which bit of I'm the Alpha are you having trouble understanding?"

"Jaxon, we need to get this done. Like you said we don't know what he is, or even if I can still contact him?" Destiny looked at the stairs as Carlton came down them. Placing her hand on Jaxon's chest she stood on tip toe and whispered. "I love you Alpha."

"Okay Carlton, we are going in to see William. Lock the door behind us and if anything happens get Destiny out."

"NO! I'm staying in there with you." Destiny grabbed Jaxon's arm. "If we are going to die then we die together."

"They can't get you Destiny, they will use your power. Now you keep away from him, I'll stand in between you. Okay Carlton, unlock the door."

Destiny entered the cell behind Jaxon, she kept her eye on William as she moved into place. "Do not interrupt me once I start." Content when Jaxon nodded, Destiny closed her eyes and searched for William in her mind. She was transported into a black space. There was no light, she could barely see in front of her. "William?" She called out. "Where are you?" No reply came. Destiny walked on further into the darkness and called again. "William?" In the distance she saw a faint glow. The glow shone brighter the nearer she got. "William?" In the middle of the light there standing on its own was an old leather chesterfield chair. As she made her way around it, she saw a little girl sitting, swinging her legs. "Hello." Destiny said gently. "Who are you?" The little girl didn't look up, instead she started giggling, the sound echoed around the void, causing Destiny to hold her ears. "I said who are you, I demand an answer."

The laughing stopped and the little girl stood up and faced Destiny. "Are you scared?"

Destiny shook her head, as she studied the girls features. She had dark brown hair, put up in bunches. Her skin was white, with a bloodied marbled effect covering it. Although she looked like something from a horror movie, it was her eyes that startled Destiny the most. She had pools of fire where the pupils should have been, surrounded by black. Destiny could feel the heat coming from them.

"Well you should be." The little girl started laughing again.

"I said tell me your name." Destiny took a step nearer and noticed the smell. It was the same as the rogue vampires, the same as the black blood that seeped from their bodies.

"Very well but first you tell me something. A question for a question…. Why do you wish to save the vampire they call William?" The girl sat back down on the chair and continued kicking her feet against the leather upholstery.

"A question for a question? No. I don't think so. Dya know what, I don't care what your name is. Take William, keep him. Your name is of no concern to me. You will die just the same." Before Destiny could continue the girl flew at her, floating right in front of her face. Destiny could feel her skin blistering from the heat. "You are irrelevant. Now leave."

The cackling came once more, filling the space they stood in. "A question for a question first. That's the rules."

"News flash, there are no rules bitch." Destiny turned and headed back to the darkness.

"No. You can't go." The girls voice drifted off into the distance.

When the glow had disappeared Destiny stopped and looked into the darkness. "William. Can you hear me?"

It was faint at first but gradually William's voice drifted through the darkness. "Destiny. Somethings wrong."

"Can you see anything William?"

"No. Everything is black."

"Can you walk towards my voice?" Destiny spun around as she tried to find the direction William's voice was coming from.

"No. I can't move. I'm suspended in time."

Destiny smiled. "I've got to go, but I'll be back for you." Destiny closed her eyes and when she opened them she was staring at Jaxon who was bathing her face with cold water.

"What the fuck happened? Your skin started to blister." Jaxon checked Destiny over before allowing her to get up. "I forbid you to ever do that again."

"I'm fine." As Destiny continued to stand she felt her legs go from underneath her.

"Fine my arse." Jaxon scooped Destiny up and took her up to their bedroom. "You are to rest until I say otherwise."

"My bossy mate." Destiny laughed. "Lay with me, that way you can make sure I do as I'm told."

Jaxon smiled as his body filled with warmth, It was the first time she had called him her mate and meant it in a nice way. "So if I lay with you and start undressing you, you will let me?"

"Undressing is fine, it's the rest of it that's off limits." Destiny watched Jaxon's face drop. "It's only a couple of weeks to wait Jaxon."

"It's killing me, being so close to you and being unable to touch you. Two weeks is a lifetime away." Jaxon replied stroppily. "I've got things to do. I'll check on you in a little while." Storming out of the bedroom Jaxon cursed the situation. He was sure no other Alpha's had this trouble.

Watching as he left, she could feel his frustration. She was frustrated too. Rolling over onto her side she thought back to William and the little girl. She was missing something. It was staring her right in the face, but she couldn't see it. Reaching for her bag she pulled out the magic book. "Let's hope you've got the answers otherwise we are all in trouble."

CHAPTER 26

Every pack member assemble by the lake, ready for Jaxon to address them. "You all know what happened to Lucas. Now we need to decide what to do with Rose."

Lucas jumped in before Jaxon had finished. "Banish her. That's the law or is she going to get a free pass because the witch likes her."

Jaxon leapt at Lucas pinning him to the ground. "Disrespecting the Luna as punishable by death, remember that before you open your mouth."

"By rights Gene should have been Luna and you know it." Lucas pushed back at Jaxon.

"What's going on?" Approaching, Destiny placed her hands on her hips. Staring down at Jaxon she started shaking her head. "Can anyone join this public lynching or is it just for your pack?"

Standing up, Jaxon took Destiny by the arm and tried to lead her away. Shaking him off Destiny glared at Lucas. "You were the cause of this. You."

Lucas stood up and walked towards Destiny. "Cut my own head off, did I?" Lucas smirked.

"Your head was taken because of the way you treated Rose. You talk to her like she's rubbish, and to actually kick her is disgusting. You're supposed to be an elite fighter, not a woman beater."

"Destiny. You need to keep out of this, it's pack business." Jaxon turned his back on Destiny and attempted to readdress the crowd.

"Yes you're right Jaxon. This is pack business. It's just as well I'm not a part of it. Rose, come with me." Grabbing Rose's hand Destiny lead her away to the pack house.

Jaxon sighed; he knew he had hurt Destiny. This was her pack as much as his. She was his Luna. Focusing back on business he continued. "Okay, let's vote. All those in favour of Rose being banished raise your hands." He didn't need to count, there were only a few pack members that didn't raise their hands, it was virtually unanimous. "Okay she goes." Turning, Jaxon made his way in to give Rose and Destiny the bad news. "DESTINY?" Climbing the stairs up to Rose's room in the attic, Jaxon stopped at the door. All Rose's things had gone.

DESTINY CURTSIED while smiling at the queen. "I need a favour aunt, and as we are family I figured you wouldn't say no."

The queen rose from her throne and walked towards Destiny. "Well that remains to be seen. Now who is this?"

"This is Rose, she was housekeeper for the pack. They have banished her because she didn't tell them about the Goblin. I need a place for her to stay, just until I make them realise how much they need her…. Please?" Clasping her hands together Destiny considered begging on her knees.

"And what do I get in return?" The queen studied Rose. "You never get anything for nothing."

"You're going to charge me?" Destiny's jaw dropped open at the thought.

"This is a magic realm. All magic comes at a price. Just like a head for a head, for example." The queen smiled as Destiny's face lit up.

"You are a genius! I've got to go, but please look after Rose until

I come back for her." Destiny held the ring out and disappeared through the green light instantly.

"Has anyone seen the Luna?" Jaxon was pacing the floor as Destiny came into view. "Where have you been?"

"I took Rose to her new home. And I hope you've informed this lot that from now on they will be doing their own cooking and cleaning." Laughing at all the shocked faces, Destiny turned and made her way down to William, with Jaxon following.

"You've taken her to the fae realm. Don't you think you should have asked me first?" Jaxon grabbed Destiny and pulled her around to face him.

"Yes I did and no I didn't. As you've made it perfectly clear that this is your pack and I'm not a part of it. I've at long last realised I'm on my own. I will of course fight this battle that's coming and then I'll be gone. As for the mating ceremony, that's a no go I'm afraid. Now if you don't mind I have work to do."

"I'll wait for you to calm down before we sort this out." Jaxon stormed out of the packhouse, trying to calm his temper as he did so.

Destiny sniffed back her tears. She had a job to do, and she needed to focus. Turning her attention to Carlton she pointed her finger and ordered him to sleep. Content when he slumped back in the chair she turned to the cell. "Open." Once the door swung open Destiny stepping in and ordered the door to close. "I'm coming to get you William, be ready." Closing her eyes Destiny opened them to find herself standing in the dark. Tapping her pocket to make sure she had what she needed, she started the long walk towards the soft glow.

"You've come back, do you want to play a game?" The little girl asked as she kicked her legs into the leather chair.

"Yes, I'd love to. What game would you like to play?" Destiny saw the girl's eyes burn brighter.

"Questions and answers." Standing up the girl skipped around the chair and then sat down again. "I'll go first."

"Wait. What's the prize?" Destiny stepped back as the girl spat fire at her.

"Why does there have to be a prize?" Annoyed the girl kicked harder at the chair, causing small dents to form in it.

"Because the winner always gets a prize. So what prize would you like?" Destiny asked hopefully.

"If I win, I get to keep you here, for ever." The girl clapped her hands together in delight at the thought of a new playmate. The others were boring. They didn't like games.

"Very well. If I win I want William released." Destiny jumped as the girl screamed.

"NOOOOOOOOO." The girl's eyes misted over replacing the fire with blood.

"What do you mean no. I thought you were powerful?" Sighing Destiny turned as if to walk away. "I'll find someone else to play with, someone who is powerful."

"Stop. This is my domain. I am the only power here." The fire started to return to the girls eye.

"If I win I want William to come with me. Otherwise games off. So what's it to be."

"Fine, but I'm going first and its sudden death, if you lie or can't answer, I win." The girl ordered.

"And if you lie or can't answer, I win. Now begin." Taking a deep breath, Destiny placed her hands behind her back.

"Why do you want William so badly?" Smiling the girl showed a set of blood-stained teeth.

Destiny chose her words carefully before replying. "I like William. He's been kind to me, now it's my turn to be kind to him, after all we have to pay our depts. Now it's my turn.... What realm is this a part of?"

The girl started cackling loudly before stopping dead and staring at Destiny. "It's Hell.... My turn. Who are you. No wait. Who am I?"

It was Destiny's turn to smile. "You are all the lost souls that walk this realm. Those that have never been laid to rest. You are the bad and the evil. You are the devils daughter. You are Lilith." Destiny watched closely as the girls head started to wobble. Gradually it got faster and faster. "What the hell!" Turning Destiny ran into the darkness. "William it's time." Returning to the spot where she had entered the realm, Destiny pulled the salt pot from her pocket and sprinkled it around on the floor, leaving a small gap for William to pass through. "WILLIAM?" Destiny saw the faint glow getting brighter. Lilith had regained her composure, and she was coming to stop Destiny from leaving. "William. Now."

Lilith's eyes burned with rage; the fire was spreading to her hair. She raised her hands out and let flames shoot from them just as William joined Destiny. "You was cutting that a bit fine." Without waiting for a reply Destiny tipped the rest of the salt to complete the circle. The flames hit the invisible wall and bounced back towards Lilith. "Ready?"

"You bet, let's go." William grabbed Destiny's hand and then they were gone.

Destiny opened her eyes to find herself standing in front of William, she was still holding his hand. "William, wake up." Letting go she turned around when she heard Carlton waking up. "Go and get your Alpha. William's back."

Jaxon jumped down the narrow staircase seconds later and glared at Destiny. "Get away from him now."

Before Destiny could answer William opened his eyes. "Destiny?" William tried to move his arms, but they were chained above his head. "Why am I chained up?"

"Do you remember where you've been?" Destiny reached up for the lock holding William in place.

"Open this fucking door now." Jaxon shook the handle until it broke. "Destiny, I'm warning you, open it."

"Not until I know it's safe." Turning her attention back to William, Destiny undid the chains and took a step back as William dropped to the floor. "William look at me. Do you remember where you have been?"

Nodding slowly William looked up. "The darkness. The voices.

There were 100's of them, all calling out for help. They wanted to be saved."

"Destiny, unlock this door now." Jaxon took a step back and kick the door as hard as he could, but it didn't budge.

Kneeling down, Destiny reached out to William, placing her hands either side of his head. She closed her eyes and listened. "I can hear, the voice." Dropping her hands Destiny stepped back. The loudest voice in Williams head was his own and only his own. Begging, pleading, and screaming for redemption. "It's William, there's nothing else inside him." Pointing to the door, Destiny released the spell holding it shut.

Running into the cell, Jaxon grabbed Destiny. "You're coming with me. Carlton lock the door until I get back."

"Alpha calm down." Destiny struggled against Jaxon's grip, but it was too tight.

"Calm down! This is calm. And stop struggling." Jaxon threw Destiny over his shoulder and ran up to the bedroom. Placing her down, once he had slammed the door shut, he stood staring at her. "What was you thinking. Going in there alone like that, and let's not forget the use of magic."

"Jaxon I have a job to…"

Jaxon held his hand up stopping Destiny from talking. "I have a job to do and that's to keep you and the pack safe. You're not making it easy Destiny."

"I realise I'm in the way Jaxon and as you pointed out in front of the entire pack, I'm not part of it, then I need to do my job by myself. I think it's best if I move out. That way you can concentrate on what's important to you."

Sighing, Jaxon pulled Destiny towards him. "When are you going to realise you are what's important? You keep putting yourself in danger and I'm here pulling my hair out." Jaxon placed his finger under her chin, lifting her head up to look at him. "I'm sorry I said that about the pack. I didn't mean it. You're my Luna and you are very much a part of this pack."

"Then why did you say it?" Destiny's eyes sparkled with unshed tears.

"Because I'm an idiot…. Look I will put this right. All I ask is that you tell me what you're planning, and we do it together. Deal?" Jaxon slipped his arms around Destiny's waist pulling her closer.

"Okay. Deal, but I'm not putting up with Lucas's snide comments, or anyone else's." Destiny felt Jaxon's lip's brush her ear as he started to kiss down her neck to her collar bone. "Jaxon." She whispered as her breathing deepened.

Gently kissing her Luna mark, Jaxon felt himself shudder. He needed to finish the bonding. It was in his blood, his birth right, to mate with Destiny. He didn't know how much longer he could wait. "It's getting harder Destiny. To be so close to you without mating…." Jaxon stopped as Magnus burst through the door. "Magnus. Haven't you heard of knocking. It's customary in a civilised society."

"There was no time. You need to come down to the kitchen. Now." Magnus turned and rushed out back down the stairs with Jaxon and Destiny following. "Look, they are going to kill each other."

Watching the chaos unfold in front of his eyes Jaxon bellowed at the top of his voice. "ENOUGH!" Once everyone had turned to look at him, he continued. "What's going on and more to the point why is this place a tip?"

Destiny smiled as she looked at Lucas. "This is what happens when you get rid of your Omega. You are all responsible for your own cooking and cleaning."

"Alpha. May I suggest the town people cook and clean for us. After all they are living on Pack ground." Lucas returned Destiny's smile.

Jaxon let out a low growl. "The town's people are not coming in here. Destiny's right, you all clean up your own mess. Or maybe you would like to do it for everyone Lucas?"

Standing, Lucas pointed to Destiny and Magnus. "And yet you let a witch and warlock in here. Maybe they should earn their keep."

Jaxon was on top of Lucas before anyone had time to blink. He brought his fist back and smashed Lucas in the face. The sound of cracking bones rang out around the kitchen as the two men shifted.

"Everyone out." Destiny stepped back as the pack members made their way out. "That includes you Magnus." Stepping back as the table tipped over, Destiny grabbed Magnus, leading him out. "This is between them. Come, we have work to do." Continuing down to the dungeon Destiny winced as the noise of crashing came from the kitchen above.

"Why are we coming down here?" Magnus asked.

"We need to talk to William. He's back." Smiling at Carlton, Destiny grabbed a chair and placed it in front of William's cell. "How are you feeling William?"

"I've had better days. How did you know where to find me?" William nodded to Magnus, then returned his attention back to Destiny.

"Lucky guess. Now can you remember anything else from down there?" Swiping at her face as a spider crawled down her cheek, Destiny then continued. "Anything at all. No matter how irrelevant it may seem, It may still help?"

"Everything seems hazy still…. There was a girl. She was singing a song that my mother used to sing to me, when I was a child." Williams eyes clouded over, as the memory of his mother came back.

"What was the song?" Magnus asked now interested in the conversation.

William smiled. "Greensleeves. My mother loved it."

"Greensleeves? I don't think I've heard of it." Destiny looked at Magnus. "Have you?"

William spoke before Magnus had a chance to open his mouth. "It was written in 1580, the composer remained anonymous. It's a very famous ballad Destiny."

"1580! Just how old are you?" Studying William's face for signs of age Destiny wondered how long his human life had been. He looked around twenty-five maybe twenty-eight. Certainly older than Jaxon.

Laughing at the concentration on Destiny's face, William winked. "Old enough to know better, young enough to do it anyway."

Magnus intervened. "He's a vampire Destiny. From the point of transformation he stays that age for ever."

"Okay. So Lilith knew…" Destiny was cut off when Magnus shouted.

"YOU WENT TO HELL?" Taking a deep breath Magnus thought the urge to ring his daughters neck. "Have you any idea how dangerous that was. I can't allow you to continue with your involvement in this war. You are grounded."

Jaxon's wolf landed on the floor behind Magnus. Shifting back he rose to his full height, on two legs. "Why is she grounded?"

Destiny's eyes wandered down Jaxon's body. She could feel her cheeks heating up as her inside's tingled. "Jaxon. You're naked."

"Don't change the subject." Jaxon smiled when he caught the smell of Destiny's arousal. "What's going on?"

"Did you know?" Magnus asked him. "Only the Alpha I knew would never allow his Luna to go into the depths of hell."

"Magnus what are you talking about?" Jaxon pushed his hand through his hair. He knew he wasn't going to like what he heard.

"My daughter. Your Luna and soon to be mate, decided to go to hell and rescue a vampire."

"What?" Jaxon looked at Destiny, she had guilt written all over her face. "Is this true?"

"I had no other choice." Destiny took a step back as Jaxon approached her.

"And why was that?" Jaxon was now so close; Destiny could almost taste his anger.

"Because that's where I need to go to kill Galdreola." Destiny flinched when Jaxon punched the wall above her head. "Jaxon, calm down."

"I'm trying, but my Luna is making it extremely difficult as she took a little trip to hell without telling me." Turning, Jaxon looked at Magnus. "You're right, she is grounded. Do whatever you have too, to keep her safe." Jaxon took one last look at Destiny before leaving the dungeon.

Destiny wiped the tears from her eyes. "Magnus, you have no idea what you've just done. Now we all die."

CHAPTER 27

Sitting at the back window in her bedroom, Destiny could see the pack training. Every so often Jaxon would glance up at her and then shake his head. It had been three days since she had been grounded. Magnus had put a spell on the bedroom so she couldn't leave. The final insult was when Jaxon took her magic book, bag, and ring, and gave them to Magnus to look after. The only things they had allowed her to keep were a pen and note pad. She had started jotting down notes on how it might be possible to kill Galdreola, but without her magic book she didn't know if she was on the right path. Without realising it, Jaxon and Magnus had given Destiny a death sentence. Walking to the other end of the room Destiny looked out over the lake. The water looked alive with the slivers of light that reflected off of it. The sun was high in the sky and the day had turned out to be the warmest so far this summer. Picking up the note pad she started fanning herself. She could just dive into the lake now and have a refreshing swim. Water always made her feel better, whether it was a nice bubble bath, a shower or a swim, water was always the answer. Throwing the note pad down onto the table, Destiny jumped up. "Water is the answer!" Running into the ensuite, Destiny turned on the tap, cupping her hands underneath the stream of water, while they filled with the cooling liquid. "Magnus Black, you're not as clever as you think you are." Focusing on the water Destiny summoned the queen. She knew the queen would be pissed at her, but time was running out. A bright flash filled the room and there standing only a few feet behind her, in the doorway, stood the queen.

"Destiny!" The queens mouth was turned down into a grimace and her eyes shone brightly with anger. "One cannot simply summon the queen."

Curtsying slightly, Destiny smiled. "Your majesty, I wouldn't normally do something so disrespectful, but I wasn't summoning the queen. I was summoning my aunt."

The queens eyes darted around the large room. "This room has a spell on it. Why?"

"I've been locked in by Magnus." Before Destiny could continue the queen jumped in.

"At a time like this. I knew he was no good. Why has he done that to his only daughter?"

"Because he thinks he is keeping me safe. He doesn't realise what's coming. Please aunt, I need your help." Destiny walked to the window at the back of the bedroom. "Look, they are all going to be slaughtered and they have no idea.... I need to go and kill Galdreola, but to do that I need to go into the lost realm of hell. That's where she is, stuck between the underworld and this one."

"Destiny you do realise how dangerous that will be?" Watching the pack train the queen paused. "Why do you care about these wolves, I sense they don't care for you."

"Because I'm part of their pack and as Luna it's my responsibility to keep them safe. Now will you help me?" Walking closer to the queen Destiny smiled. "Please, I haven't got my mum to ask so I'm asking my aunty."

"You certainly have a way with words.... Okay, I'll help. First you need to call a meeting. I will inform them all of what's coming. I will need Magnus and Edna to form a tripod with myself. It takes three people with magical abilities to form a wall of magic. That way we should be able to drag you back out if things go wrong, and of course stop anything from escaping. Now, shall we go." The queen pointed to the door but before she cast a release spell, Destiny stopped her.

"Allow me aunt." Destiny filled a glass with water and tipped it along the bottom of the door. After waving her hands, the door sprung open. "After you, your highness."

"Well done Destiny. You're a quick learner." Making her way down the stairs, Destiny marched with the queen, out onto the training ground. "ATTENTION. ALL PACK MEMBERS ARE CALLED TO AN EMERGENCY MEETING TO TAKE PLACE IN TWO HOURS AT THE EDGE OF THE LAKE." Destiny closed her eyes as Jaxon came storming over.

"How did you get out of the room?" Jaxon noticed the queen standing by the door. "Ahh, I see you called for backup."

"Jaxon, listen to me. This is serious, we are running out of time." Destiny pleaded.

"You are not putting yourself in danger Destiny. I'm not having you going off fighting demons or devils or whatever the fuck they are. It's my job. Not yours."

"You're right. It is your job. That's why you will be coming with me. In fact you all will be." Turning to the queen Destiny continued. "This way your majesty." Grabbing Jaxon's hand Destiny walked to the front of the lake. "Can you tell Jaxon everything while I get Magnus and Aunt Edna." Without waiting for a reply, Destiny turned on her heels and headed off towards the pack house.

Returning minutes later, Destiny held her bag whilst taking her place next to Jaxon. "Okay?" She asked, looking up at him.

"I don't know." Shaking his head Jaxon motioned to Magnus. "What does he think?"

Staring at the lake Magnus sighed. "We need a plan; I presume you have one Grace?"

Looking around the group Destiny laughed. "Who's Grace?"

"I am. And I'll thank you to call me your highness, Magnus. Now can we get back to the subject in hand." The queen continued to address the group. "Galdreola comes from the demon realm, it's also known as the fire realm. That is where her power lies. You need to drawer her out into this world and kill her quickly." Destiny put her hand up. "You are not in school Destiny. Speak."

"How do we kill her?"

Magnus interrupted Destiny. "Galdreola wants to come to this world and you're suggesting we bring her here. That doesn't sound too smart to me."

Destiny jumped in. "It's not too smart to sit around waiting for her either. She comes on our terms before she gets too powerful."

Jaxon stepped forward. "Destiny's right. That thing won't be ready for us. So how do we get it here?"

"You go and get it, lead her here and Destiny will do the rest." The queen pointed to Magnus and Edna. "We will protect you while you are in the Demon realm and pull you back out, along with Galdreola."

"I'm going with him." Destiny grabbed Jaxon's arm. "I've been in there; I know where to look."

Turning to Destiny, Jaxon shook his head. "No you're not. I can't fight and protect you at the same time. It's too dangerous."

"Well you ain't going down there on your own." Destiny looked up when she heard Carltons voice.

"He won't be on his own, we will be with him." Carlton jogged over and joined the group, followed by Alex.

The queen clapped her hands together. "Wonderful. Now this is what we must do. Magnus, Edna, and I will form a triangle, by joining hands. This will contain the portal to the other realm. Destiny will be able to see you, so when you are ready to come back, we break the triangle and let you through. We must however join hands again once Galdreola comes through otherwise more of her kind will be able to freely enter. Now Destiny. You asked how to kill her. This is your task, yours alone. You can do this Destiny, think back to the bedroom. Now I must be off. I will return tomorrow just before midday. That will be the best time to strike, and Jaxon, prepare your army. Just in case." The queen vanished into thin air.

"She always did enjoy the sound of her own voice." Magnus said as he turned and walked back to the packhouse.

Glancing at Jaxon, Destiny could see the worry on his face. His brow was creased, and he was looking at the ground. "Jaxon. Can I talk to you in private." Destiny slipped her hand in his. She felt his hand tighten around hers as he looked at her.

"Let's go to our room." Stopping, Jaxon turned. "Alex, continue training the pack, they need to be ready by late morning and make sure they all eat well and rest tonight."

Climbing the stairs together, Destiny squeezed Jaxon's hand. "It's going to be okay."

"Shouldn't I be reassuring you?" He replied as he pushed the bedroom door open. Jaxon pulled Destiny in and onto the bed. "I wanted one night with you, just one fucking night."

"Lock the door Jaxon." Watching as Jaxon jumped up, she pulled her dress over her head, laughing when Jaxon turned around and stopped dead.

"I thought we couldn't, you know." Grinning Jaxon wiggled his eyebrows.

"No we can't. But I'm sure we can find something else to do." Rolling over Destiny tapped the bed. "Well, are you going to join me?"

Jaxon grabbed his t-shirt, pulling it over his head, he then dropped it on to the floor. As he undid his jeans Destiny watched his muscles rippling at each movement he made.

For the first time she allowed herself to study him. Every contour was perfect, even the battle scars blended into his body, making him sexier.

Slipping out of his pants, Jaxon threw them down and then walked to the bed. Lying next to her, he breathed in the familiar scent of cupcakes and wild honey suckle. "Come here." He whispered as he slipped his arms around her, pulling her on top of him. Their lips met as the electricity surged between them. It was like the first kiss all over again. The passion. The longing. The desperation to own each other's bodies as their hands wandered, touching and caressing. Jaxon flipped Destiny over and began kissing down her body, unclipping her bra as he went. His breathing became heavy as he looked down at Destiny's breasts. They rose and fell with each breath she took. Cupping one in his hand he placed his mouth around the other, sucking and licking. Both nipples hardened immediately.

"Jaxon." Destiny murmured as she ran her hands through his hair. Destiny held her breath as Jaxon kissed down her stomach, further down he went until he reached her thighs. Pushing her legs gently apart he ripped off her briefs, and then ran his tongue along Destiny's lips before pushing it deep inside her.

Destiny bucked as his tongue hit the spot. "Jaxon!" She panted. As his rhythm increased, Destiny tried to push his head away. She had no control as the feeling of euphoria started in her groin and exploded over her whole body. Shaking Destiny could feel Jaxon drinking her in as her orgasm peaked. The scream left Destiny's mouth as she grabbed Jaxon's hair. Pulling him up to face her she kissed him, tasting herself on his lips. Pulling away she smiled. "My turn." Pushing Jaxon over, Destiny started kissing down his neck as he caressed her bum, roughly kneading the soft skin in his hands. As Destiny kissed down further she felt Jaxon tense as her mouth teased his throbbing errection.

Blowing out slowly, between his lips Jaxon looked down as Destiny licked the full length of his shaft. "Jesus Destiny, don't stop."

Destiny cupped her hand's around Jaxon's testicles and slowly squeezed, as her mouth slid around his penis. Using a gentle sucking motion she took more of him into her mouth, using her tongue and teeth to tease him a little more. Gradually she built up speed as Jaxon started moving in rhythm with her movement.

Placing his hand on the back of Destiny's head, Jaxon pushed himself into her mouth, deeper and faster as he felt himself about to cum. As his body started to shake Jaxon let out an almighty roar as he exploded into Destiny's mouth. "Fuck!"

Destiny swallowed down the creamy liquid as it shot into her mouth, gulping for air in between, as Jaxon watched breathlessly. Licking her lip's Destiny looked up shyly. Her face flushed with embarrassment as she was met with Jaxon's unblinking eyes.

"That was fucking amazing. You are fucking amazing." Pulling Destiny up, he kissed her softly on the mouth. "You're mine and I will never let anyone hurt you. Not ever."

Wrapping her arms around Jaxon's neck, Destiny breathed in his scent. "And you are mine Jaxon King." Sighing she propped herself up on one elbow. "You need to go and talk with Carlton and Alex. Make sure they are ready for what's to come."

Nodding Jaxon closed his eyes. "I know, why don't you stay here and rest. I won't be long."

"I was going to cook a meal for everyone, the pack, and the town's people. I will take the shield down in the morning and they can return to their homes. They will be safer in town.... Jaxon?"

"Hmm." Jaxon lazily opened one eye and focused on Destiny.

"You will be careful. It's dark down there, and you won't see her coming."

"I'm a wolf Destiny. I can see in the dark, I also have the ability to smell things coming from a distance and let's not forget my hearing.... I have a plan. Now stop worrying and concentrate on cooking a feast for your mate." Swinging his legs over the side of the bed Jaxon stood and grabbed his clothes. "And then tonight, I want a repeat performance of that." Pointing to the bed Jaxon grinned. "That was perfect." Pulling on his jeans, Jaxon pecked Destiny on the lips then left the room.

Destiny smiled as the door closed. He was right, it was perfect. She turned to her bag and pulled out her magic book. She also had to make plans. Plans on how to kill Galdreola. Opening the book she ran her finger down the index of demons, stopping at Galdreola's name. Reading the same paragraph over and over again, Destiny slammed the book shut. "I know she's the serpent of fire. I need more info." Grabbing her bag she closed her eyes. "Give me a clue." Suddenly the tap in the ensuite turned on. Destiny peeked around the door to see who was there, but the room was empty. Slowly she made her way to the ensuite and watched the tap as the water gushed into the sink. Destiny frowned as she turned it off. Was that the sign? She wondered. After staring blankly at the tap, Destiny's eyes lit. "Waters always the answer!" Everything now made sense.

CHAPTER 28

Destiny waved off the last of the towns people as they left for the safety of their own homes. Jaxon came up behind her, slipping his arms around her waist, he watched as the procession of cars and trucks drove off into the distance.

"It's nice to have the place back to normal." Jaxon nuzzled into Destiny's neck. "Once todays over, we can finally concentrate on us."

Closing her eyes Destiny savoured the feeling of his mouth against her skin.

"Destiny, is everything ready?" Magnus asked as he approached them.

Turning his head Jaxon glared at him. "Magnus. Impeccable timing as always."

Destiny laughed as she pushed Jaxon away. "We don't have time for any shenanigans Alpha." Holding her hand against his chest, she stood on tip toe and kissed his cheek, noticing the annoyed glint in his eyes as she did so. "After battle, I'm all yours."

"Spending time with my mate doesn't class as shenanigans. And later, you won't have the choice." Turning, Jaxon marched away, back towards the pack house.

"You know he's growing on me." Magnus told Destiny as he stopped by her side. "I can see he loves you."

"Can you stop winding him up them please?" Destiny asked. "Because I'm not sure how much longer he's going to put up with it Magnus."

"Oh come on Destiny, I'm allowed a little fun, besides, once this is over I'll be returning to my cabin…. I don't suppose I'll see very much of you then." Magnus sighed. He had loved being here with Destiny. Getting to know her, her little quirks. Not so much her temper, but even that was a part of her.

Sensing the sadness in his voice Destiny reached for his hand. "You're wrong. You're my dad, and I need you…..I know Jaxon's my future, but so are you." Destiny felt Magus's grip tighten on her hand. "Why can't you move your cabin here? Well the back of it at least. That way I will get to see you every day and as a bonus I will be able to walk straight through your cabin and into town." Destiny laughed. "Sounds like a win for both of us."

Magnus watched the smile spread across Destiny's face, but he wasn't convinced that would be the answer, not with Jaxon anyway. "And what do you think the Alpha would say about that?"

"I think the Alpha would do anything to keep his mate happy. At least consider it dad?"

Just hearing the word dad made Magnus feel magnificent, like he used to, before Destiny was gone. Looking at her hopeful face he nodded. "Okay. But first let's get today over with, and remember, I'll be with you every step of the way."

Walking back towards the pack house, Destiny spotted Jaxon sitting on the porch. He was staring out at the lake vacantly. "Magnus I need a word with Jaxon. I'll see you in a little while." Without waiting for an answer Destiny sprinted over to join him. "Hey! Are you okay?"

Grabbing Destiny, he pulled her onto his lap. "I am now."

Wrapping her arms around his neck, Destiny studied his face. "What's wrong, you looked a million miles away?"

"I heard what you said to magnus. About him moving his cabin here, and yes, I would do anything to make you happy."

"You were thinking about your parents. I'm sorry Jaxon. I know how hard it is, I think about my mother too." Resting her head on Jaxon's shoulders, Destiny sighed. It was hard for both of them, possibly harder for Jaxon, he had lost both his parents.

"I miss them. My dad always knew the right thing to do. Sometimes I feel like an imposter playing at being the Alpha." Kissing Destiny's forehead, Jaxon wrapped his arms tightly around her. "The only light to come out of this is that I now have you."

"And I you…. You know not only do I think you are a good Alpha, but I also think you are pretty damn hot too."

"You can show me how hot I am later." Laughing, Jaxon slid his hand down to Destiny's bum and gave it a little squeeze. "And on the summer solstice, I'll show you how hot I really am."

"Well Alpha, I shall look forward to that. Now shall we prepare for battle?"

Jaxon's face dropped. "Why do you have to fight, It's not right. You should be somewhere safe."

"Jaxon, all your pack members fight, I'm no different. Tell me, did your mother ever fight?"

"Yes, but she was a wolf." Jaxon replied without realising this was going to turn into an argument.

"Oh right, so I can't fight because I'm not a wolf?"

"Destiny you're my Luna…"

"Stop Jaxon. We have a battle to win, I don't intend wasting my energy on quarrelling with you. I am a witch, and I can hold my own." Pushing herself up, Destiny glared down at Jaxon. "I suggest you make sure you're ready."

"DESTINY!" Calling after her as she stormed away, Jaxon cursed himself. She didn't even look around when he called her.

"Trouble in paradise?" Magnus took a seat next to Jaxon and starred out at the lake.

"I bet you're loving this Magnus." Jaxon replied with his eyes still on Destiny.

"No. No I'm not Alpha. You know she's just as worried about you as you are her." Magnus pulled an old photo from his pocket. "And I'm worried about you both too."

"I can understand you being worried about your daughter, but don't pretend you're worried about me."

"Look at this photo." Magnus held out the photo and flinched when Jaxon grabbed it. "Gentle. Its precious."

Jaxon could tell straight away it was Destiny. She was wrapped in a long white shawl that hit the floor, despite a woman holding her. "Destiny?"

Magnus nodded. "She was only a few hours old there. Look at her face purple with anger." Magnus laughed. "We were trying to get a family photo. That's her mother, holding her. Destiny wouldn't stop screaming, her face grew more purple by the second. Anyway, that was the best photo we could get. I left Venessa to feed her while I came here on pack business with your father. When I returned home, they were gone." Magnus closed his eyes as if to blot out the pain. "You know it still hurts to this day. The only consolation I have is having my daughter here, now."

"Magnus I'm sorry for what you went through, but I don't see how this helps with me and Destiny."

"I'm making two points Jaxon. The first is, she has always had a temper on her. Sometimes I wonder if she knew her mother was going to take her?" Magnus shook his head as he tried to focus on the present.

"And what's the second?" Jaxon asked, now interested in the story.

"The second is, I love my daughter and I will do everything in my power to keep her safe. That includes keeping you safe because I don't want her to experience the grief of losing someone she loves.... I also know that you love her and will do the same for her. Now go and make up with her. You both need to be focused for what lies ahead."

As Jaxon stood, the ground started to shake as a large green glow came across the lake towards them. "Magnus what's happening?"

"If I'm right, this will be the queen and her minions entering from the fae realm." Magnus stood and walked closer to the light just as Destiny dashed around the corner.

"What the hell is that?" Pointing to the green glow, Destiny saw the queen emerging, followed by Sir Gideon, Willow, Magnolia, Raymond, and an army of Snodlin's. Wide eyed Destiny turned to Magnus. "I see she's brought the cavalry."

The pack members came running from all directions, shifting as they did so. "Stop them Jaxon!" But it was too late. The pack all lined up around the group, snarling and bearing their fangs.

Immediately the Snodlin's started popping into spikey balls, showing their defensive armour. Rolling around the queen and her companions, they formed a barricade and readied themselves to strike.

Jumping in front of Destiny Jaxon roared at the top of his voice. "ENOUGH!" As the area fell silent Jaxon looked between the pack and the Snodlin's. "All of you shift back now." The sound of cracking bones and popping bodies filled the ground.

Watching Jaxon in action, Destiny's heart raced at the authority he showed, taking control of not only the pack but also the Snodlin's. The tiny flutter inside her spreading down her body to where it really shouldn't have gone. Feeling the moistness between her legs, Destiny's blushes were made worse when Jaxon looked over to her and smirked. He could smell her arousal.

'Later cupcake.' Jaxon mind linked. Turning his attention back to the crowd he focused on the queen. "You didn't tell us you were bringing an army."

Irritated by the lack of disrespect, the queen ignored him and spoke to directly to Destiny. "Have you worked out how you are going to kill Galdreola?"

"I'm working on it. Now if you would be so kind as to answer the Alpha, then we can all get on with our jobs." Destiny moved over towards Jaxon and held his hand.

"Fine. They are here to fight anything else that may come though the portal. Occasionally demons piggyback one another to realm hop. It's just a precaution really." The queen looked around the crowd for Edna. "Where is the other witch?"

"I'm here your majesty." Edna replied as she appeared out of the packhouse. "I've made these for Jaxon, Carlton, and Alex. They are charms used to ward off evil. You place them around your wolf's neck. They will only give the wearer a small amount of protection, but even so, do not lose them."

"Thank you Edna." Jaxon took the chain and studied the small charm that hung from it. It looked like a tiny eagle. Puzzled Jaxon looked at Edna who smiled.

"It represents safe flight, for when you leave the fire realm. Carlton has a dolphin, which represents water. It will help you with the intense heat down there, and Alex. You have a chameleon. That represents camouflage. So it will help you remain hidden. Now all three of you must stay close together for the charms to work on all three of you. Any questions?"

Jaxon shook his head. "No, I think we've got it…. So when do we go?"

"Midday when the sun is at its highest. It will give some light down there which will disorientate Galdreola for a few minutes, which should give you time enough to start the journey back." The queen stopped as Jaxon interrupted.

"So we jump down there and then jump back up. Is that it?" Jaxon knew it couldn't be that easy.

"No, that isn't it. Once you've jumped down the portal will have shifted, you head straight back towards the light. You all run for your lives and lead Galdreola out. Now Destiny, you really need to come up with a plan. Once she bursts through the portal we will close it again. Raymond, Sir Gideon, Willow, and Magnolia will protect us while the Snodlin's will assist you. Jaxon your pack will have to defend against anything else that might appear. Now we have 15 minutes until the sun peaks. Places everyone. Chop. Chop."

Pulling Destiny towards the packhouse Jaxon moaned. "She is so bloody bossy, now I know where you get it from."

"Jaxon slow down, I cant's keep up." Almost running to keep up Destiny sighed. "Look we haven't got time for this."

"What. We haven't got time to say goodbye, just in case?" Jaxon pulled Destiny into the packhouse and kicked the door shut.

"Please don't say that." Destiny felt her breath go as Jaxon pushed her against the wall. Smashing his lips into hers, she savoured the feeling only he could give her.

Pulling back Jaxon ripped off his t-shirt and jeans. "Right, I'm going to get that bitch and kill her myself. You stay somewhere safe and out of the way." Pulling the door open, Jaxon shifted before Destiny could answer.

Jaxon bounded towards the queen. She stood next to Magnus and Edna. Signalling to the rest of the pack to shift, Jaxon stopped as he was joined by Carlton and Alex. Turning Jaxon noticed Destiny emerging from the pack house. 'I told you to stay somewhere safe.'

'I will be safe when you return. So make sure you come back to me.' Placing her hand to her mouth, after kissing it she blew it to Jaxon. 'I love you.'

'I love you too, now please, go inside.' Watching Destiny head back inside, Jaxon mind linked with Carlton and Alex. 'Let's make this bitch pay.'

The queen, Magnus and Edna joined hands as the three of them started reciting the spell. A cloud of dust rose in the centre as the ground started to shake and open. Magnus looked at Jaxon. "Now!" Pulling his hand away from the queens, he stood back as the three wolves dived into the hole.

CHAPTER 29

Destiny emerged from the pack house just as Magnus took the queens hand, forming the wall to guard the passageway to the fire realm. She had changed into the clothes the queen had given her and she had her bow and sword. Making her way to the lake Destiny starred out. Water was the answer, played through her mind over and over again. Turning to the queen Destiny suddenly had questions. "Magnus told me a witch can only master one of the elements. Is this the same for all creatures?"

Nodding the queen tightened her grip on Edna's hand, she could feel the ground trying to pull them in. "Yes even demons only get one power."

"What happens if they try to master them all?" Destiny paused. "Would that be like a magic overload?"

"Only one witch had tried it, she was greedy. The court of Salem took her powers and banished her before she had the chance to complete all four. She had mastered the elements of Fire and water. Those two alone started to drive her mad. No one knows what would happen if a supernatural succeeded. But my guess is they would become so insane that they would rip themselves apart.

Quite literally. Now Destiny, whatever you are thinking, it's a bad idea. Concentrate on the sword and bow."

Nodding politely to the queen Destiny thought back to her book. Galdreola wanted all the magic it contains, but she cannot have it because its Destiny's. Unless she were to die and get eaten. No there had to be another way. "How much longer will Jaxon be Magnus?"

"They should be back any minute." Starring at the hole, Magnus could feel something was wrong. The hairs on his body were standing on end. Looking at Edna, he knew she could feel it too. "I think we should shut the passage. Somethings not right."

"No, you are not leaving them in the fire realm to die." Closing her eye's, Destiny focused on Jaxon. When she opened them she could see the light shining from the human world in the distance. Mind linking with Jaxon she called his name. 'Jaxon. Can you hear me?' Looking out into the darkness Destiny scanned the area. She could see a faint glow ahead. Turning when she heard the pounding of paws, Destiny rushed towards the shining light. Carlton was the first to come into sight followed by Alex. "Where's Jaxon?"

Carlton's mind link was weaker down here, she could just about make out what he said. 'Behind us…. Its…. Where Jax…'

Destiny pointed to the sunlight. "Wait underneath it. I'll find Jaxon." Running in the direction the wolves had come from, Destiny stopped and took a deep breath. She could smell him, he was close. She could also smell blood. Jaxon's blood. Hurrying further into the darkness, Destiny heard the voice of a woman, she was talking to Jaxon. As she neared the voice Jaxon's wolf lay on the floor wounded, while a woman knelt beside him, telling him everything would be alright, now he had found her.

"Get away from him." Destiny barged forward knocking the woman back.

'It's okay Destiny, she's my mother.' Jaxon told her through mind link.

'That's not your mother Jaxon. Think. Why would your mother be in the fire realm of hell. She was a sweet caring Luna. She will be with the moon goddess, not here. Now listen to me. I need you to get up and run towards the sun light. Can you do that?'

'It's my mom, I can smell her.' Rising to his feet Jaxon growled at Destiny. 'I'm taking her with me.'

'Jaxon no. She's not your mom. Please, we need to go.' Looking back to the sunlight that was now fading, Destiny tried one last time. 'That is a demon, Jaxon please.'

Jaxon lowered himself as the woman climbed onto his back. Taking off before Destiny could react, she screamed out. "Carlton, Alex. Get out now." Closing her eyes and then opening them she was back at the packhouse just in time to see Carlton and Alex emerge from the hole. "Be careful. Jaxon's carrying a demon, he thinks it's his mother. Wolves, get ready."

As Jaxon jumped into the air, Magnus, Edna, and the queen were pushed back. The link was completely broken. Before they could stand another demon flew out of the hole. Galdreola landed on the ground with a loud cackle. The other demon still looked human, as she slid off of Jaxon's back, she raised her hand, as talons appeared at the tips of her fingers. Swiping at Jaxon, the talons dug deep into his flesh, ripping away his fur and skin.

Jaxon yelped as his body slumped to the ground, motionless. His eyes focused on Destiny. 'I'm sorry.'

"NO." Destiny ran to Jaxon and knelt down beside him. "Jaxon?" Shaking him gently she studied the wound. It was deep. Too deep. Grabbing her sword, she slit her palm and let the blood trickle into Jaxon's wound. "It's not working."

"It's magic Destiny, you need to kill the thing that did this. It's the only chance Jaxon will have, and hurry, he's dying." The queen called over as she joined hands with Magnus and Edna once more.

Looking up in all the confusion, Destiny watched as Galdreola lunged towards the pack. The Snodlin's flung themselves at her, but their spikes couldn't penetrate the thick scaly skin. The human looking demon started to shake and convulse as eight long legs protruded from the woman's body. The human flesh fell away as a large black hairy ball emerged, It had twelve large eyes on the head, and two long pincers at the edge of its large mouth. She had transformed into a giant spider. Destiny's eyes flitted around the chaos. She sat starring at the commotion all around her, all she could hear was death. Destiny placed her hands over her ears. She could smell blood, wolf blood. Looking down at Jaxon she let out a sob.

"DESTINY!"

Turning, Destiny looked at Magnus.

"GET UP NOW!" Magnus demanded. "I NEVER HAD YOU DOWN AS A QUITTER."

"I can't do this." Shaking her head Destiny rose and walked towards the packhouse, as flames flew over her head. She watched as the packhouse as it started to burn; Destiny stopped. Turning she looked around. The dead bodies of wolves lay on the floor. Snodlin's lay squashed on the ground. Shaking her head she felt the tears falling. What was she thinking, she was a 17-year-old girl, not some great witch.

Carlton appeared at her side and shifted to his human form. "Luna. We need you. Jaxon needs you. Please."

Destiny looked up as Raymond came bounding towards her holding Jaxon's limp wolf. "Only you can do this Destiny." Laying Jaxon at her feet, he then turned and ran towards Galdreola. Letting out a piercing scream Raymond hit the ground. His body was smoking from the fire that Galdreola had blasted him with.

Looking around in a daze Destiny crumpled. "It's all my fault." She closed her eyes tightly; she didn't want to see it. "Everyone's going to die and it's all my fault." The noise of every ones screams and shouts filled the air. It was carnage. Destiny opened her eyes and looked down at Jaxon.

'Destiny, run.' Jaxon opened his eyes and then closed them again.

Watching Jaxon's breathing slow, Destiny felt the fire grow inside her. How could she do nothing. This was her plan, her Alpha, her family. She jumped up and ran into the burning packhouse, she made her way up to the bedroom and grabbed her magic book. She took it into the ensuite and turned on the tap in the bath. Standing in the stream of water she opened the book at the middle she then balanced it on the side of the bath. Placing both hands on the pages, she closed her eyes and took a huge breath in. The spells from the book spiralled up her arms and into her head. As her knowledge grew the pages of the book emptied. Breathing in one last time Destiny opened her eyes. She could feel the power, her body was pulsating with it. Throwing the book down she ran from the room, down the stairs and out into the grounds.

Galdreola cackled. "The coward joins us once more." Blowing out a huge fireball towards Magnus, Galdreola suddenly started choking as the fireball came back towards her, hitting her in the face.

Destiny marched towards her, her eyes like shining beacons of pure energy. Her hair was blowing behind her, as if in a storm. Raising her hands she directed them towards the giant spider. With a clap of her hands the spider started to shrink. Standing over the now tiny spider, Destiny brought her foot up and squashed it. Next she focused on Raymond, raising her hands again, water from the lake rose up and splashed down onto his smoking body.

Galdreola grinned, "I see you've decided to use magic after all." Rising to her full height, Galdreola started reciting an incantation, as she slithered closer to Destiny.

"If you want my power have it!" Raising her hands towards the demon, Destiny felt her power start to flow along her arms and into the air, towards Galdreola. "I give you the gift of fire… I give you the gift of water." Destiny faltered as she heard the queens plea.

"Destiny no. Please." The queen tried to pull away from Magnus, but he tightened his grip.

"Your majesty, Trust her." Watching Galdreola as she inhaled the magic, Magnus realised she was growing bigger. "I hope you know what you're doing Destiny."

Ignoring everyone, Destiny continued. "I give you the gift of air…I give you the gift of earth." Falling to the ground Destiny felt her connection to Jaxon breaking. Looking over she realised he wasn't breathing. "No, Jaxon stay with me." Scrambling across the scorched grass Destiny held onto Jaxon's body. "You said killing the demon that wounded him, would save him."

The queen shook her head. "The magic may have been too strong. Destiny, concentrate on Galdreola."

Turning back towards Galdreola, Destiny felt the hate course through her veins. Grabbing her sword, she ran towards lake, ducking under Galdreola's body as she attempted to swipe at Destiny. Diving into the lake, Destiny swam towards the rock island as she called to Galdreola. "Come and get me snake lady."

Edna turned to Magnus. "What is she doing?"

"What she has to. Now concentrate on your grip. I can feel more demons trying to push through."

Galdreola, slithered her way to the edge of the lake and stopped. She had never liked water. She was a demon of the fire realm after all. "Do you think I'm that stupid little girl…. I think I'll just destroy everyone here."

"Who's the coward now, and to think, I just gave you the power of water." Destiny pulled herself out of the water and onto the rocks. "I Destiny Black, challenge you Galdreola of the fire realm to battle."

"And why would I bother myself with such an insignificant little girl?" Galdreola snaked her way around the front of the lake.

"Because you need me dead, remember. I have the book inside me, and if you want it, come and get it." Destiny placed her sword onto the ground and held her arms out at the side of her. "I'm all yours."

Galdreola stopped and stared at Destiny. "Why would you give yourself freely?"

"A life for a life. You may have mine so Jaxon may live." Watching Galdreola, Destiny smirked. She really did think she was all powerful.

"NO DESTINY." Magnus felt his insides crumble as he listened to his daughter. "IF YOU DIE JAXON WILL DIE ANYWAY. SAVE YOURSELF."

"I LOVE YOU DAD." Destiny called out across the lake before turning her attention back to Galdreola. "So what's it to be?"

"I'm going to kill you Destiny." Diving into the water, Galdreola shot like a missile towards the rock island. As she approached she surfaced, ready to take a deep breath and cover Destiny in a fire ball. As she breathed out nothing happened. "What have you done witch?"

Laughing, Destiny raised her sword as Galdreola lunged at her with her mouth gapping, ready to swallow Destiny whole. "Not today demon, today you return to hell in pieces." Floating up above the demon, Destiny used all her might to swing the sword at Galdreola's neck.

Magnus, Edna, and the queen looked on stunned as did the surviving members of the pack. Sir Gideon raised his bow and shot an arrow into Galdreola's head, just behind her ear. As she let out a loud scream, Raymond picked up a boulder and threw it at her tail.

Destiny swung her sword again and managed this time to strike. "For someone as ancient as time you're not very bright. An eye for an eye. A question for a question. A life for a life and a spell for a spell." As Destiny spoke Galdreola thrashed around knocking Destiny into the water.

All the eager faces watched in anticipation to see where Destiny would surface, but she didn't. Galdreola dived into the water where Destiny had fallen, pulling her down into the dark depths of the lakebed.

"She needs help!" Carlton called to Magnus, as he ran to the edge of the lake.

"NO. Stay away from the water. If you want to help, check on the Alpha." Magnus didn't take his eyes from the water. The lake surface was completely calm now, not even a ripple appeared.

"Jaxon's dead." Carlton replied as he watched the lake for signs of movement. "We have no Alpha." Before he could continue a whirlpool appeared near the island, as the water rose up, Galdreola's body parts were thrown onto the ground in front of Carlton's feet. Stepping back as a severed arm dropped where he was standing.

At the top of the whirlpool Destiny appeared holding Galdreola's head aloft. As the water formed a bridge for Destiny to cross onto dry land, she marched towards Carlton. "Pick up all the body parts, they need to go back to the fire realm."

Carlton signalled to the remaining pack members as he grabbed a piece of the demons body. Following Destiny towards Magnus, he watched as Destiny spoke. "Break the circle." As Magnus let go of the queens hand, Destiny motioned to the others to throw the body parts into the hole. As they did she began to speak once more. "I give you the body of the demon known as Galdreola. A life for a life." Throwing the dismembered head in Destiny stood back. "Close the hole." Running towards Jaxon, Destiny knelt down beside him. "I know you're in there, come back to me Jaxon."

"It's not working." Carlton knelt next to Destiny. "Why isn't it working?"

"Wait." Destiny whispered. Bending forward she kissed Jaxon on the lip's. Feeling her tears swell, Destiny started to sob. She was so sure it would work. It had to work. There was a price to pay for everything. Squeezing her eyes shut, the tears continued to fall from her cheeks and onto Jaxon's lips.

Jaxon's eyes opened slowly, as if he had woken from a dream. Looking up at Destiny's face he reached out to touch her. "Destiny?"

"Jaxon." Throwing her arms around his body, she half sobbed, and half laughed. "I thought I had lost you."

"It will take more than death to take me from you. Help me up." Jaxon stood with the help of Destiny and Carlton. Looking around where the battle had commenced he shook his head slowly. "So much death."

"And also life.... You need to rest. Carlton stay with him while I speak with the queen." Turning Destiny made her way towards Magnus.

"You did it, Destiny." He smiled.

"We did it." She replied, before focusing on the queen. "I want to thank you for your help. We couldn't have done it without you."

Nodding, the queen studied Destiny's face. "You know you're so much like your mother Destiny. Not only in looks but also you have her stubbornness. Tell me, how did you manage to kill Galdreola?"

"She thought she had all the power, but you can't take it all if it's given freely. I've learnt if you give something you also take something. It's funny really, she taught me the first lesson. A question for a question. Them Grimly the goblin, A head for a head. It's give and take. So I figured why not a life for a life. I was banking on her diving into the water. She thought she had the power of fire, water, air, and earth, when in reality each time I gave her a power she returned it back to me. Without knowing, of course. So when I gave her fire, she gave me the fire that she already had mastered. When I gave her water, she gave me the fire I had given her. When I gave her air, she gave me water and finally when I gave her earth, she gave me air. She couldn't breathe under water without that. The hardest thing was holding her down there. I had to think of a spell to seal the water. Once she was trapped it was easier to kill her. Anyway, the rest, as they say, is history." Destiny looked around for Willow and Magnolia. "Where are the fae?"

"They have gone back to our realm. You wouldn't have seen them; they were invisible as the battle broke out. I'm glad you're safe Destiny, but I fear there will be a price to pay with the witches council. You have taken all the power from the book and that is not allowed. Right Raymond, Sir Gideon, we must leave now." The queen held her hand out and immediately a green glow appeared. "Visit soon Destiny, after all, you are family."

Destiny turned to Sir Gideon and threw her arms around him. "Thank you for your help."

Pulling away red faced, Gideon bowed. "It was my pleasure your majesty."

Destiny then turned to Raymond. "Raymond, my brave friend, thank you so much for everything." Kissing him on the cheek as he knelt in front of her, Destiny smiled as his cheeks blushed. "I will see you soon."

As they walked through the green light with the remaining Snodlin's, Destiny waved, they were all heroes to her. Turning back towards the packhouse, Destiny took in the fire damage and sighed. She would have to use her magic. Raising her arms in the air, she closed her eyes as she imagined the packhouse as it was before the battle. Opening them again, she was shocked to see the fire damaged shell was still there. "What the hell?" Before she tried again there was an almighty clap of thunder as four hooded women appeared in front of her. "Who are you?"

The four figures spoke in unison. "Destiny Black, you have been found guilty of greed. You will be stripped of your powers fourth with and you will lead the life of a mere mortal."

With another clap of thunder they were gone.

CHAPTER 30

"Calm down Destiny. What do you mean they have taken your powers?" Jaxon watched as Destiny paced in front of the burnt out packhouse porch.

"They just appeared. From nowhere. Four old ladies. They must be the witches council, the queen warned me about them." Destiny stopped abruptly. "I need to speak with Magnus."

Jaxon jumped up and grabbed Destiny's shoulders. "We will sort this out, but first." Jaxon motioned to the packhouse with a nod. "We have other priority's, like where are we all gonna sleep."

"My priority is my magic." Destiny pushed Jaxon away. "I understand the pack comes first. You deal with that." Turning, Destiny walked away in search of Magnus.

Destiny's temper bubbled as she walked to the back of the packhouse. Of course Jaxon wouldn't know how she felt. How could he. He hated magic, but it was good enough for him when it saved the pack. She felt empty. Like there was a big void inside. It was her magic, and they had no right taking it. Spotting Magnus at the edge of the grounds, Destiny called out. "Magnus."

Magnus turned as his daughter came towards him. "Destiny. What's wrong, you have a face like thunder."

"They have taken my magic. I need to know how to get it back. Please Magnus, help me?" Wiping at her tears, Destiny crumpled into Magnus's arms.

Magnus held Destiny in a tight grip as her legs buckled. "Shh, now don't get upset, we will sort this out."

"How?"

"We will have to go to Salem. That's where the witches council reside. Now have you spoken to Jaxon?" Magnus flinched as Destiny pulled away in temper.

"Of course I have. All he cares about is the pack, to him, losing my magic is no big deal. Look I'm going to get my magic book and bag. I'll meet you out front in ten minutes." Destiny turned and ran towards the packhouse. She would go to Salem and make those four old hags pay.

Magnus watched as Destiny disappeared around the side of the packhouse. He would have a word with Jaxon himself. He knew Destiny would need him now, more than ever, and Magnus would remind him of that. Strolling over to Jaxon, Magnus smiled. It was always better to smile when you were about to have words with the Alpha. "Can I have a word Alpha?"

"Magnus." Jaxon sighed. "Can't you see I'm busy."

"This is important. It's concerning Destiny." Without waiting for an answer Magnus continued. "I don't expect you to understand Jaxon, so I'm going to make it simple for you. Destiny has had her magic taken. She will be feeling like some part of her is missing. She will feel confused and most likely empty. Now try imagining how you would feel without your wolf. It's a part of you, it's who you are. I should imagine you would feel only half the man you are now."

Jaxon pushed his hand through his hair. Losing his wolf was unimaginable. The thought alone left him feeling cold. "Where is she?"

"She has gone to get her book and bag. Destiny is going to get her magic back. We will travel to Salem and seek council with the witches." Magnus turned and made his way to the front of the packhouse with Jaxon following.

"Where is she?" Jaxon looked at the sun as it began to set. "You said she was getting her bag and book."

"Let me go and get find her." Magnus walked up to the porch and looked at the packhouse. It didn't look safe.

"ALPHA!" Carlton jogged over to Jaxon. "Your pickup truck has gone."

"Magnus. Can Destiny drive?" Jaxon already knew the answer to that question, but he thought he would give her the benefit of the doubt.

"Not as far as I know. We need to find her, before she kills herself." Magnus shook his head. "You should have listened to her Jaxon."

Jaxon shifted and took off along the road before Magnus had time to stop him.

DESTINY PULLED over to the side of the road. She had managed to go three whole miles in first gear. Bunny hopping all the way. She was starting to feel sick from the jumping motion which was only made worse by the crunching sound of the gear stick every time she tried to get it into second. "Come on Destiny. You just saved the world. It can't be that hard to drive. Now that's the brake, that's the accelerator so this one must be the clutch." Destiny pulled away slowly, while she kept her eyes on the pedals. Content she grabbed the gear stick and attempted second gear again. As it shifted into second, Destiny smiled. "There, not so hard after all." Slamming her foot on the brake, Destiny swerved as Jaxon's wolf stood in the middle of the road, right in front of her. She ground to a halt half in and half out of a bush, Destiny jumped when Jaxon pulled open the door. "You idiot. I could have run you over!"

"I doubt it. You were only going five miles an hour." Jaxon blew out slowly, he didn't want to upset her any more than she already was. "Destiny what were you thinking, taking off like that?"

"You wasn't interested remember, and put some clothes on, for

Christ sake." Destiny's eyes grew wide as Jaxon pushed her over so he could get in.

"I'll put some clothes on when we get back. And just for your information, I was. I am interested. We will sort this out together." Jaxon started laughing uncontrollably.

"What's so funny?" Destiny asked as she folded her arms.

"The speed you were going it would have taken you a year to get to Salem." Starting the truck, he reversed out of the bush and made his way back to the packhouse. "We go together Destiny, but may I suggest we take the Porsche. It's faster and we only have a week till the wed…mating ceremony."

"Fine. But how long will it take?"

"Only a couple of hours. Now come on, pack a bag, if your clothes ain't too smoke stained." Jumping from the truck, Jaxon pulled Destiny out and dragged her into the packhouse. Everything was burnt. The staircase looked like it was about to fall down any minute. Jaxon felt the lump in his throat as he surveyed the damage. "It's gonna take some doing to get this place back to liveable."

"Get Carlton to go into town and ask the townsfolk for help. They owe us." Destiny continued up the stairs. Why hadn't she noticed the extent of the damage earlier?

Jaxon slipped on his jeans and a t-shirt. "Pack a change of clothes for me too. I'll go and let Carlton know what's going on. Meet you downstairs in 20 minutes."

Nodding, Destiny looked up as Magnus walked in. "Magnus."

"Destiny." Standing in the doorway, Magnus looked around the room. "Not much damage in here. You were lucky."

"Yeah, I'm feeling really lucky." Letting out a bitter little laugh Destiny walked to the window and watched as Jaxon gave orders to the pack. "You know they took my bag and book. They even took my ring. The ring that the fae queen gave me. They had no right to take that. It was a gift from my aunt."

"Destiny you will get over this." Magnus perched himself on the edge of the bed. "I know it seems hopeless…"

"Hopeless? No Magnus. It's not hopeless. They took what doesn't belong to them and they are going to give it back." Destiny pulled open a drawer and rummaged through her clothes. Grabbing a pair of jeans and a couple of T-shirts, she placed them in the holdall along with Jaxon's. "Now if you don't mind, I need to get going. I'll see you in a couple of days."

"Destiny, be careful. The council of Salem can be.... difficult." Magnus warned.

"Yeah, well they haven't met a 17-year-old teenager that just saved the world. I'll show them difficult." Destiny smiled at Magnus. "Don't worry, I'll be fine." Kissing Magnus on the cheek, Destiny turned and ran down the stairs and straight into Jaxon.

"Whoa.... We wanna get there in one piece." Jaxon held onto Destiny as she started to fall backwards.

"I've got the clothes; can we go now?" Starring up at Jaxon, Destiny felt the warmth from him as he gripped her. It would have been calming if she hadn't of been so on edge.

Sensing her mood, Jaxon nodded. "Yeah. Let's go." Leading her to the Porsche, Jaxon opened her door and watched as she climbed in, he then threw the holdall into the boot and climbed in next to her. "Ready?"

Destiny nodded, "Ready." As the words left her lips, Destiny grabbed onto the seat as Jaxon hit the accelerator, immediately the speed pushed Destiny back in the seat. The scenery became a blur as it flashed past her window. "Jesus Jaxon, slow down."

Laughing Jaxon changed gear and pressed the accelerator harder. "We are in a hurry cupcake. Now sit back and relax."

MAGNUS STOOD in the doorway as he was joined by Edna. "Did you warn her?" She asked.

Magnus watched as the car drove out of sight. "Yes, but I don't think she took any notice. I just hope Jaxon doesn't lose his temper because that will cause a whole other shitshow."

Rubbing Magnus's arm Edna sighed. "We best be ready then."

CHAPTER 31

Jaxon pulled the car into a 24-hour diner and looked over to Destiny as she glared at him.

"What are you doing, why are we stopping?" Destiny released her grip on the seat and rubbed her knuckles. They were still white from the force of holding onto the seat.

"I've spent the last hour listening to your stomach rumbling. You need to eat, and I need coffee." Unbuckling his seatbelt Jaxon threw open the door and marched around to Destiny's side. "You need to keep your strength up, come on."

Entering the diner the delicious smell of food wafted over Destiny's senses making her stomach rumble louder. She hadn't realised how hungry she was until now. They took a seat in a booth next to the window. Destiny grabbed the menu just as a waitress came over.

"What can I get you guys?" Holding her pen above her tiny note pad, she smiled. "Coffee to start?"

"Please, and I'll have a couple of steaks. Rare. Eggs, bacon, sausages, and toast. Destiny?" Jaxon looked at Destiny, who was now starring at him with her mouth open.

"I thought I was the hungry one!" Turning her attention back to the waitress, she pointed to the menu. "Can I have a cup of tea and a cheese and tomato omelette please?"

When the waitress left, Destiny continued to stare out of the window. "How much longer will it take to get there?"

"Only another hour. The sun will be up by then.... Do you know how you're gonna get your magic back. Only from what I've heard the witches council don't backtrack. They are mean and punish anyone who speaks out against them." Jaxon looked up as two cups were placed on the table. "Thanks." He nodded to the waitress and waited until she was out of earshot before he continued. "I'm not going to let them hurt you." Reaching over Jaxon covered Destiny's hands with his own. "And even if you don't get your magic back, you are still my Luna and I love you."

Destiny pulled her hands away and noticed Jaxon's face drop. "I will get it back. Failure is not an option. Look, can we talk about something else. Like the pack. You lost fifteen members Jaxon; I didn't think but you must be hurting."

"Of course I'm hurting, the pack are family." Jaxon looked down at his hands. "It could also cause trouble."

"What sort of trouble?" Destiny couldn't help the panicked tone to her voice.

"Nothing for you to worry about. Look the foods coming." Jaxon grabbed the knife and fork then started to tuck into his food. He had said too much.

"Jaxon. Am I a part of your pack?" Destiny asked, a little put out.

"You're my Luna, of course you're part of my pack.... Our pack." Jaxon corrected himself.

"Then tell me. What trouble?" Destiny picked up her fork and started to push the omelette around the plate.

Jaxon sighed. "I don't want you to worry."

"And those are the exact words that will make me worry. Jaxon, tell me, please." Destiny dropped her fork and folded her arms.

"Fine. I don't know if you had noticed but there's no pups at the packhouse. No one has been able to find their true mate. And only true mates can breed. We've just lost fifteen pack members, which puts us down to thirty-five. With only thirty-five pack members it will make us a target for bigger packs to take over." Jaxon rubbed the back of his neck. "Magnus should be able to form an illusion to outsiders, make it look like there's more of us than there really is, but it will only fool them for so long."

"I'm sorry Jaxon, I hadn't realised how you were feeling. The worry you carry for the pack every day must be hard." Destiny sighed. "You should have stayed at the packhouse. You were right, that was more important for you…. I just want you to understand that I need to do this, I need to get my magic back."

"No. We need to get your magic back, or at least try…. The pack should be fine for a couple of days. Anyway eat up so we can get going." Jaxon shoved a large piece of steak in his mouth and chewed loudly. "This is good."

Watching as blood smeared Jaxon's mouth, Destiny picked up a serviette and wiped it. "I'm glad you're enjoying it Alpha."

Jaxon grabbed Destiny's hand and kissed the back of it. "And just for the record Luna, there's no place I'd rather be right now, than with you."

Once they had finished eating, Jaxon threw some dollars on the table and waved to the waitress, before heading back to the car. "So any thoughts on how you're gonna handle this?"

"Beg. Plead. Oh I don't know. I'm sure I'll think of something when the time comes." Destiny gripped the seat readying herself for the rest of the journey. She glanced at Jaxon as he clipped in his seatbelt. He looked irritated. "What's wrong?"

"Why are you gripping the seat like that? You were the one that said we needed to hurry." Starting the car Jaxon pulled away, forcing Destiny back in the seat.

"That's why Jaxon. Slow down a little, please. We need to get there in one piece." Destiny's anxiety eased as Jaxon placed his hand on her knee. "How do you do that?"

"Do what?" Jaxon grinned; he could feel her relaxing. Squeezing her knee a little, he felt himself relax too.

"Make me feel better, just by touching me." Destiny placed a hand on his.

"It's the mate bond. I know we haven't mated properly yet, but even so, we both have the power to soothe each other. And once we do mate properly, these feelings will be stronger." Jaxon laughed. "You won't be able to keep your hands off me."

"In your dreams Alpha." Destiny blushed. She knew what he was saying was true. Even now when she looked at him she wanted to jump his bones.

"We'll see cupcake." Jaxon's concentration turned to the road. "We should be there in about 20 minutes."

"I suppose I should come up with a plan, and regarding the mate bond, I've got to be honest, I like it." Smiling at Jaxon she turned and continued to look out of the window.

IT WAS JUST after 7am when Jaxon pulled up in Salem. After finding somewhere to park, the couple made their way to Liberty street. "This was where the witch trials were held. Have you any idea where we're going?" Jaxon stopped and stared up at a stone monument. "I must admit, I thought it would have been bigger."

"As a reminder that witches are evil?" Destiny asked with a tinge of sadness. "Or as a celebration that they were executed?" She added.

Jaxon placed his arm around Destiny's shoulders. "No....as a reminder of those lives lost. I'm sure many of them would have been just humans and for the record not all witches are bad." Jaxon placed a comforting kiss on Destiny's forehead and pulled her closer.

Destiny allowed the comfort it brought and smiled before focusing back on the mission. "I guess we should find the entrance to the coven."

"Have you any idea where it is?" Jaxon asked as he scanned the area.

Destiny closed her eyes and took a deep breath, on opening them she pointed towards the opposite side of the road. "Down that alleyway, I can feel the magic flowing from the opening."

"What alleyway, what opening?" Jaxon asked as he scratched his head.

"Can't you see it?" Destiny stared at the small opening between two old buildings, both made of old stone. "It must have a spell on it so others can't see it. Come on, let's go."

"I'll go first." Jaxon replied as he pulled Destany behind him.

"How can you go first if you can't see it?" Destiny laughed. She was starting to find it endearing, the way he always wanted to protect her.

"Lead me to it then get behind me." Jaxon replied a little put out.

Destiny did as he had asked and walked behind him until they emerged into a very old square. It was surrounded by high stone walls that shimmered with energy. Destiny could feel the magic flowing all around her. It was strong and old. Old magic to protect the coven from being detected. There was a grass area with beautiful flowers in neatly kept borders and in the middle stood a huge stone statue of a woman, tied to a stone stake with stone flames surrounding her feet and lower legs. Destiny looked up at the woman's face. It perfectly showed the pain she would have felt. Her mouth was twisted in horror and her eye's bulged. Destiny turned away as the image came to life in her mind. She could hear the woman's screams and smell the fire as it burned into the woman's flesh. Squeezing her eyes shut Destiny shook her head and let out a whimper.

"What is it Destiny, what's wrong? Jaxon asked as he grabbed her and pulled her to him.

"It's, it's…." Destiny pointed to the statue before burying her face in Jaxon's chest. How could they do that…. I can feel her pain Jaxon, I can feel it all."

"Humans are cruel cupcake, anything they don't understand they destroy." Jaxon pushed Destiny back so he could look at her. "I won't let anyone hurt you."

"I love you Jax…." Before Destiny had finished speaking Jaxon had pulled her behind him as movement had caught his eye. Destiny peaked around his body and watched as a black cat came stalking towards them. "We are close. I can feel the magic. In fact it's getting stronger as the cat approaches."

In the blink of an eye the cat turned into a young woman. "We have been expecting you Destiny. Follow me."

"And you are?" Destiny inquired, slightly miffed at the lack of information. "And where are you taking us?"

"I am Lolly. One member of the witches council, and I'm afraid only you may follow."

Jaxon gritted his teeth and let out a low growl. "I go where she goes."

Lolly inspected the wolf man. She disliked his kind. Always fighting and causing trouble. Before she answered Destiny cut in.

"Jaxon comes with me. He's my mate." Grabbing Jaxon's hand, Destiny stayed glued to the spot.

"Oh very well, but the others won't like it. Now follow me and don't speak unless you are spoken too. Raven can get a bit cranky with outsiders." Glaring at Jaxon she shook her head and walked towards an old stone monument. Whispering a few words, the monument moved, revealing a stone staircase that led deep underground.

As the three descended the staircase the monument moved back, surrounding them in darkness. Jaxon squeezed Destiny's hand as he guided her down into the depths of the coven. Once they reached the ground, everything lit up in a blaze of light. Crystals hang from the stone ceiling, sending slithers of multi-coloured lights twisting around the passageway. The further they walked the larger the passageway got.

Jaxon could hear the whispers, there were 100's of them all speaking at once, calling for help. His head was beginning to spin. Within seconds, Jaxon's body crashed to the floor.

"What have you done to him?" Kneeling Destiny tried to pull him up. "Jaxon. Jaxon, wake up."

"It's okay Destiny, he is only sleeping. I will get someone to look after him. He will be fine. Now please, follow me. It's not good to keep the council waiting." Lolly grabbed Destiny's arm and led her to a great hall. It was filled with witches and war locks, all muttering as they turned and stared at Destiny. As the hall fell silent, Destiny swallowed down her nerves, and slowly approached the five golden thrones. Lolly took a seat on the far right one and smiled at Destiny. "Destiny. This is Raven. She holds the power of earth."

Raven sat back in her throne and studied Destiny briefly before standing. Flicking her long black hair behind her she walked towards Destiny, circling her once, until stopping dead in front of her. "She's just a child." She called back to Lolly and the other two. "How is it possible she could control so much power."

"She has strength, sister. I could feel it in the air before she arrived here." Lolly smiled again at Destiny. "I'm certain she is the one…. Destiny this is Allegra. She has the power of fire."

Allegra rose and joined Raven, her hair trailed down her back in waves of copper and red.

Destiny could feel the heat radiating from her. Taking a step back as Allegra took a step nearer, she blinked, Allegra's eyes lit up like two fire balls. "It's true, I can feel it too." Reaching her hand out, Allegra stroked Destiny's cheek. "We need the supernatural council here. Someone call them now."

"They are already on their way. Now Destiny this is Esmée, she has the power of water. Which is why she insists on dying her hair blue." Lolly let out a little giggle as Esmée rolled her eyes.

Standing, Esmée bowed slightly towards Destiny then clapped her hands. "Prepare a feast for our guests. They will arrive soon." With a flick of her head, Esme disappeared.

"Guests?" Destiny asked, aiming her question towards Lolly.

"The supernatural council will have to meet to decide your fate. It concerns us all Destiny. Now let me take you to your room."

"I have a room?" Destiny followed in a daze. Was she going to be tried without anyone defending her? This was wrong, so wrong. "Where's Jaxon, I want to see him."

"He's in your room waiting for you, now Destiny don't worry. It will all be over soon enough." Lolly opened a door and ushered Destiny in. "Someone will come and get you when we are ready."

"Wait! Please. There was a fifth throne, where is the witch that sits on that one?"

"That's why you are here. All will become clear at the feast. Now spend time with the wolf before he leaves. It will be the last chance you get." Lolly vanished, leaving Destiny in shock.

"What do you mean before he leaves. Where's he going?" Turning Destiny spotted Jaxon lying on a large bed in the middle of the room. "Jaxon!" Running over to him she watched as his eyes opened.

"What happened?" Rubbing his head, Jaxon sat up. "Where are we?"

"Shh, lay down." Destiny crawled up onto the bed and cuddled into Jaxon's solid body. She felt the comfort as she wrapped her arms around him.

"As nice as this is, we need to find a way out. It's not safe here Destiny, I heard voices, somethings wrong."

"It's too late for that Jaxon." Stroking his face, Destiny felt the sting of tears. "I love you. More than life."

"I love you too…. What's going on?" Jaxon pushed Destiny away and stood up. "Have they hurt you?"

"No. Look I don't know what's going on. I just needed to tell you how I feel." Tapping the bed next to her Destiny smiled. "Please Jaxon, just five minutes."

Jaxon frowned as he sat back down on the bed. "Five minutes and then we leave." He lay back as Destiny placed her arm over him.

Destiny closed her eyes and breathed in Jaxon's scent, relaxing in the familiarity of his arms. Breathing in again she started to panic, something was wrong, Jaxon's scent was fading. Opening her eyes, she sat up. Jaxon was already gone. "NO. NOT YET. I'M NOT READY!"

CHAPTER 32

Sitting on the now empty bed Destiny sobbed. She hadn't had long enough with Jaxon. He was her mate. Her one true love. How could they take him from her. Sniffing loudly Destiny looked up as the door opened.

"We are ready for you now." Lolly looked sadly at Destiny. "It will get better child. Now come."

Following Lolly back into the giant chamber, Destiny looked at the four new faces, although one of them she already knew. "What's going on?"

"We ask the question's here." Raven replied snappily. "You would do well to remember your place."

"You've taken everything from me. Kill me, I really don't care." Destiny looked over and pointed towards the fae queen. "Nice to know you can't be trusted." Destiny turned and looked at all the faces in the great chamber. They were all starring back at her. "So what do we have here…. I take it this is the supernatural council. The fae queen…. A vampire…. And if I'm not mistaken a wolf. So I'm guessing you four witches make up the fourth. So now tell me, what do you want from me?"

"You should be careful with that mouth of yours girl. We are the four and you will respect that." Raven pointed at Destiny. "You live here now so get used to it."

"I am the four and you will live to regret this." Destiny laughed in defiance at the shocked faces. "I am fae. I am witch. I am princess and I am Luna…. So tell me Raven, what do I have to get used too?"

The gasps went up around the chamber as Raven turned purple and raised her wand. Before she cast her spell the wolf king bellowed, making everyone jump. "ENOUGH!" He looked around to make sure everyone was paying attention then continued. "Destiny. I am the wolf king, but you may call me Adolphus. You are here because of the remarkable strength you have shown. No one has ever taken all the magic of the book and lived. Now the coven needs a fifth member, and they would like it to be you."

"But what if I don't want this. I want Jaxon. Where is he?" Feeling the tears fall again Destiny swiped at her eyes.

"You love this wolf?" Adolphus asked.

"Yes." Destiny took a shaky breath. "With all my being."

"You know he had to go back. He will be challenged for his pack in the next few days. Now that it's so weak and carries fewer members, it doesn't look good for him. Adolphus shook his head. "I'm sorry child, you will never see him again."

"Does he die?" Destiny walked towards the king and dropped to her knees. "Please. Help him."

"I can't. It's beyond my control. I can only see what will be, I cannot stop it I'm afraid."

"Then let me stop it. Tell me what I have to do?" Destiny turned to Lolly. "A life for a life. Take mine and let him live."

Raven stepped forward and pulled Destiny up. "There's only one way. We can make it that you never met. He will not remember you, but you will remember him. You will carry his pain as well as your own."

"Will he be happy? Safe?" Destiny swallowed down a sob.

"Yes. He will live his life as he should. All the pack members will be restored, and he will live his life with another. Do you consent to that…. I must warn you the pain will be great."

Nodding Destiny closed her eyes. "Yes. I consent."

Adolphus looked at Destiny with respect. "Then so it shall be."

The first wave of pain hit Destiny like a recking ball. She fell to the floor holding her heart. The pain intensified as Jaxon's memory was wiped clean. Destiny rolled from side to side as she screamed out in agony. Wave after wave of Jaxon's memories hit her. The first meeting in the bar. The first kiss in the truck. The night's spent in bed, not being able to touch one another. The Luna ceremony. The night they did touch, the explosive electricity that shot between them. Every memory of Jaxon's was now hers.

The fae queen ran to Destiny and hugged her, trying her best to ease the pain. "Can't we do something to help her?"

Raven shook her head. "I'm sorry, this was her choice." Looking at Lolly she pointed to Destiny. "Take her too her room."

The wolf king stood and swooped Destiny up in his arms. She was the bravest human he had ever met, and she deserved to be treated with respect. "You seem to be enjoying this a little too much, Raven." The wolf king breathed in Raven's scent. It wasn't quite right. "Make sure you look after her. We shall return in one week, if she survives, to speak about the other matter."

MAGNUS AND EDNA sat in a stone circle, surrounded by salt. Edna and himself had done the spell just after Destiny had left. They had been sitting here for 24 hours now. "Do you think it's safe to leave?" He asked Edna.

"I'm sure the spell will be strong enough to ward off any evil magic. Take a handful of the salt, earth, and pine leaves and place it in your boots Magnus. It will give a stronger protection. I shall do the same." Edna removed her shoes and scooped the ingredients up into her hand and covered the inside of her shoes before slipping them back on. "The pine leaves are a little uncomfortable, but this will keep us grounded."

After doing the same, Magnus stepped out of the circle and closed his eyes. "There's dark magic in the air. I can feel it. We should take a bag of the potion with us; we may need it for others."

Edna magically produced a bag and filled it with the salt, earth, and pine needles. "Let's get back to the packhouse and see what's happened." Edna picked up her old spell book and walked through the trees. "There's something wrong Magnus. I can't feel Destiny."

"Yes. There's something very wrong." Magnus agreed. He searched for Destiny in his mind, he could see her, but not feel her presence. Something was blocking her.

As they approached the packhouse, Magnus looked up at the burnt-out shell. Why weren't the pack fixing it?. They were carrying on as though everything were normal. Jaxon was stood next to Carlton watching the pack members train. Magnus nudged Edna. "Do you see what I see?"

"If you are talking about the fifteen dead wolves training, then yes, I do. Look, there's Gene." Edna pointed. "Her body is rotting."

Magnus nodded. But his thoughts were on Destiny. Where was she? Why was Jaxon here without her? Just what was going on? Magnus had a hundred question's spinning around in his head. "Things are worse than I first feared Edna."

Jaxon came marching over and growled at the uninvited guests. "What are doing here?"

"Alpha. Where's Destiny?" Magnus watched the flicker of irritation flash across Jaxon's face.

"You do not come to the pack's grounds without an invite Magnus, you know that. My god, are you actually sober?"

"He's memory has been wiped." Edna glanced at Magnus and then back to Jaxon. "Alpha. Please beg our pardon but we need your help. Please, where is Destiny?"

"I don't know any Destiny. Is she one of your lot. A witch?" Jaxon snarled. He hated witches.

"We need to go to Salem, Magnus. We need to find who has cast this spell and get them to reverse it." Edna glanced at Jaxon. He looked more confused than ever. Edna tried one last time to see if she could jog Jaxon's memory. "Alpha, what happened to the packhouse?"

"What is wrong with you two. The packhouse is fine. Look." Jaxon pointed to the packhouse. "Have you been eating those magic mushrooms again Edna, I thought you would have learnt your lesson last time. Now go, leave the pack grounds."

Magnus pulled Edna's arm and led her away. "This is pointless…. I think we should speak with the fae queen. She may have an idea what's happening as she's on the supernatural council."

"Can we trust her though Magnus?" Edna sighed. "I know she's Destiny's aunt but why would she be a part of this." Edna threw her hand in the air. "Surely she would have warned us. Warned Destiny even."

"I don't know Edna, but we've got to start somewhere, and she's the one with the closest link to Destiny. I fear the wolf king and the ancient vampire will have no interest in helping unless we get her on side first…. Right, let's get back to my cabin, we can grab what we need and leave from there."

"Oh Magnus, I hope Destiny is okay." Edna looked into the distance. "Someone has set this all-in motion. From the very beginning. I can feel it now."

ADOLPHUS PACED AROUND in his room, while his Luna, Otsana, looked on. "Somethings wrong. I can't put my finger on it."

"Alpha. Will you please sit down, Your making me dizzy." Otsana took his hand and guided him to a chair.

"Since when did Raven have the power to bring back the dead. And then there was the smell, her scent was all wrong….Raven was always the sensible one, the one with compassion. For supernatural's as well as humans. It doesn't make sense that she enjoyed Destiny's pain so much, I could smell it. The pleasure and satisfaction wafted off her in waves…. Things haven't been right since they banished Faith."

"Alpha, this is something you cannot get involved in. You cannot go against the supernatural council. It will bring trouble for us all." Otsana warned.

"I fear trouble is already on the way and if I do nothing it may spell the end for all of us. I need to speak to Grace, she is not only the fae queen but also Destiny's aunt. She must have sensed it." Adolphus stood; he had decided. "I will leave in the morning."

CHAPTER 33

The fae queen sat on her throne, starring into space. Replaying the previous day's events in her mind. Why hadn't she put a stop to it? She could see the pain in Destiny's face, she could see it in her whole body. The way she dropped to the floor wreathing in agony. The queen closed her eyes tight, trying to blot out the vision.

"Your majesty, you have visitors." Willow called as she curtsied.

Pleased at the distraction, the queen nodded. "Show them in." Watching as Magnus and Edna were brought before her she sighed. "What do you want?"

"We want to know where Destiny is?" Magnus replied abruptly.

"And if she is okay, your majesty." Edna added.

Looking at the two worried faces, the queen shook her head before replying. "She is with the witches council in Salem. I thought you would have known that as you're her father Magnus."

"I know that's where she went but I can no longer feel her. Something's wrong Grace." Ignoring the queens glare, Magnus continued. "She went to get her magic back after the witches council stole it. Now I know how these things work. They would either give her the magic back or not. You would have been there, you would know. So where is she now and why hasn't she returned?"

Before the queen could reply Willow returned following the wolf king, as he bounded in. "I'm sorry your majesty, I told him you were busy."

"I can speak for myself fae." Adolphus looked at Magnus and Edna. *More damn witches,* he thought. "And you are?"

Ignoring the Wolf king, Magnus returned his attention back to the queen. "If you know what's happened to Destiny then I demand you tell me. Please Grace. She is my daughter."

"You're Destiny's father?" Adolphus asked.

"Yes I am. Do you know what's happened to her?" Magnus walked towards Adolphus. "Somethings wrong. I can't feel her presence anymore and Jaxon has no memory of her."

Adolphus studied Magnus for a moment. "She is at the coven…. You say you can't feel her presence. And what about you Grace, she is your niece; can you feel her presence still?"

Shaking her head slowly Grace looked at her hands. "Something is wrong. Very wrong."

Magnus glared at Grace. "And you left her there. On her own?"

"She is with the witches council" Grace stood and walked towards Magnus. "No one can hurt her there."

Adophus intervened before Magnus could answer. "Unless it's one of them. I noticed Raven's behaviour, it was…. odd."

"Odd in what way?" Edna asked.

"When Destiny took the memories from Jaxon, she liked the pain it caused, delighted in it even. And there was the bringing back the dead. No witch alone has that power." The king stopped as Magnus jumped in.

"That explains it."

"Explains what?" Grace questioned.

"When Destiny and Jaxon left for the coven of Salem, Edna and I protected ourselves in a truth circle. After 24 hours we emerged to find Jaxon back, oblivious to recent events, and the pack members that perished in the battle with Galdreola, all walking about as if they were still alive, only they were walking corpses.

Quite literally." Magnus sighed. "This is all connected to the very first incident."

"Which was?" Adolphus huffed. "Can you start at the beginning, so we can piece everything together."

"Destiny's mother was killed on all hallows eve, the same as Jaxon's parents. Both fluke car accidents. Then Destiny was brought here, by Mr's Richards, who turned out to be Galdreola. Now, Galdreola was after the magic in Destiny's book, but only Destiny can access it as it's her birth right. So Galdreola had to get Destiny to soak up the book to enable her to get all the magic, by eating her. However Destiny defeated her, ending her plan." Magnus finished with a proud smile. The thought of his daughter being a mighty witch warmed him. His smile fell immediately when he thought of her alone in the Salem coven.

Adolphus started to pace the floor, he held his hands behind his back and walked to and fro whilst unravelling the events in his mind. Stopping he turned to Magnus. "Tell me, how would a demon escape from their realm?"

"They can't. It would take magic of some sort." Magnus realised in that moment they had all been played. "Someone else has caused this."

Adolphus nodded. "This is all linked to Raven."

"We need to get Destiny back, she's not safe there." Magnus stomped towards the door.

"STOP!" Adolphus yelled. "You can't simply go in there without a plan. Destiny will be safe for the next five days. The supernatural council are due to meet then. Now I suggest we put our heads together and work out what we are going to do."

Destiny spent five days in bed, her brain was absorbing all the memories and trying to store them in the deepest depths of her brain. Somewhere she wouldn't find them. But her body was still calling for Jaxon. She still had the mate bond, even if he didn't. Climbing from the bed, Destiny walked to the door. She still felt weak, as her knees gave way she slid down the wall and sat with her back resting against the cold stone. She could feel the power through her skin. It was sucking up the magic that surrounded her. Placing her whole body against the wall, she breathed in. She could feel it. Her magic was coming back to her. Breaking away as her head swam with incantations and potions, Destiny stood. This time much steadier. She wanted to see Jaxon, just one last time. Opening the door Destiny made her way to the great chamber, running her hands along the stone walls as she went. The magic was pulsating its way around her body. Destiny stopped when she heard her voice called.

"Destiny!" Raven said, surprised that Destiny was already up and walking. "How are you feeling?"

"I want to see Jaxon. One last time. Please Raven." Destiny placed her hands together in a begging motion.

Placing her finger to her lips Raven shushed her. "Follow me." Leading her to a small room full of mirrors, Raven pulled her in before shutting the door quietly. "I'll get into trouble if the others find out. Now pick a mirror and think of the wolf. Picture him in your mind, and he should appear. He won't be able to see you, but you will see him. And Destiny, you may not like what you see." Raven warned.

Destiny stood in front of a large mirror and nodded. "Okay." She thought of Jaxon, his chiselled jaw line. His black hair. His bulging muscles. Jaxon's face came into view and Destiny took a sharp breath, He looked happy. Laughing and joking with Carlton. Gene walked over to him and threw her arms around him. Jaxon kissed her on the lip's, just like he used to Destiny. Destiny saw movement in the corner, looking over she saw Magnus. He was staring straight at her. Unsettled by this Destiny turned back to Jaxon and stroked his face. Jaxon pulled away from Gene and turned towards Destiny. His face wrinkled as he placed his hand where hers had been. He was touching his cheek exactly where Destiny had stroked it.

"Okay. That's enough. We need to go." Raven pulled Destiny

away from the mirror and out of the room. "Promise me you won't go in there again."

Destiny nodded, there was no way she was going to promise. The nod seemed to pacify Raven and they made their way to the great cavern.

"Look who I found." Raven announced to the others. "Are you hungry Destiny. I mean you must be. You haven't eaten for five days."

Destiny thought back to her last meal, in the diner with Jaxon. "A little I guess."

Destiny sat waiting, with her head down. Magnus had seen her; she was sure of it. Jaxon had felt her, why else would he have touched his cheek. He looked happy though, maybe she should leave things be. Let him have his life with Gene, who was dead. Dead? How could they bring all the dead back, wasn't it a life for a life? Something didn't make sense.

"Here we go Destiny, a nice bowl of broth, with crusty bread. Now tuck in." Lolly sat next to her and watched as Destiny picked up the spoon.

"Do you always watch people eat? It's very off putting." Destiny pushed the bowl away. "I want the meeting tonight. I want to know what's going on."

"One does not simply summon the supernatural council Destiny. They will be here in two days, so in the meantime, I suggest you get used to your new home." Raven pushed the bowl back towards Destiny. "Now eat."

Destiny looked up at Raven who was standing over her. She was a little forceful with the food. Too forceful. Something was wrong.

EDNA STARED at Adolphus and Magnus in disbelief. "How on earth do you expect me to get Jaxon away from the packhouse?"

"He has respect for you Edna, and you know we can't talk to him on pack ground. It's cursed. Whoever cast this spell will sense somethings wrong. We need to get him to the coffee shop where no one will be able to pry." Magnus folded his arms in annoyance. "I can't do it. He hates me."

"Magnus is right, I can't go there either. They will know we are onto them." Adolphus reached out and touched Edna's arm. "It's in all our best interests to save Destiny, but to do that we need Jaxon."

JAXON REACHED the packhouse and shifted back to human form. He needed that run; his wolf needed that run. He'd had a strange feeling since Magnus and Edna had visited. And then he felt like he was being watched, touched even. Jaxon raised his hand to his cheek and rubbed it. It was strange, he had a warm feeling. Pulling on his sweatpants he sighed as Gene came out of the packhouse.

"Hey handsome, did you enjoy your run?" Gene asked as she sat on the packhouse steps. "You know I would have come, if you'd told me."

Jaxon looked at Gene and breathed in her scent. Her sweet smell was mixed with death or was that rot. Rotting flesh. Breathing out he smiled at her. "I needed to stretch my legs and my mind. You can come next time." As Jaxon was about to head in when he heard the sound of an approaching car. It was Edna. "Go inside, I'll be in shortly." Walking to the now stationary car, Jaxon leaned into the open window. "Edna."

"Alpha. How are you?" Edna replied, not knowing what to say.

"I don't believe you came here to see how I am. What do you want?"

"I've made a load of cakes for the packhouse, would you be so good as to come into town and collect them?" Edna felt her heart rate increase. She was glad she had put a spell on herself so Jaxon wouldn't notice.

"I'll collect them tomorrow." Jaxon turned to walk away.

"NO! I mean no they will spoil, please Alpha, now would be good, I need space in the shop." Edna smiled. "I've just had a big order come in."

"Fine. I'll follow you in the truck." Jaxon watched as Edna pulled away. What the hell was going on with everyone?

'Jaxon'

The voice filled his mind and senses. It was so familiar. Calling out in his mind he waited for a reply. 'Who are you?' But none came.

CHAPTER 34

"He's here." Edna opened the door as Jaxon approached. "Can we make this quick Edna; I'm needed back at the packhouse." Jaxon's eyes went wide when he spotted Adolphus standing in the middle of the coffee shop. "Your majesty." Jaxon bowed his head slightly.

"Jaxon sit down. We need to talk." Adolphus pulled out a chair and motioned to Jaxon. "You best sit for this."

DESTINY LAY ON HER BED, her stomach was rumbling loudly, making it difficult to sleep. 'Jaxon' she called out in her mind, but she couldn't reach him. She was so sure earlier he had heard her, but she must have been mistaken. Destiny's magic was off too. The magic she had picked up from the cavern wall was bad. It made her angry, like she wanted to hurt someone. So she emptied her body and allowed it to flow out. She turned her attention to the crystals that hung from her ceiling, Destiny sighed. Why hadn't Magnus come to save her? Didn't he say he loved her? Words came easy to some people. And then there was the fae queen, Destiny should have known better. Closing her eyes when she heard the door handle move, she kept still, pretending to sleep.

Raven looked down at Destiny and stroked her hair as she smiled. She was just a child. Pulling the cover over her Raven bent down and kissed Destiny's forehead. Turning she made her way back out, closing the door gently behind her.

"None of this makes any sense. I don't know a Destiny. Don't you think I would remember making this woman my Luna?" Jaxon stood aggressively. "I'm surprised at you." Jaxon pointed to Adolphus. "You are the werewolf king; shouldn't you be on my side or are you suffering from lunacy?"

"Jaxon please sit and take your boots off." Edna stood in front of him with the bag of salt, earth, and pine needles."

"Edna, are you mad too?" Jaxon sat and run his fingers through his hair.

"Humour me Alpha." Edna kneeled and waited for Jaxon to slip his boots off. Once he had, she placed a handful of the spell inside each boot. "Now, put them back on."

"Ouch, that's digging in." Jaxon pulled his foot out and removed a pine needle. "I don't know what this is about, but I think you're all mad."

"Alpha please." Edna pushed Jaxon's foot back into his boot, then stood and looked at him.

"Is it working?" Adolphus asked as he studied Jaxon's frowning face.

"It will take a minute or two." Edna replied. "Jaxon, did I tell you Destiny is going to be working here?"

"Destiny? But I don't know...." Jaxon trailed off. "Cupcakes and wild honey suckle."

"What's he going on about?" Magnus looked around. There were cupcakes but no wild honey suckle.

"He remembers her scent." Adolphus smiled. "It's working."

Jaxon closed his eyes as a vision filled his head. 'Destiny' He raised his hand to his cheek and got the same warm feeling he did earlier. 'Jaxon!' He heard back. It was faint but he heard it none the less. "What's happened, it's confusing."

"Listen Jaxon, you need to go back to the packhouse. Everything will come back to you gradually. You will be reminded of things, when you see a certain place or maybe a time of the day. But listen carefully. You must carry on as normal, whoever has done this spell will know." Edna carried a large box of cupcakes to the table. "You will need these to keep your cover."

"What about the dead wolves, which might be too much of a shock for him." Magnus looked at Adolphus and then Edna. "Should we do a spell, to keep him safe?"

"No. The pack may sense it…. Jaxon do you remember the battle with Galdreola?" Adolphus asked as he sat opposite Jaxon.

"I don't know, I can't think straight…. Death. So many dead." Jaxon shook his head.

"Jaxon look at me." Adolphus grabbed Jaxon's chin. "The packhouse has been damaged and you lost fifteen wolves. Also Gene died at the battle with the rouge vampires."

Jaxon laughed. "I was with Gene last night. I think I would have noticed if she were dead."

"Very well, this he will have to see for himself." Adolphus looked up at Magnus. "Tomorrow is the supernatural council meeting, to see what Destiny has decided. I fear she won't get a choice, so we need to be ready."

Jaxon drove back to the packhouse. As soon as he was back he would get rid of this spell in his boots. They thought they could trick him. Well he had other ideas. Pulling up, Jaxon looked at the burnt-out front of the packhouse.

Turning his head as Gene approached he shuddered. She was rotting. Her flesh was grey and her once sparkling eyes had magots crawling out of them.

As the sickness hit, Jaxon threw open the door and let the contents of his stomach empty onto the floor.

"Jaxon, what's wrong?" Jean grabbed Jaxon's arm and helped him out. "You need to lay down."

Shrugging Gene off, Jaxon made his way to the back of the truck. "I'm fine, something I ate. Here take these into the kitchen." Passing her the box of cupcakes he watched as she walked away.

"Hey. Free cupcakes." Carlton laughed. Stopping when he noticed Jaxon's pallor complexion. "What's wrong?"

"Nothing. Be ready for seven, you me and Alex are going for a beer." Jaxon slammed the door shut and headed towards the packhouse.

"I take it the future Luna will be accompanying us." Carlton stated. He never got to spend time with Jaxon without her present. It was starting to piss him off.

"No. Boys only." Jaxon informed him. "Be ready for seven and let Alex know."

THE BAR WAS ALREADY full by the time Jaxon walked in, followed by Carlton and Alex. As Jaxon approached the bar he was hit with the memory of the first meeting with Destiny. The way she walked in nervously and then called him a dog, right in front of his pack. The feeling he got from her, like she was his and no one else would do. 'Destiny' He called out in his mind, but there was no answer this time. "We need to find Magnus and Edna. We'll have one drink and then head out."

"Jaxon what's this all about, you've been off all afternoon." Carlton motioned to the bartender and perched on a stool. "Is something wrong?"

"You'll find out soon enough. Now drink up." Jaxon knocked back his drink in one and then walked to the door.

Carlton and Alex looked at each other as they followed. They could tell something was wrong. "Where are we heading?"

"The coffee shop." Jaxon crossed the street and stood looking in the window of the coffee shop. He could smell Destiny, cupcakes and Wild honey suckle. Taking a deep breath he caught another smell. Rotting flesh. "Quick. Gene's coming." Pushing hard on the door, the lock broke, and the door swung open.

"Jeez Jax, what's going on with you?" Carlton stood watching as Jaxon marched inside.

"Get inside quick, they can't smell us in here." Jaxon pushed the door closed behind him then bent down. "Get down, don't let her see you."

"Who?" Carlton and Alex asked in unison.

"Gene." Jaxon crawled to the bottom of the staircase. "Magnus, Edna, you up there?"

Edna came running down the stairs with Magnus in tow. "Alpha, why are you on the floor?" Looking up just as Gene was about to walk in, Edna waved her hand sealing the door. "Come upstairs, she can't see you now."

Carlton stood up, placing his hands on his hips. "Since when do we hide from Gene?"

"Carlton do you trust me?" Jaxon waited for him to nod. "In that case, just do as Edna tells you. Edna have you any more of the pine needles?"

Edna smiled at Carlton and Alex, then she nodded to their boots. "Take them off."

Carlton slipped out of his first and watched as Edna placed a handful of dirt in them. "What the hell?"

"Now put your boots on and go and look at Gene, she's out there somewhere I can smell her." Jaxon watched the two men go then turned to Magnus. "Everything's starting to come back to me, but I noticed the bite on my collar bone has gone, will that come back?"

"I don't know, sorry Jaxon. If it doesn't, you'll just have to mark each other again." Magnus thought for a moment, before continuing. "Have you been able to feel her at all?"

"I keep getting the weirdest feeling, like she's calling me, but I'm not sure, maybe its wishful thinking." Jaxon spotted Carlton and Alex walking up the stairs. Their faces both green. "You saw her then."

"What is that thing?" Alex asked Magnus.

"It's Gene. In her true form. She died when you fought the rogue vampires, or rather the Alpha killed her to save Destiny."

Jaxon closed his eyes as the memory hit him, he could see Destiny fighting, unaware that Gene was lunging towards her with a sword. The feeling of wanting to protect her even stronger than before. "How do we get Destiny back?"

Carlton flinched. "Wait a minute. Jaxon did you…. with Gene?"

Jaxon nodded. "Thanks for reminding me. Edna I hope you can do a spell to get rid of that memory."

"Of course Alpha." Edna turned her attention to Magnus. "Should we make our way to Salem tonight or in the morning?"

"Morning. Jaxon, Carlton, and Alex must return to the packhouse. Everything must appear as normal." Magnus watched Jaxon's face drop. "You'll have to tell Gene you have a headache." As Magnus started to laugh he stopped immediately when he heard Jaxon growl. "Well you had better get going. Meet us here at 7am. We can head off together but for goodness sake, please make sure you are not followed."

"What happens if they follow us?" Alex asked.

"It will put Destiny's life more in danger than it already is." Magnus motioned to the stairs. "Off you go and if you are not here by 7am, we will leave without you."

"Come on Alpha." Carlton slapped Jaxon on the back. "I don't know how you're going to escape Gene's clutches tonight."

Jaxon walked down the stairs; he didn't know either.

CHAPTER 35

Magnus and Edna watched as the SUV approached. "Looks like we're travelling in style." Edna remarked.

"I don't care how we travel as long as we get there." Magnus made his way over to Jaxon, as he exited the vehicle. "You're cutting it a bit fine Jaxon."

"We had trouble getting away." Jaxon growled at the memory of Gene's rotting arms around his neck. The kiss was worse. He tried a peck on the cheek, but she wasn't having it. As she stuck her rotting tongue in his mouth, Jaxon had to fight the urge to push her away. Carlton was the one that saved him though, demanding they had to go on urgent pack business, so they could get back and enjoy the sunshine with the pack. He had arranged a BBQ in celebration of the mating ceremony that night. So Gene was content to stay home and organise the party. She was walking around shouting orders to the remaining pack members, like she was already Luna. Jaxon sighed. "It's the summer solstice tonight. Will we have Destiny back by then?"

Magnus looked at Edna and then back at Jaxon. "I should hope so, however there is a chance we may not make it back at all Jaxon.

This is strong magic and none of us really know what we are dealing with."

Destiny ran her fingertips along the crystals in her room. They seemed to be multiplying if that were at all possible. Before she had finished, Raven barged into her room, holding her head.

"Stop that!" Raven's eyes closed as the pain in her head receded.

"Stop what, oh you mean this?" Destiny once again ran her hand along the crystals and listened to the chimes.

Raven held her hand aloft and blasted Destiny to the wall. "I said stop…. you are trying my patience."

Winded Destiny pushed herself off the wall. "No need to get cranky, if I can't touch them take them out."

"No. They are here for your protection." Now get ready for the council. You have two hours." Raven turned and left, slamming the door for good measure.

Destiny looked up at the crystals. So they were for her protection. That didn't sound right, they seemed to have an adverse effect on Raven. Causing her pain like that meant only one thing. She was connected to them. Destiny pulled out a chair and stood on it, as she reached up she started to take them down, one by one. Making sure not to let them touch each other. Once she had covered her bed, she started to wrap each one in cloth and place on a tray. The best way to protect herself was to get rid of them all together. Her final job was to take them out and find somewhere to hide them, somewhere safe. Heading to the room of mirrors, Destiny held her breath while trying to avoid eye contact with the passing witches and war locks. She shouldn't have worried, they walked past as if she weren't there. She couldn't understand why they all had vacant expressions. It had been the same since she had arrived. No one spoke to her, no one made eye contact. They just seemed to walk about as if in their own world. Destiny stopped abruptly when she noticed a witch walking towards her. As the witch neared she simply turned around and walked back the way she had come. Destiny realised whatever dark magic was in the coven walls was also inside these witches. Someone was controlling them. She didn't have time for another mystery though, she needed to finish her task. As she made it to the entrance of the room, she checked to make sure no one was around. The door was locked, of course it would be. Destiny could feel the magic surrounding it. Rethinking, she turned and made her way back to her room. She would place them in the cupboard until she could safely dump them. Her next job was to start collecting the crystals from the entrance. If she stood any chance of escaping they would have to go.

ADOLPHUS SAT in a small coffee shop, just outside the main town of Salam. He stared out of the window as the sun glistened on the small river that ran opposite. Being a wolf, he loved all things nature. The rivers, the forests. Everything that the humas had yet to destroy. That's why he had bought so much of the countryside, all around the USA he owned large areas of forest's and nature reserves. To protect it from the concrete jungle's that seemed to be popping up everywhere. He nodded to his two most fierce fighters that accompanied him, as Jaxon's SUV pulled up outside. "They are here." Standing he made his way out to greet them.

Jaxon bowed his head as Adolphus emerged from the coffee shop. "Your majesty. This is Carlton, my Beta, and Alex my Delta."

Adolphus nodded to the two then turned his attention to Magnus and Edna. "Have you been able to come up with anything that might help?"

Stepping forward, Edna held out the bag of pine needles, salt, and earth. "This will help keep you grounded and stop any spells that may make you hallucinate. All you need to do is put a handful in each boot."

"Won't it be detected, I though witches could smell magic?" Adolphus asked as he kicked of his boots.

"No. I purposely used pine needles in the spell to cover any traces of magic. So whoever's cast this dark magic, they will not notice." Edna dug her hand into the bag and proceeded to fill the boots. "There, that should do."

"So what's the plan?" Jaxon asked, as he watched Adolphus pull on his boots.

"I am due to enter at noon. My two guards here will be with me. The fae queen should already be there, she was bringing two of her fighters. We couldn't risk bringing anymore. They would know immediately that we are onto them. Edna, can you do a spell to get Jaxon, his beta and delta, inside?"

Edna nodded. "I can put an invisibility spell on them, but the witches council will be able to feel their presence, if they are close by. May I suggest that as soon as we get in there, Jaxon finds Destiny, while we keep the council distracted. Magnus has every right to ask to see Destiny. Of course they won't let him, but we can stand there and argue, hopefully it will give Jaxon time to sneak her out."

"I carried Destiny to her room; I will draw a map so you can find it." Adolphus rubbed his chin. "You will need to be quick Jaxon, before the council smell trouble."

"How do we get out though, everything is guarded by magic. I can't see brute force doing the job." Jaxon frowned. "And then what happens when they realise they've been tricked?"

"Hopefully, you will be out before that happens. Now shall we have a bite to eat before we go?" Adolphus headed back into the coffee shop followed by his two men.

DESTINY SAT at the bottom of the steps that lead to the entrance of the coven. She had been unable to grab any of the crystals as Lolly had ambushed her as she had made her way there. "Lolly what exactly do you want from me?"

Lolly smiled. "We want you to join us. To become one of the sisters of the council. It's quite an honour Destiny. Most witches would be made up to be asked."

"Choose one of them then." Destiny looked at the floor. "I want

Jaxon. I want my dad and I want my life back. I hate it here. Its full of evil."

Lolly's mouth dropped open. Taking a minute to recover she took a deep breath. "This place is not evil Destiny, it's magical. We do a lot of good here you know."

"You can't even feel it. Can you?" Destiny shook her head in dismay. "You're one of them. I shouldn't be talking to you."

"Now just hold on a moment young lady, you do not get to talk about us like that.... Raven would have a fit if she were to hear. Quite literally." Lolly took a seat next to Destiny and sighed. "You know everything changed when Faith was banished. Raven had always been close to her and when she tried to destroy the world, it was Raven that stepped up. You see all these crystals that hang from the ceilings." Lolly pointed. "Raven put those up. To protect us."

"And what exactly do they protect you from?" Destiny asked with a roll of her eyes.

"Danger of course." Lolly replied a little too quickly.

"What danger. You live in one of the safest places on the planet. No one can get in, or out, without you knowing." Destiny stood up and pointed to the crystals. "They are evil, I can feel it, just the same as the coven."

"Destiny, you have no magic, so you won't feel anything." Lolly reached out and touched Destiny's arm. "Please sit."

Destiny sat back down and looked at Lolly. "When did Faith get banished?"

"New hallows eve. It was horrible. She had tried to master the elements. As you should know we only get one each. It is like a safety valve to stop any one witch from being too powerful. Anyway, we were alerted when her power spiked. She had mastered two, which is not allowed. Raven stopped her and banished her. Raven has kept us safe ever since." Lolly looked at her hands, they were shaking at the memory.

"So, I mastered all of them, I've had my power taken because of it and now you want me here, but I'm not a witch, so this doesn't make any sense." Destiny thought back to her mother and Jaxon's parents all killed on all hallows eve. The same day Faith was banished. Mr's Richards said we, but she was really Galdreola. So Galdreola was not working alone. Raven was the common link. For anyone to get the full magic of the book Destiny needed to learn it all and then be killed. Everything suddenly clicked into place. "I'm feeling tired, I'm going for a lie down." Jumping up Destiny made her way back to her room. She now had to come up with a plan.

"ARE YOU ALL READY?" Adolphus asked. "Jaxon. You three stay close and follow us in, they will not smell you if you are with us. Magnus, you, and Edna ask for entry fifteen minutes after we are in. That will give Jaxon time to get to Destiny's room. Right. Let's go."

Jaxon looked at Edna. "Okay make us invisible."

"You already are Alpha." Edna replied with a wry smile.

Grunting, Jaxon followed Adolphus to the monument. There in front of it stood Lolly. "Adolphus. Welcome." Signalling to the stone steps that lead down, she turned and started to descend into the darkness.

Once Jaxon hit the bottom step he looked around. Watching as Adolphus walked into the distance with Lolly and his two fighters, Jaxon glanced at Carlton and Alex. 'This way' He mind linked. Making their way down a long corridor, Jaxon breathed in as Destiny's scent hit him. Almost running, he made his way to a door and stood starring at it. He knew she was in there.

Destiny looked up as the door opened. "Who's there?" Jumping off the bed she stood watching as the door closed, by itself.

Jaxon walked up to her and smiled. 'Destiny' checking the mind link worked he watched as the surprise hit her.

'Jaxon?"

'Yes it's me. Now listen I am standing in front of you. Edna made me invisible so I could get into the coven. We need to get you out. Carlton and Alex are here too.'

Destiny reached out and felt Jaxon's face. 'I want to see you.'

'Not yet cup cake. Soon' Jaxon grabbed Destiny's hand and pulled her towards the door.

'No. I can't go, not without my magic book and bag.'

'Don't you think they have caused enough problems? I need to get you out of here now' Jaxon did the best to contain his annoyance.

'You don't understand' Destiny stopped when Jaxon growled.

'You don't understand. Destiny they are going to kill you' Jaxon gripped Destiny's hand and dragged her to the door.

'Jaxon. If I don't stop Raven we are all dead anyway. Please listen to me' Destiny begged.

Maybe it was because of the urgency in her voice or maybe it was because he loved her, he released his grip. 'What can I do?'

'The crystals hanging from all the ceilings have a direct link to Raven. Earlier I ran my hands through them causing them to jingle, Raven came in holding her head and demanded I stopped it. Now if we can do enough in different rooms, it will disorientate her enough for me to get into her room. I am sure that's where she has my book and bag. If I can get the book I should be able to get some of my magic back. Then can you get Alex to take them and get out of the coven?'

'I don't like it but okay. Magnus and Edna will be here soon. They were going to cause a commotion so I could get you out. If we strike then the confusion will be greater. I'll let the others know' Jaxon mind linked with Carlton and Alex.

Once all the men knew what they were doing, Destiny lead them out towards different areas of the coven. 'Jaxon as soon as you hear Magnus you go for the crystal's, I'll meet you at the entrance in five minutes.'

Destiny headed towards Raven's chamber. The nearer she got the stronger the dark magic. As she approached the door, she noticed it was partially open. She pushed the door slowly open.

There in the middle of the chamber stood Raven. Just standing, with her eyes closed. Sensing Destiny she opened her eyes. "You shouldn't be here Destiny."

"Why shouldn't I?" Destiny was sure she saw a glimmer of sadness in Raven's eyes.

"It's not safe. Please go to your room. She will call for you soon."

Raven walked past Destiny towards the door, pausing for a moment. "Things are not as they seem child. I'm sorry."

Destiny watched as Raven left her chamber, noticing the crystals hanging from her ears. She also wore a crystal necklace and had a crystal bracelet on both wrists. Something was off. Ignoring her thoughts, she then began her search. After going through all the drawers and cupboards Destiny stood and looked around. Looking at the ceiling she spotted the same crystals that hung from her room. But why, why would Raven have crystals in her own room when they caused her so much pain. Why would she wear crystals? Leaving the room Destiny made her way to Esme's chamber. If she were right, there would be crystals hanging in there too.

CHAPTER 36

Adolphus, Grace, and the ancient vampire took their seats at the large stone alter. Adolphus looked at Esme, who was as white as a ghost. "Why is there a sacrificial alter where the council table should be?"

Esme put her head down and shrugged her shoulders. "We moved things around."

Lolly intervened before Adolphus could reply. "The table broke, so Raven thought it would be a good idea to use this. Don't you think it's beautiful? So much history in one thing so precious." Lolly ran her hand over the alter and smiled. "Now shall we get down to business?"

"You're a little too eager Lolly. Shouldn't we wait for Destiny?" Raven asked. "We do need to all be here for the council to proceed."

Annoyed Lolly glared at Raven. "Go and get her and be quick. After all we shouldn't keep the supernatural council waiting."

Raven nodded and made her way out. As she walked into Destiny's chamber she looked up at the ceiling and smiled. Destiny may have lost her magic, but she still had her brain.

Magnus knocked loudly on the stone monument and recited the incantation for entry.

Seconds later the monument moved, and Lolly stood there, with her face like thunder. "Magnus. What do you want?"

"I demand to see my daughter." Magnus took a step closer and smiled. "I do believe it is in the coven rules that before any decision is made on a new coven member, the family get to see her one last time." Magnus watched Lolly closely, she was the newest coven member, only having been here a couple of years. He was surprised that she had so much clout here. Normally you worked your way up, and that could take years. Magnus tilted his head and studied her eyes. They held a power he couldn't quite pinpoint. "Well?"

Lolly nodded; it was too late now for Magnus to stop the ceremony. "Follow me."

Magnus bowed his head slightly and motioned for Edna to go first.

Raven walked into Esme's room and watched as Destiny rummaged through a cupboard. "You won't find what you're looking for in there."

Spinning around Destiny studied Raven. "You know I thought it was you."

"That's what you were supposed to think. Now what you seek is in Lolly's room, but you have no chance of gaining entry. Even I cannot break the magic that guards it." Raven sighed. "It's time Destiny. You must follow me."

"Wait. Lead me to her room, I have an idea." Destiny mind linked with Jaxon, 'I need you to come with me, bring Carlton and Alex. I'm in the main corridor' Destiny walked out of the room and waited for Jaxon.

"Destiny, it will do no good." Raven grabbed Destiny's arm as she walked past. "You should never have come here. Now we must go before she finds us here."

"Don't you want to at least try?" Destiny shrugged Ravens hand off. "Your life as well as every other supernatural's will change. There will be war, famine, natural disasters, all the things you read about in the bible and let's not forget the humans. They don't deserve what's to come."

"Don't you think we've thought about that." Raven snapped.

"Wait a minute, you banished Faith.... She's inside you. She is, isn't she?" Destiny studied Raven's face.

"It was the only way to keep her safe. Lolly would have killed her. You see Faith was on to her, she discovered an old scroll in Lolly's room. That's when Lolly gave Faith the power of water. She then notified the rest of us, but I knew something was wrong, so before Lolly had the chance to banish Faith, I did."

"Why didn't you say something to the others?" Destiny frowned. "There were four of you against her."

"Do you see these crystals; we all wear them apart from Lolly. That's how she controls us. Through pain. We woke up one morning and we all had them on. So if we do anything Lolly doesn't like, we suffer. Look I know you mean well but…" Raven trailed off.

"What's the power of the four?" Destiny asked as soon as the thought came into her head.

"It used to be the power of the five, but Lolly changed it to four when Faith disappeared."

"So four is a powerful number?" Destiny watched Raven nod. "Take me to Lolly's room, we haven't got long."

"MAGNUS, WHAT A PLEASANT SURPRISE." Grace said with a smile, as Magnus entered the great chamber.

"Grace." Magnus returned her smile and then focused on the witches. "I demand to see Destiny. NOW!"

"You do not come to the coven of Salem and make demands

Magnus. And you certainly do not shout." Allegra looked at Lolly. "Why did you let him in?"

Adolphus stood and looked at Lolly. "He has a right to see his daughter. Do we no longer honour traditions Lolly?"

Magnus held Edna's hand and bellowed at the top of his voice. "DESTINY IS MY DAUGHTER AND I DEMAND TO SEE HER!" The chamber started to shake as Magnus's voice crescendo.

Next Grace stood and joined in the shouting, calling for her niece to be brought to her father.

The noise was so great, Lolly couldn't focus. Holding her head she took a deep breath. Something was wrong.

"This is her room. The magic seems to be weakening. What is all that noise coming from the great chamber?" Raven turned to walk away but stopped when she collided with Jaxon. Looking in front of her, she couldn't see anyone, but she could feel his presence. "What is this?"

"This is Jaxon. My mate. Now four is all powerful. So we have Jaxon. You and Faith and me. That's four. Carlton and Alex, I want you to burst through the door once the incantation has been said. Right, we need to put our hands on the door, leave room for Carlton and Alex to kick the door in. Start Raven and hurry."

As the last word left Raven's lips, Carlton, and Alex both leapt at the door feet first and watched as it fell inwards.

"Hurry Destiny, I can feel her watching." Raven grabbed her head and sank to the ground. "Search the dresser." She mumbled through the pain.

Destiny ran into the room and tried the first drawer. "It's locked."

Jaxon pulled Destiny to one side and yanked the drawer out, watching as the contents fell to the floor. "Here. One magic book, ring, and one bag. Now what?"

"You need to get these out of here. Carlton take them, they will be invisible if you hold them. Now get them as far away as possible." Destiny turned to Raven. "We need to get those crystals off of her."

Jaxon knelt down and pulled at the necklace. "It won't break. Destiny, she's not breathing."

"Give me the book." Reaching up to Carlton, Destiny grabbed the book and searched for a release spell. "Here." She said pointing to a spell. Placing her finger on it, she breathed in and felt the tingling sensation as the spell mixed with her blood. "Stand back." Holding her hands over Raven's body she staired at the crystals. "I release you." One by one the crystals broke away from the chains, until finally the chains themselves crumbled.

Raven gulped a huge lungful of air. "Destiny you need to run."

"No not yet, my dad is in there and I'm not leaving without him." Looking down at the book, Destiny placed her finger on the fire spell and breathed in. "Take the book and place it in the bag. Now go Carlton."

Jaxon nodded and turned to Alex. "Protect him. Make sure no one touches the bag."

Raven stood shakily and clung to the coven wall. "I'll let them out, but you must hurry before Lolly banishes your father. Jaxon, you will have the element of surprise, use it wisely." Raven made her way to the entrance, leaving Jaxon and Destiny alone.

"I'm sorry cupcake." Jaxon looked at Destiny, how could he have forgotten her?

"You know it's very off putting when you can't see who you're talking to, and just for the record, you have nothing to be sorry for." Destiny closed her eyes and felt Jaxon's face. "I missed you." Leaning forward Destiny brushed her lips against Jaxon's. "That feels good." She pulled back and sighed. "Okay, I guess we better finish this."

MAGNUS WAS THROWN to the floor when Lolly erupted into a mass of anger. Her eyes blazed with malice and the air began to whip around the chamber. "I SAID SILENCE."

Magnus reached out for Edna and held her hand. "Well we have definitely got her attention. Now what?"

"Magnus, look." Edna motioned to the door as Destiny walked in.

"They were supposed to get her out of here." Magnus pulled himself and Edna up using the stone alter.

Adolphus roared as the wind blew him against the wall. "YOU WILL PAY FOR THIS." Watching Destiny out of the corner of his eye he continued to keep Lolly's attention on him. "What do you expect to gain. The whole of the supernatural world will rise up against you."

Destiny strolled into the cavern and smiled. "Looks like I'm missing all the fun." She glanced at Magnus and then Lolly. "My, you've whipped up quite a storm in here, who'd have thought you were such a windy person."

Before Destiny could continue she was dragged towards the alter by an invisible force. It was Lolly's turn to smile. "At last. The guest of honour."

Destiny rose into the air and ended up laying on the sacrificial alter, unable to prise herself off. 'Jaxon stand at the side of the room near Adolphus, she won't smell you there.'

Magnus rushed to Destiny's aid, trying to pull her up. "You'll pay for this."

"ENOUGH!" Lolly clicked her fingers and watched as everything stopped. Everyone was frozen to the spot. "Now, Destiny. We have a little ceremony to perform." Looking around, Lolly searched for Raven. "Where is Raven Destiny?"

"Why are you asking me? She's your lap dog." Destiny tried to wriggle free, but the invisible force was to strong.

"Never mind, I'll get her myself." Lolly marched from the cavern and vanished from sight.

"Is everyone okay?" Destiny called out.

"You were supposed to get out of here Destiny. Why can't you do as you're told." Magnus asked, slightly irritated by his daughters wayward actions.

Destiny pulled her hand up slightly and turned it towards herself. "I release you." Sitting up she stared around the cavern. "Right, get ready to leave here and don't come back." Waving her hands around the room Destiny repeated the words. "I release you. I need you to get everyone out. Get as far from the coven as possible." Destiny turned to Allegra and Esme. "You two are very quiet, have you nothing to say?"

"We can help get everyone out. Follow us." Esme replied.

"I'm not leaving you on your own." Magnus stopped when Raven walked in.

"She's not on her own. Now everyone leave." Turning to Allegra and Esme, Raven motioned to Destiny. "How do you both feel knowing a child is cleverer than both of you?"

Destiny blushed as everyone looked at her. "I don't think this is the time for recriminations. Lolly will be back any minute. Now please, get everyone out safely." Destiny turned to where Jaxon was hopefully standing. 'Are you ready for this?'

'I'm always ready cupcake.' Jaxon watched as the last of the group left. 'Whatever you have planned, make it quick, we have a mating ceremony to attend.'

'I wouldn't miss it for the world, Alpha. Now concentrate, she's coming.' Destiny sat on the edge of the alter and smiled as Lolly walked in.

"Raven. Where have you been. And where's the council?" Turning to Destiny Lolly shrugged. "Never mind, I don't need them for the last part. Raven give me the book."

"I don't have it." Raven watched as Lolly's face turned purple.

"What do you mean you don't have it. I sent you to get it twenty minutes ago." Turning her attention back to Destiny she glared. "What have you done with the book Destiny?"

"What book?" Destiny yawned and started swinging her legs backwards and forwards into the alter. The noise had the desired effect. 'Get ready Jaxon pull her down and jump out of the way.'

Lolly raised her hands ready to send a blast towards Destiny, just as Jaxon lunged towards her. Pushing her backwards, the blast shot from her hands and hit the ceiling. Before she had time to right herself, Destiny sent a blast of fire towards her, then ran and joined hands with Raven.

Lolly laughed. "You stupid girl. you need three with magic to form a tripod."

Before she had finished Faith parted from Ravens body and joined them to form the triangle.

"We banish you to the demon realm. Your power will fail as you fall through the depths of the earth." Faith looked down at Lolly and shook her head. "We were sisters."

All three watched as Lolly's body faded into the ground until there was nothing left. Faith turned towards Destiny and pulled her into a hug. "Thank you. You know I'm going to enjoy getting to know you."

"Oh no you're not" Jaxon growled. "She's mine and she is coming home with me."

"I thought I could smell wolf." Clicking her fingers, Jaxon appeared. "You are a very lucky wolf to have such a wonderful witch. Now tell me do you think you deserve her?"

Jaxon starred at Destiny before answering. "No. I most likely don't, but I love her, and I will always keep her safe."

"Destiny, the choice is yours. Would you like to stay and be a part of the Salem coven or would you rather go and live with this…. wolf man. We need another member now and I think you would love it here." Faith already knew what the answer would be, so Destiny's words were of no great surprise.

"Thank you for your kind offer, but my place is with Jaxon. I don't think I could live without him. Not now." Destiny saw the smile erupt on Jaxon's face and felt her own spreading. "I do know someone else who would be suitable though."

"Really, and who may that be?" Faith asked, puzzled.

CHAPTER 37

The drive back to the packhouse took longer than expected. Especially when Jaxon had to stop off to use a phone. After twenty minutes Destiny went to search for him. He looked guilty to her, just what was he up to?

They had to hire a car as Carlton and Alex took the SUV. So now someone would have to drop this one back tomorrow, she suspected Magnus would offer.

As they drove through the town Magnus put his head down. He would miss Edna, even though they said he could visit often. Still she was now on the witches council of Salem. They couldn't have picked anyone better, and he really was pleased for her, but still, she was the one that kept him going when Destiny and Vanessa disappeared, and he would forever be grateful.

As the packhouse came into sight Destiny's eyes lit up. "Why are there white roses everywhere?" Destiny thought of her mother and the roses that filled every windowsill of her old home.

"They are for the mating ceremony, or had you forgotten about that?" Jaxon grinned. Tonight was going to be perfect, for himself and his Luna.

"Well I guess the Luna ceremony was a bit rushed but still, I wasn't expecting this." Looking at the burnt out packhouse, Destiny swallowed down. It was her fault it wasn't fixed.

"It will be okay cupcake." Jaxon looked over and winked at her. "We can fix it tomorrow. Tonight is for celebrating."

Destiny smiled; she still couldn't get used to him reading her mind.

Pulling up, Jaxon jumped out of the motor and walked around to help Destiny out. He watched Magnus from the corner of his eye. He could sense the sadness rolling off of him in waves. As soon as Edna had said yes to the witches council his demure had changed. "Magnus, you need to choose the spot for your cabin, maybe you could do that while everything is being prepared for the ceremony?"

Magnus stared at Jaxon with his mouth open. He didn't think in his wildest dreams Jaxon would allow him onto pack land.

"Dad? You do still want to move here?" Destiny asked, irritated by his silence.

"Yes. Yes of course…. I didn't think…. Yes." Magnus laughed.

"Then I'll leave you to sort that Magnus. Destiny we have things to sort out too." Jaxon grabbed Destiny's hand and lead her to the packhouse and up to their room. "The bedrooms are still habitable."

"I could use magic to fix it." Destiny replied.

"No. I've had enough of magic for now. The pack can fix it; besides, you need to get ready for tonight, but first my Luna." Jaxon pulled Destiny onto the bed.

"No Jaxon. You can wait until tonight." Destiny felt the sheet beneath her. "Jaxon, I can sense Gene. Did you…. You know, in our bed?"

"Look Destiny, you need to remember my memory was wiped clean." Jaxon sat up. "Yes. I fucked a corpse. Thanks for reminding me."

"Well obviously we can't spend the night here. In this bed. It's tainted." Destiny crawled off the bed and walked over to the window.

"It's our mating ritual tonight Destiny, we have to complete the ceremony by physically mating. So where do you suggest we do that?"

"I am not doing anything in that bed." Destiny crossed her arms in defiance. "In fact it needs to go."

Jaxon blew out slowly. He had forgotten just how pig headed she could be. "Fine…. Get your stuff, I'll take you to Magnus's. You can get ready there, while I sort this out."

Jaxon helped Destiny with her bags and then headed back to the pack house. He made his way up the stairs then stood there. As he pushed the door open he looked at his parents' bedroom. It had remained empty since they had been killed. The room was bigger than his. Not only did it stretch from the front of the house to the back, but it also had balcony's at either end too. He didn't know how he would feel moving into here. The room was a happy place, full of so many good memories. His mother reading to him as a child. His father teaching him about being the Alpha. Snuggling in his mother's arms when he was unwell. It was a room full of love. Smiling he pulled the door shut and went to find Carlton.

"I'M TELLING you Magnus something is going on. Jaxon's been acting weird since we got back from Salem, and he was too quick to pack me off to yours. Oh my god. Do you think he's changed his mind?" Destiny felt the panic rising up by the second. "It was the bed thing; Surely he doesn't expect me to sleep in that after what's happened, I mean, seriously."

"Destiny calm down." Magnus took Destiny's hand and guided her to the sofa. "Now sit down, I'll make you a cup of tea."

"I don't want tea. I want to know what's going on…. I need to talk to him. Make sure he still wants me." Destiny stood but didn't move as Magnus stopped her.

"Sit." Pointing to the seat as he raised an eyebrow. "Jaxon love's you, that's all you need to remember."

"Wow, since when did you become his biggest fan?"

"Since he was prepared to sacrifice his life to get you back. And also may I add young lady, he only went with Gene because you asked for his memory to be wiped." Magnus shook his head. "Poor bloke. When Edna gave him the truth spell and he could see what Gene really looked like, you know on account of her being a corpse, he still went along with it to keep you safe." Magnus trembled as Genes image flashed through his head. "Horrific."

"I still can't sleep in that bed." Destiny closed her eyes as she thought of Jaxon and Gene together, in her eyes it didn't matter what Gene was, it still tainted the bed.

"And Jaxon is sorting that now, as well as all the other stuff, ready for tonight. In fact I should be helping. You can get ready at your aunts."

"What, Aunt Edna's?"

"No. Aunt Grace's. Now go." Magnus stormed out of the cottage, straight into the pack grounds. Spotting Jaxon he made his way over.

Jaxon looked up as he approached. "Where's Destiny?" Panicking Jaxon looked over to the Cottage.

"Don't worry, I've told her to go to the fae queens and get ready. She still has no idea what you've planned." Magnus stared at Carlton and Alex who were manoeuvring a large bed out of the packhouse. "Ah the dreaded bed. Glad you're getting rid of it; I don't think I could take anymore of her moaning."

"She had a point. I don't want to sleep in it again, not after…. you know." Jaxon winced. That was one memory he would bury.

"Hmm, I don't blame you. Now what can I do to help, I have an hour or so before I need to get ready." Magnus looked at the packhouse. "Are you sure you wouldn't like a little magical help with the repairs?"

DESTINY WALKED through the green light and straight into the palace gardens. There, already waiting was the fae queen. "Were you expecting me?"

"Of course. Now let us prepare for the ceremony." Grace

clapped her hands together and immediately Willow and Magnolia appeared, giggling. "Now take Destiny to the royal suite and run her a nice hot bubble bath. Destiny when you are done we will go to the dress room, I'm sure there will be something there for the occasion. Right. Chop. Chop."

Destiny followed the two fae up to the royal suite, gasping at the shear luxury. "Gold taps. Isn't that a bit over the top?" She guessed not, the queen did like all the finer things in life.

"It's a palace Destiny, only the best for the fae queen." Willow replied as she started running the bath while Magnolia attempted to undress Destiny.

"I'm not a child." Pulling her top off she stood staring at the two fae as they stared back. "And I don't need an audience."

"She's shy Willow." Magnolia whispered.

"She's embarrassed. Look she's gone red." Willow giggled back.

"I can hear you. Please leave and let me bathe in peace." Destiny stepped out of her jeans and threw them on the floor. "I said leave." Waiting until the fae left, Destiny took off her underwear and stepped into the bath. As she sank down into the steamy bubbles her body started to relax. All the worries she had been carrying, without knowing, simply evaporated. Her mind emptied as she drifted off to sleep.

"Destiny!"

Destiny opened her eyes and came face to face with the fae queen. "What?"

"I said you need to have your hair washed. Now sit up.... Willow, will you do the honours please. And then you can get out. Wrap this robe around you and come through to the next room."

Destiny sighed; her aunt Grace was bossy. Fae queen or not, she had no right to order her around. She hadn't asked to come here, in fact she had been banished here, by Magnus. Wrapping the robe tightly around herself, Destiny made her way into the next room. There hanging on a mannequin was a white, pure silk dress. It had diamantes sew into the tight bodice, and a train of lace stretching behind. It shimmered in the sunlight. "Who's is that?"

"It was your mother's. She wore it on her wedding day to

Magnus. Magnolia, dry Destiny's hair…. I think you should have your hair up; it will show off your slender neck."

"Aunt Grace. Your majesty, this is a mating ceremony, not a wedding." Destiny ran her hand along the soft silk material. "It's beautiful." Destiny closed her eyes and pictured her mother in the dress. She would have looked every inch the princess.

"The mating ceremony is one that joins two people…. erm wolves, or supernatural's, together that love each other. No different from a wedding. Now sit down while Magnolia does your hair."

"Okay places everyone, she should be here in a minute." Magnus smiled as Edna approached him. "I'm so glad you were allowed to come Edna."

"I wouldn't miss it Magnus. It's going to be quite a ceremony. The grounds look beautiful." Edna replied as she gazed at all the white roses. "I have a gift for Destiny." Edna reached into her bag and pulled out a long slim box, as she opened it, Magnus smiled.

"Was that our mothers?" Magnus asked as he touched the necklace tenderly. "The three stones of Orion…. such beautiful diamonds." Magnus marvelled over the intricate platinum chain that bound the diamonds in a straight line, just like the stars of Orion's belt. He knew this was a powerful piece of jewellery although he had never seen what it was capable of.

Edna nodded. "She wore it on her wedding day…. As I will never marry I thought it would be fitting to pass it down to Destiny and hopefully one day she will pass it down to her daughter." Edna closed the box. It was more than just an heirloom it was also a protection charm. The power of Orion was to fight off all Evil and Edna knew it would be needed, if not now then soon.

"They will be arriving at the back of the packhouse, we can wait for her there and then you can give it to her." Magnus replied.

Edna nodded and then grabbed Magnus's arm. "We mustn't tell her what it does Magnus, not yet, let her enjoy her wedding, mating ceremony…. There will be plenty of time to tell her the rest."

"Okay." Magnus confirmed with a nod of his head. He watched Edna closely. What a weird thing to say, he thought.

Jaxon stood underneath a giant arch of white roses as he waited for Destiny. "Shouldn't she be here by now?" He asked Carlton nervously.

"Isn't it normal for humans to be late?" Carlton shrugged. "Hang on look, the fae queen and is that the troll?"

Jaxon smiled. "They helped in the battle, remember. They are her friends; they should be here." Jaxon's mouth dropped open when he spotted Destiny walking with Magnus towards him. He had never seen a more beautiful vision in all his life. She looked exactly like what she was…A princess. Jaxon held out his hand as she walked to his side. "You look stunning." He whispered.

Destiny held his hand and smiled. "You look hot." She whispered back.

Magnus stepped back and took his seat next to Edna. "What aren't you telling me." Magnus asked as he looked at Edna's worried expression.

"Not now Magnus, lets enjoy Destiny's special night." Edna refocused on the happy couple as the ceremony began. There would be time for talking later.

CHAPTER 38

Jaxon carried Destiny up the two flights of stairs and headed to their new room. After pushing the door shut with his foot, he laid Destiny on the bed. "Alone at last Mrs King."

Destiny giggled. "Mrs King…. I can't believe we got married and mated in one night. It was perfect."

"Well it's about time something went right, anyway enough talking and more action." Jaxon looked at the dress and scratched his head. "How do I get it off?"

Destiny rolled over, revealing a row of tiny buttons along the back. "Start by undoing them."

As Jaxon reached for the first button a tiny ray of electricity shot from the necklace. "Ouch."

"What's wrong?" Destiny spun around and looked at Jaxon's finger, it was smoking. "How did you do that?"

"I didn't, it was that necklace. Take it off." Jaxon replied as he blew his finger.

Destiny pointed to his finger and splashed it with water. Then she reached for the necklace. "I can't find the clasp, help me."

As soon as Jaxon attempted to touch the necklace, another blast hit him, causing him to jump up and shake his hand. "Where did you get that from, it's cursed."

"My aunt Edna gave it to me, go and find her, I'm sure there's a reasonable explanation.

Jaxon threw open the door and jumped down the stairs. His temper at breaking point. Why would Edna give Destiny something so dangerous? Marching out towards the party goers, Jaxon looked around. As he spotted Magnus he made his way through the crowd of dancers and grabbed Magnus by the arm. "Where's Edna?" He growled.

"I think she's over there, with the fae queen.... Jaxon?" Magnus watched Jaxon as he pushed his way through the crowd, stopping in front of Edna.

"You need to come with me." He grabbed Edna by the arm and lead her into the packhouse.

"What's wrong Alpha?" Edna asked as she was marched up the stairs, as she looked behind she noticed Magnus following.

"You'll see what's wrong when you get in here." He pushed Edna into the bedroom and pointed at Destiny. "Get that thing off of her now."

"Aunt Edna there's something wrong with this necklace. It keeps attacking Jaxon and I can't get it off." Destiny fiddled with the necklace and then tried to yank it off of her neck.

"I don't understand, it's supposed to protect you from enemy's. Not your mate.... It must be faulty." Edna walked over to Destiny and studied the necklace. As she reached out to touch it the necklace sent a ray of electric to her hand causing her to jump back and yelp. "Magnus?"

Magnus walked forward and inspected the necklace with his hands placed firmly behind his back. There was no way he was getting zapped. "I can't see a clasp."

"You do know this is our mating night. The night we can actually touch each other." Jaxon roared. "I don't care how you do it, but you." Jaxon pointed to Edna. "Get that fucking thing off of my mate."

"Yes Alpha." Edna replied as she continued to rub her hand.

"The electricity seems to be coming from the diamonds Magnus, is there a way we can prise them out?"

"It would have to be done with magic.... your magic, as you were the one to give it to her." Magnus looked over to Jaxon, as he paced the room. "Maybe you would like to go and get a drink Alpha, while we sort this out.... thirty minutes should suffice."

Jaxon growled. "I'm not leaving Destiny here with that thing on."

"It's okay Jaxon, I'll be fine. Go and have a drink and when you come up bring some champagne with you." Destiny smiled at Jaxon and watched him leave. He wasn't happy. "Right you two." Destiny glared between Magnus and Edna. "What's going on?"

"I don't know Destiny, the necklace was our mothers, it's supposed to be lucky." Edna replied, still holding her hand.

Destiny clicked her fingers and the necklace fell of." I'm not talking about the necklace; I'm talking about the weird looks you've been giving each other. What's going on?"

"You mean you did that." Magnus asked as he pointed to the necklace.

"You wouldn't talk to me downstairs, so I had to think of some way of getting your attention." Destiny sighed. "What is going to happen now?"

"It's your wedding night Destiny, you should be enjoying yourself with your mate. We can discuss this tomorrow." Edna replied. "Magnus, go and get Jaxon."

Destiny raised her hand and the door slammed shut. "You have twenty minutes to fill me in. Now what is it?"

"Okay." Edna replied. "It seems that the events that have happened here are part of a bigger prophecy. It states that a witch, that's you. A vampire, we don't know who she is yet and a werewolf, we don't know who she is either, join together to defeat the biggest threat to our world. Its written in ancient scrolls that were buried in the coven many years ago. No one believed in the prophecy, which is until they met you."

"So this may not even happen?" Destiny replied flatly.

"No, which is why I never said anything." Edna smiled. "We will hear if such a vampire or werewolf exists, so you needn't worry. But if it did ever arise, you must wear the necklace."

Destiny studied her aunt Edna's face for a few seconds, she looked serious. "Why?"

"Destiny I really don't want to go into this now, as I've already said, it may not happen." Edna shrugged. "It's your wedding night after all."

"Aunt Edna, why must I wear the necklace?" Destiny asked once more.

Edna looked at Magnus who nodded his approval. "Because it will amplify your powers when you most need it."

"And how will I know when I most need it?" Destiny replied, annoyed that she wasn't getting a straight answer.

"The necklace will know…. Now promise me you will wear it when you feel danger." Aunt Edna pleaded.

"Okay, fine. Now if you don't mind I would like to spend the rest of my evening with Jaxon." Destiny watched closely as Magnus and Edna left. Minutes later Jaxon popped his head around the door and held up a bottle of champagne. "Lock the door Alpha, I don't want any more disturbances."

Jaxon placed the bottle and glasses on the side and then perched on the edge of the bed. "He undid his tie and threw it onto a chair. Slowly he crawled onto the bed and kissed Destiny on the lip's. "If there's any more interruptions I'm going to lose my shit."

Destiny pulled him closer. "Well Alpha, I'm all yours." It was Destiny this time that kissed Jaxon, her hands pulling at his clothes.

Jaxon slid his arms out of his jacket and tossed it onto the floor. Destiny proceeded to undo his buttons while Jaxon undid hers. As he reached the waist, he pulled down the dress exposing Destiny's breasts. At this point Jaxon couldn't contain himself. He ripped his shirt off followed by his pants, and then ripped Destiny's dress in half. He looked down at her tiny briefs and licked his lip's. Ripping them off he positioned himself on top of her and rubbed his throbbing cock against her wetness. With one push Jaxon had entered her, he felt the ping of her virginity leave her as he pushed in deep. With each thrust he thought he was going to explode. Destiny's moans were making him thrust harder. He needed this; he needed her. He felt her hands on his bum, massaging him. He took her left nipple into his mouth and sucked on it; her moaning was getting louder as she bucked her hips in time to his thrusting. With one last push Jaxon and Destiny let out a scream so loud, that it rang out around the forest.

Magnus looked up to Destiny's window and sighed. "Well that's it, the Orion prophecy has been set in motion."

THE END

About the Author

Carol McDonald lives in Essex where she spends her time working, writing and spoiling her grandchildren.

Her normal genre is gangland fiction and has two books published. Dolly King – The Gangsters Daughter and The Stepney Feud.

This is the first fantasy novel she has written and is working on the next book in The Orion Prophecy trilogy.

 facebook.com/carolhellier
 instagram.com/author_cahellier

Also by Carol McDonald

The Orion Trilogy

In the Shadows

WRITING AS CAROL HELLIER

Dolly King – The Gangsters Daughter

The Stepney Feud

Printed in Great Britain
by Amazon